I0629204

MASKS

MBK Global Security

Kenzie Macallan

Copyright © 2019 Kenzie Macallan

Published by Steel Butterfly Press

ISBN No.978-0-9973492-5-2

All rights reserved. No part of this publication may be reproduced, distributed, or transmitted in any form or by any means, including photocopying, recording, or other electronic or mechanical methods, without the prior written permission of the publisher, except in the case of brief quotations embodied in critical reviews and certain other noncommercial uses permitted by copyright law.

Please Note

The reverse engineering, uploading, and/or distributing of this book via the internet or via any other means without the permission of the copyright owner is illegal and punishable by law. Please purchase only authorized electronic editions, and do not participate in or encourage electronic piracy of copyrighted materials. Your support of the author's rights is appreciated.

No part of this book may be reproduced or transmitted in any form or by any electronic or mechanical means, including photocopying, recording, or by any information storage and retrieval system, without the written permission of the publisher, except where permitted by law.

This book is a work of fiction. Any references to real people or real places are used fictitiously. Other names, characters places, and events come from the author's imagination, and any resemblance to actual places or persons, living or dead, is coincidental.

Cover design © 2022 teblackdesigns.com

Praise for Kenzie Macallan

"Michael (Misha) and Raquelle may be my new favorite couple in this series!"~*April, Goodreads review*

"Once I started Masks I couldn't put it down. As the story unfolds and the secrets started coming out it made it harder to put down. The emotion in this book felt so real...Definitely recommend this book!" ~*Tiffany, Goodreads review*

"Filled with tantalizing chemistry and unnerving suspense, this impressive story and well-written characters made for an exceptional read!" ~**Sarah,** *Goodreads review*

Deception may give us what we want for the present, but it will always take it away in the end.
~Rachel Hawthorne

Chapter One

RAQUELLE HAD no idea how much of her soul she would have to sell to solve the mystery of her papa's death. She coiled up in the corner, avoiding the sharp edges of the cracked vinyl seats that could snag her custom-tailored dress. The cab smelled of stale cigarettes combined with someone's last-night backseat romp. Her nerves were on edge and thoughts scattered. Had she thought far enough ahead, she would have ordered a car and avoided the dirty, uncomfortable ride. But cabbies navigated New York City like NASCAR drivers. Trapped at the mercy of the driver, she was determined to be punctual for an appointment in lower Manhattan's financial district.

Surviving in the steel jungle required strength and was challenging but not impossible. Only the tough survived in this brutal, unforgiving city. Compromises and sacrifices were necessary to flush out the true identity behind the mask everyone wore. Her body had served as a negotiating tool, of sorts, to get what she wanted out of life. Sometimes that meant allowing another faceless man to use her. *Use* was such a harsh word. Who was she kidding? She enjoyed most of them, just not all of them. From an early age, she understood how men viewed her and how to make it work to her advantage. But this time, she wouldn't cave to her sexual appetite. She needed this commission to be strictly by the book, no sex as a bargaining chip.

The cold spring rain coming down in sheets served as an appropriate backdrop to the memories of her dark childhood. A shiver ran under her skin, assaulted by the black-and-white film of memories of the first set of hands to handle her innocence, the result lacked compassion. She hugged her coat, wishing she had had the courage to change things, to say no, instead of giving into her cravings. *Weak and stupid* were her excuses then, but never again. Her experiences had turned her into a fighter. Dread crept through her veins as she thought about where she was headed in the channel of clogged traffic.

Her fingertips streaked down the condensation on the cold window, leaving them chilly and numb, two familiar feelings. She blew out a heavy breath, anxious about her destination. The one time she had visited CZR Investments, she had met her sister Mara's husband, Brock, a junior investor. She had recognized him as a user from the minute she'd laid eyes on him. On vacation in Mexico, Mara had shared her story of his abuse behind closed doors. Raquelle had never felt rage like that before and wanted to kill him for causing her sister so much pain.

This time she was going to CZR for a different reason. She hoped it proved to be a lucrative one that would put her on the map as an artist. Raquelle was born to be a great artist, and nothing would get in her way. At twenty-four, her time had come, and she would take advantage of it.

The cab lurched forward and came to a stop, slamming her face into the Plexiglas partition. The driver yelled at another cabbie in a foreign language, beating his hands on the steering wheel.

"What the hell?" She rubbed the side of her face.

He opened the divider. "I'm sorry, madam. The traffic's completely stopped. I have nowhere to go." He shrugged.

"Here." She shoved a wad of bills through the window at him. "Keep the change."

She could see the skyscraper through the window and would have to make a mad dash for it in torrential rain. Her dress would get drenched, her hair would be ruined, and her makeup would streak down her face, but she would not be late. She grabbed her portfolio and Birkin bag and opened the door. Raindrops pelted her like damp needles. Using her portfolio as cover, she jumped over the puddles to the revolving glass doors leading to the lobby. She tried to fit her portfolio through the doors, but her three-thousand-dollar purse got stuck in the gap, ripping the handle off. Someone jammed the rotation, crushing her between the door and the frame.

"Goddamn it," she muttered.

She stumbled into the polished entrance, came to a stop, and righted herself, making eye contact with a man leaning over the security desk. Dark hair and skin with hazel eyes gave him an air of danger. He peered up at her, held her stare for a minute, and turned his attention back to the guard. Goose bumps formed on her arms and her cheeks burned as she picked up pace to the elevator. A sea of people pushed her from behind and into the next available car. She found space in the corner and called out for the 108th floor. Small confined spaces provoked anxiety for her, but she wasn't walking up a hundred and eight flights of stairs. She used her relaxation strategies to breathe and focused on the surrounding details. Smashed up against the mirrored back wall, she looked like she'd been in a dunk tank. Checking her watch, she hoped she might have time to make a detour to the bathroom. First impressions were everything.

Stepping off the elevator, the other passengers scattered, leaving her confronted with a sterile-looking lobby. Warm and fuzzy weren't words to describe this company. Black floors offset cream-colored walls. Whoever put this together didn't have a soul. A huge curved gray desk stood at the other end. Above it were the words *CZR Investments* highlighted in a brushed-nickel finish.

Head held high, she walked toward the empty front desk as several phones rang at once. She looked at her watch. Waiting wasn't one of her strong suits, but she could use the extra time. Hallways verged off on either side, and the left one looked worth pursuing. Young interns scurried around but paid no attention to her. She headed for the end of the hall, looking for the name of the CEO. All the bigwigs had end offices with a view. As predicted, the last set of massive doors, in dark bold letters on a gold satin-finish plaque, read *Michael Raines*. She knocked, but there was no answer. The door opened with little effort.

"Hello?" Her voiced echoed in the empty front office.

She went to the next set of doors and knocked again with no reply. Letting herself in, she peeked around the corner looking for a bathroom. She stepped inside, closing the door behind her.

The lack of decor continued from the hallway into the office. Walls were a muted tan without a single piece of artwork or family photos. A gray area rug covered the black floor and a huge black desk sat at the apex of the windows. Floor to ceiling bookshelves were to the left filled to the brim with books save for one space. Her eyes lingered on the sculpture of an African elephant showcased with a spotlight.

A fancy coffee maker with more buttons than a spaceship sat on top of the credenza. The room was a decorator's worst nightmare or soon-to-be wet dream.

She hung her head, having the sudden revelation that this commission might not work out. Her portraits were bright and colorful. They would stand out like a sore thumb in this room.

She slid her portfolio between the leather couch and end table that sat in the middle of the room before she hurried into the executive bathroom. Standing in front of the mirror, she scrunched her curls, wiped away streaked mascara, and straightened her suit. She cursed at the small red blotch forming under her eye from the cab ride and searched for the perfect concealer. Even as her imagination painted a picture of the executive to be fat, bald, and boring, she unbuttoned the top button, making her La Perla lace demi-bra visible from any angle. Her mind and actions were on automatic pilot. She dropped her hands, stood back from the mirror, and buttoned up her blouse, one button shy of the top. *No, not this time.* She hoped this was going to be her big break, but she fought the urge to use sex appeal to get the job. Her portfolio needed to speak for itself.

She came out of the bathroom and was drawn to the massive windows. Clouds hung like curtains as raindrops landed on the window, racing to the bottom. On a sunny day, the view over the Hudson must be magnificent. The scene was fit for a king overlooking his domain.

The door clicked shut. She held her breath but stayed facing the window.

"I find it rude when someone comes into my office unannounced." His deep voice held authority.

An icy chill hit her, and she turned around, staring at the handsome man before her, recognizing his eyes. His cool judging glance at her in the lobby didn't go unnoticed. "Maybe, I'm not just anyone," she retorted.

His eyes held a flicker of recognition. "Look, maybe I wasn't clear when I made my request. Are you even capable of presenting yourself to me properly—like on your knees?" He remained stoic with his hands stuffed in his pockets as a slight crease formed between his brows. Arrogance rolled off him. It became clear that the décor of the office reflected its owner.

Her heartbeat kicked up a notch. What crazy shit was he into and who did he think he was? Just because he was a CEO didn't mean women needed to be on their knees for him. The #metoo era had erased those days. *This commission may end before it even starts*. She assessed her new challenge. His steel gray suit fit him to perfection, the markings of high end and tailor made. His hand-painted tie was an interesting addition.

Her nails pressed into the palm of her hands as she rounded the couch and stood in front of him. "I rarely get on my knees for anyone. That has to be earned. Besides, I don't need to be on my knees to paint your portrait." She used a quiet voice to get his attention. Handling this type of man required a special touch.

His eyes widened slightly. The smallest wave of acknowledgement crossed his face and the crease left his brow. "I apologize." He rubbed his forehead. "I must have mixed up my appointments." His arm fell to his side and worry made a brief appearance.

She didn't even want to know. "God help the woman that disappoints you," she muttered under her breath.

"I'm sorry. I didn't catch that." He tilted his head and cupped his ear.

Inhaling deeply, she collected herself and extended her

hand. "Let's try this again. I'm Raquelle Luccenzo. I'm here to see if you want me to paint your portrait without ever being on my knees."

Her delicate artist's fingers disappeared in his handshake. Warmth traveled up her arm despite his hard demeanor. "I'm Michael Raines. You can call me Misha." His lips formed a tight line while his eyes bored into her.

She looked at him with curiosity.

"It's my mother's nickname for me. When I started playing ice hockey at a young age, the other kids thought it was cool and the name stuck."

Her hand slipped out of his. She needed to take control. The raging bull that had entered the room needed taming, but he didn't appear to be backing down.

"You're Antonio Luccenzo's daughter."

She swallowed the lump in her throat. "Yes. But that's where it begins and ends. My work is nothing like his if that's what you're expecting." She gripped her hands in front of her to the point of pain.

People around the world knew her papa's artwork from his portraits to his huge installations. She craved the spotlight and wanted to be the next big hit in the art community, out from under his constant shadow.

"Let's see if talent runs in the family," he said, assessing her.

She turned to get her portfolio. "I brought my portfolio for you to look at."

"Please." He motioned to the couch.

She sat down next to him, trying to get a better gauge of his mixed vibe. He opened the portfolio and spread it out over their laps. One page after another exhibited photographs of beautifully painted portraits with bright colors, intense eyes, and captured personalities. She enjoyed seeing her own work but was hypercritical with each piece, seeing mistakes or improvements that needed to be made in everyone of them. The hazards of being an artist. The term "an artist's work is never done" always applied to her.

She had followed in her famous father's footsteps and became a portrait artist. She shared that with her sisters, who were artists in their own right. They were all trust fund babies, but her papa expected her and her sisters to make something of themselves. She would do what it took to propel herself into the limelight of the art world.

Misha examined each portrait without a change in expression. "Beautiful. You seemed to have captured their essence. How do you do that? I know some of these people. You've allowed the viewer to see who they really are. I guess talent is in the gene pool. These are complex pieces with a lot of color," he said hesitantly. His look had a trace of understanding. If granted the commission, she would have to dive deep to depict him accurately.

"Thank you. Talent is one percent of what you have to have to make it. Perseverance is the other ninety-nine percent," she paused, locked in his stare. "To be honest, as I look around your office, I may not be the best choice for you. You may need something in a more classic style." Her hands gripped the edge of the couch underneath the portfolio, willing him to take a chance on her. This commission could be the avenue to greater things, allowing her to present it to the gallery that put her papa on the map. Misha would have to agree to let her borrow it for a gallery show and she would make it part of the contract. She wanted to be the next Luccenzo the art world would beg for and pay money to have added to their collection. Nothing would get in her way.

"So you noticed the lack of color." He sighed and looked straight ahead. "This is courtesy of my father. I despise it. It's not really me." His hand skimmed over the photograph of one of the male portraits. "It's upon his suggestion that I have my portrait done. I've put it off long enough. It's meant as a gift for him. Given your style, it would be a surprise as well."

His words said one thing, but the hardness never left his face. Silence fell between them. She couldn't look away and tried to ignore the flutter in her stomach. Of all the men she had been attracted to over the years, strong and dominant were not characteristics possessed by her lovers. She liked to stay in control of her liaisons.

He abruptly closed the portfolio and stood. "I'll be in touch. I have some other artists to interview. Thank you for your time."

Not so fast. "Could you at least show me where you plan to display it?" She stood up, craning her neck toward his face.

"This wall right here." His head tipped toward the empty wall next to the bathroom opposite his desk.

"You want to look at your own portrait?" She walked toward the blank space.

He stood behind her without touching her. The heat from his body came at her like waves off concrete on a hot summer day. His fresh spring scent hung in the air around her and she closed her eyes.

"Yes. A man should know who he is at all times." His voice had an edge.

She turned to him as his eyes focused on the vacant wall. They held a touch of sadness.

He looked down at her. "I'm afraid I have other meetings to attend to. Let me—"

The door burst open. A well-put-together redhead entered the room. "The portrait artist never showed. Do you want me to schedule another one?" She stood with one hand on the door and the other on her hip. "And I've got Victoria on line one. What do you want me to tell her?" She focused on Misha as if he was the only one in the room. *Oh, hell no.*

"Hi, I'm Raquelle, the portrait artist. I didn't catch your name." She walked around Misha and extended her hand.

The redhead stood there. "How did you get back here?" Her eyes narrowed.

"No one was at the front desk or at your desk." She pointed to the vacant desk on the other side of the door. "You should really look into tightening your security. Besides, I'm on a tight schedule today. I didn't have time to wait. It was nice meeting you…?" She waited.

"Audrey."

"Audrey." She gave her a big smile and turned to gather her portfolio.

His eyes twinkled absent of any smile. "Tell Victoria I'll be in touch. Thank you, Audrey." She continued to stand there. "You can go now." She left in a huff, closing the door behind her.

Raquelle held her portfolio like a shield for what was to come.

"Well done. Audrey is a force to be reckoned with." His face shut down and the mirth had disappeared.

"So am I. I look forward to hearing from you." She turned without a backward glance.

She clutched her portfolio, walking on shaky legs to the elevator. His ice with a touch of fire was messing with her mojo. She nodded and smiled, passing by several employees. They needed to know who she was because she would be back.

The elevator doors shut and she collapsed against the wall. Something in her spun tight and he was the weaver. She couldn't wait to find out what lurked inside Mr. Dark and Dangerous.

Chapter Two

SURROUNDED BY THE QUIET, Misha smiled, thinking about the hurricane that just left his office. Her brazen attitude combined with a raspy voice made his fingers itch. Even soaked to the bone with wet hair and hints of streaked makeup, she was ravishing. Dressed in designer clothes, she demanded attention, making it clear she would decide what man would grace her orbit. He didn't miss the hidden black lace bra following the curve of her breast underneath her wet shirt. He imagined what he wanted to do to her, for her, and with her. His reaction to her was unexpected but welcomed. After his recent failure in the relationship department, he had sworn off women.

He walked over to his coffee machine, settling on an espresso instead of his usual cappuccino with a spoonful of sugar. The duel of bitter and sweet seemed to be the theme of the day. Raquelle cornered the market on both. She stirred something in him he couldn't identify.

He reached into his drawer and smoothed his hands over the silk rope. Her curves would make an excellent canvas for his rope work, the art of Shibari. He had spent years looking for the chemistry that could only be found between an artist and a willing canvas. The experience of Shibari required trust few women were willing to give to any man, a trust that had to be earned on both sides.

The small black espresso cup did little to warm his hands while he examined the blank wall taunting him from across the office. All work and no play made his world colorless, lacking any real dimension. Only one man, his father, steered his life and seemed to have his destiny carved in stone. Every time he made a move outside the perimeter, his father pushed him back into place. This was his repentance for years ago, when he had defied his father's orders and refused to be the perfect son.

He almost choked on his own words: "a man should know himself at all times." Having been brought up in the greatest country on earth, his father groomed him to run the investment firm from day one. He was the youngest man ever to be named CEO of an investment firm in the financial community. But it came at a price. Early on, he and his father were at odds with the direction his life would take. Careful orchestration by his father left him empty, a puppet. His father questioned and countered his every move, making him a robot at his father's command. Misha wore the mask of someone who called all the shots, but the only control he owned was when he used the rope to tie masterpieces onto beautiful, wanting bodies.

"Victoria's on line two," Audrey broke in through the intercom.

"Thank you." He looked at the phone, willing the flashing light to stop but succumbing to the inevitable.

He picked up the receiver, dreading what waited on the other line. "Victoria, what can I do for you?"

"Well, for starters, it would be great if you would take my calls the first time." She exaggerated her sigh.

"What do you want? I'm very busy. Last time I checked, we were done." His tone came out harsher than he wanted it to, but they had done long ago. They were in the gray area of breaking up when one person tries to save the relationship.

"I know, but I think we should give it another try. I promise I can be what you want me to be. Practice makes perfect and I've been studying at the club with Ben. He said I'm coming along. Please," she whined. Her voice bled desperation.

God, not this again. Begging was so unbecoming.

"No. You'll never be what I need, truly need. It can't be faked, learned or practiced. You've got to want it, Victoria. It needs to be in your blood." He paused, waiting for the sniffling on the line to end.

The tears stopped long enough for her to respond in a small voice. "But I need you. I don't want to live without you. I love you. Isn't that enough?"

He sat down and leaned back in his high-back leather chair. "If I were anyone else, it would be enough. But I'm not and neither are you. You're not into being tied up. You have anxiety attacks. Shibari requires two people in the same place, space, and time. You have to be able to give yourself over to it." *Lord knows, she had given it her all.* "I know you tried and I give you a lot of credit. But I need that control in my life. I want a woman who understands what that means. True surrender is a connection of trust, give and take that happens when two people really connect." He had said it so many times, it could set it to music. "I'm sorry. This isn't what I want. You deserve someone who wants you exactly the way you are."

The whimpering continued, "Okay. I'll talk to you later," she said.

Did she hear a word he had said?

"Goodbye, Victoria."

The woman before Victoria was into the pain. She had evolved into wanting him to tie her so tight it hurt, leaving deep marks. She ended up moving to Europe with a man that could deal out her kind of torture. But he had his limits, everyone did. On the pain meter, he was at the low end. Tears weren't a turn-on for him.

"Your mother's here," Audrey said deadpan through the intercom.

The impressive start to the day was in a rapid decline. "Send her in." His mother, Yvonne, loved Victoria, the daughter she never had. She had ended up with only boys, Misha and his two brothers, Adrik and Kiril.

His mother swooshed in with several bags in each hand. The clock showed eleven a.m. and she had already hit Neiman Marcus, Chanel, and Versace.

"Misha, come say hello." She gave him her cheek.

He kissed his mother on both cheeks, offering the traditional three Russian kiss greeting. "I see you've been shopping again. I would think your closets would be full by now."

Her chestnut, pin-straight hair framed her surgically enhanced face, making her look years younger and somewhat plastic. "Don't be silly. You can never have too much." His father's unlimited funds fueled her need to own the season's latest designer outfits. The void in her life was bottomless.

"What are you up to today?" The answer would the same as he had gotten yesterday. He was torn between loving and protecting his mother and not wanting to be suffocated by her needs.

Over the years, he had watched his mother cry one too many times from loneliness due to an absent husband. She would refuse his comfort, pushing him away every time. As the years went on, she comforted herself in other ways and her dependence on him had grown.

"Oh, you know, lunch with the girls, a little tennis, and a massage." She looked at her red polished nails.

He could recite it in his sleep.

"Sounds like a full day." He watched her eyes dull.

She sat down on the couch and dropped her bags, avoiding eye contact. "Did you talk to Victoria?"

"Yes." He wouldn't give into her.

"Are you two getting back together?" She gripped her knees.

They must be conspiring to break him down. His father had taught him all he needed to know about how to be strong. "No. I have made my decision, Mother. I'm not changing my mind. I know you really like her, but it's not going to work between us." His blood boiled.

"I don't understand what the problem is. She's a good girl. She comes from a wealthy family, perfect for you. You're not getting any younger and I want grand babies." She put on a pouty face.

And there it was. This was about what she wanted. Another distraction from her empty life.

He let out a breath. "This is between me and Victoria. You need to let it go, please."

"Okay. I just don't see what the problem is." She popped up from the couch, grabbed her bags, and headed for the door. "*Moy malenkiy krolik*," she said, and blew him a kiss.

He smiled at her Russian nickname for him, my little bunny. When he was a little boy, she would always complain that he ran around just out of reach from her like the bunnies

15

in the garden. It seemed she had caught her bunny. Now he was always within her reach, driving him crazy.

"I'll talk to you soon," he said without looking up. His resentment had lain dormant for years.

He turned his attention to his daily agenda. Every day at eleven thirty he had a conference call with his father to discuss business. His father acted as a puppeteer behind the scenes. His latest suggestion involved putting CZR Investments on lockdown. He demanded a freeze on hiring and was more involved in the day-to-day operations, which was odd. His father preferred to stay out of the details end of the business, letting Misha handle daily problems. The atmosphere at the office was intense.

His father called him on a cell phone designated only for their business calls. He braced his forearms on the desk and clenched his hands together, taking a deep breath before pushing the talk button.

"*Otets*." He used the Russian word for father. His father preferred to speak in his native language.

"Misha, how are you and your mother doing?" He never failed to ask about his mother, even though he abandoned her years ago, choosing his business abroad over marriage and family.

"We're fine. What do I need to know for today?" He sighed.

"I've been talking to the other two families, Cavit and Zurich, we need to start the lockdown immediately. You need to be very aware of who is coming and going. We're vulnerable until we find the missing money and get this under control."

Cavit and Zurich were the two other families that owned CZR Investments. Zane Cavit and Andre Zurich were the COO and CFO of the company. Their fathers were Russian, but the sons were all born and raised in the United States. They had not visited Russia and had it ingrained in them to never speak Russian to anyone outside the three families. Their fathers wanted the company to have the look of being American through and through with no Russian ties. They were told it was better for business. Their fathers knew best. The financial community called it Czar Investments, but the laughter died when they looked at the numbers and success of the firm.

"Didn't Brock leave a digital trace on the money so he could find it? Our security team must be on top of it. I think the lockdown is a little extreme." It puzzled him why no one could find the missing money. Brock Walker, an up-and-coming investment broker, had swindled millions from their high-end clients over a couple of years.

His father's voice tensed. "We'll keep it locked down until we have it under control. I have the top guys working on this, but Brock was very good, maybe too good. That's what you get for hiring the best." He sighed. "We need to keep this under wraps. No one should know, and for some unknown reason the FTC and FBI aren't going public. We have paid all the clients in full, but we're on thin ice for funds. I won't be in the US for a while."

Something else was going on. He was used to his father coming and going, but his visits had been regular for many years. This announcement caught him off guard.

"Why?" he demanded.

"It doesn't matter why. You need to understand what needs to happen now. That is all." His tone was clip.

Misha stood up. "If you will not be here, then I will make the decisions. I'll meet with Zane and Andre and we'll keep it tight."

"You will do as you are told," his father roared. "Remember what happened last time you took over?"

"Are you ever going to let that go? It was ten years ago. I was young and stupid. How are you going to run things from Russia? When are you going to let me be a CEO? This is what I'm trained to do, at your demand, I might add." He ran shaky fingers through his hair.

"Soon, soon. Just do what I tell you to do and it will all work out. You're a good boy, a loyal son. I'm very grateful. We'll talk soon." His father hung up.

He slammed the phone down. Damn him. His father always had the last word, and Misha was at his father's mercy once again. The word *boy* rang in his ears. The day wasn't even half over and he was already exasperated. Misha would need to fight to break out of that shell.

His thoughts floated back to Raquelle. He first noticed her pieces across the room in a small gallery. She captured a person's character through brush strokes of vibrant color, introspection, and intense portrayal of the eyes. He was somewhat of an art expert, given that he had started his college career in art history. The firm also had an impressive collection kept on the premises under his direction. Her portrait of him would brighten to his dull life.

He decided to keep her a secret, wanting his portrait to be his surprise. The less his father knew, the better. Besides, she was a portrait artist, not a security risk.

But he might want her for more than her artistic talent.

From the minute Raquelle walked into his office, she had brought fire, color, and sun with her. She came in like a commander and took no prisoners. Her confidence oozed sex appeal, but underneath it he sensed softness, questioning whether she really wanted to be a leader. She would be a challenge like none other. He would want her to submit willingly to his rope. His fingers dug into the leather armrests. It had taken everything he had not to reach out and touch her.

The sun peeked through the clouds. He turned his chair around to face the windows. The rays streaked the sky, putting on a fantastic show in between the clouds.

Vibrance.

Warmth.

Dimension.

They had taken a back seat as he fought to take his own path. Since he had almost lost the company, his father required nothing of him except to take orders. But this had gone on long enough. His parents loved him dearly, but in unique ways. Lost without a sail, he wanted to steer the ship.

He turned back to his desk as the last ray of sun hit the empty space on the wall, making it white, a color without color. He made his decision.

"Hello, Raquelle? It's Misha." He waited for her to recognize him.

"Ah, Misha. How could I forget your unique name? What can I do for you?" She spoke in a business voice with a flirty edge.

"I'd like you to come by the office tomorrow. There's something I'd like to show you. I think you'll find it fascinating." He tried to keep the excitement of seeing her again out of his voice.

"It sounds intriguing. I'll come by first thing tomorrow morning."

He cut her off. "I need you here at noon. I'll see you then." He smiled to himself.

A beat of silence lingered on the other end. "Fine. See you then."

He had won this round, but he was in it to win it all.

Chapter Three

MISHA WENT for his daily run and a couple boxing rounds before making it into work. Skipping the espresso, he made cappuccino with sugar. He didn't need to add extra caffeine to his already amped up state of mind. Many times during the night, Raquelle had entered his thoughts with her seductive blue eyes, leaving him with pent-up energy and frustration. She sparked his curiosity and he couldn't wait to see her reaction to what he wanted to show her.

The morning conference call with his father repeated like a broken record. This song and dance was getting old. His father barked the orders, and as the obedient son, Misha followed them. Resentment reared its head. The thought of never getting out from under his father clung to him. Life was a series of calculated maneuvers. Early on, his father had decided he should go to Wharton at the University of Pennsylvania to get his master's degree in business, but he was tired of being hemmed into his father's vision for him. He wanted to spread his wings and fly, but waited for the right opportunity.

He paced. How much more of his father's manipulation could he tolerate? When he noticed the imprint of his shoes on the gray shag rug, he stopped to acknowledge the irony. He didn't want to follow in his father's footsteps; he vowed to leave his own marks on his life. Raquelle would be a first step.

He had made all the arrangements for her appointment. When his portrait was finished, he thought he might redecorate his entire office around the colors of the portrait. But Raquelle had one more test to pass.

Audrey peered around the door. "Your twelve o'clock is here. Do you want me to let her in?"

"Yes, thank you." He felt jittery, like a high school teen waiting for his crush to show up at school. He needed to shut down the absurdity. This woman couldn't possibly have this effect on him after one meeting.

Raquelle walked in dressed to the nines. A tight-knit designer dress hugged her body along with over-the-knee high-heeled boots. His breath caught in his chest. She had more curves than the Autobahn. He hoped she wasn't another high-maintenance woman. His mother was all he could handle.

"Hi." She plopped her enormous bag onto the couch.

He sipped his coffee. "Will you be spending the night?"

"I have to be prepared for any situation. Oh, look. It has a sense of humor," she replied with half a smile, "unlike yesterday."

"Like getting caught in the rain?" He stepped closer and held her gaze. "Tread carefully, Ms. Luccenzo. You don't have the job yet." He held back a smile. "You should be kissing my ass. This commission could catapult you into all the right places."

She took a step toward him without flinching, holding her arms at her sides. "I'm not kissing your ass or anyone else's." She paused. "The rain was an unfortunate event out of my control." Regret flashed across her face. "Just to be clear, I can handle anything you throw my way."

"You seem to handle being out of control well. I like a woman who stands her ground. Let's see what you can handle." His words held so much more meaning as his fingers curled on their own.

"Bring it. I brought kneepads for both of us, just in case. I wouldn't want you to miss out on the fun." She smirked.

He couldn't resist a smile. This woman gave as good as she got, if not better. "Well played. You'll be happy to know you won't need your kneepads, at least not today. Please, have a seat. I would love your opinion on my collection. But you need to sign an NDA, nondisclosure agreement, before you can see it." He grabbed the document she needed to sign.

She frowned. "What kind of collection and what am I signing?"

Good. She was curious yet cautious. "Our employees and anyone who views our collection must sign an agreement prohibiting them from disclosing the secrets behind our closed doors. I don't agree with it, but who am I to argue?" There he was, bending like a young tree in a windstorm. No one knew it was his father who didn't want the collection shown to the world.

"Aren't you the CEO?" Her brows hit her hairline.

"Yes, but this comes from the partners." She needed to stop questioning him.

He sat down next to her and slid the document over the coffee table. She held it up, scanned it, and signed. "Looks pretty standard. You've piqued my curiosity," she said with a gleam in her eye.

He had to ask, "Seems odd that you would be familiar with a nondisclosure agreement."

She cleared her throat. "I've worked on nudes that were very private."

"Ah." He turned toward her as his knee touched hers. "Have *you* ever been painted in the nude?" An odd, pained look came across her face. He couldn't guess why she would have such a reaction to being painted in the nude. She was beautiful and seemed comfortable in her own skin.

"Where's the collection you wanted me to see?" She stood up and moved toward the door.

"Allow me to lead the way." He opened the door.

Once they were in the hallway, he offered his arm. He was close enough to see how blue her eyes were as they held each other's stare for a beat too long. Something flashed between them before she turned away. He hadn't that kind of spark with a woman in a very long time.

They housed the private collection on the other side of the building. Two huge, engraved wooden doors imported from an old Italian church sealed the entrance to the room.

"This is our gallery of artwork that has been collected over many generations. I wanted your thoughts on the arrangement. We're in the process of reconfiguring some pieces and I'd like to know what you think about where they should go."

They entered an enormous room linked to several smaller rooms. In the middle of the vast space were several places to sit: recliners, hammocks, rope chairs, and wood benches.

"Why do you have these types of chairs in here?" Her fingers grazed the rope on the hammock.

Interesting.

"We like to encourage our employees to come in here and sit comfortably to enjoy the art. What's the point of having all

23

this if not to be viewed by at least the people that work here?"

Her eyes went wide as she saw the first piece. "That makes sense," she whispered. "Wow. This is quite a collection. Unbelievable, actually."

She let go of his arm and drifted toward the closest painting. "We may be here awhile."

He smiled to himself. *Jackpot.* "You're free to come back anytime. I made lunch reservations for us. I hope you're available."

She turned to look at him over her shoulder. "I'm not sure if I should be flattered that you took time to make plans or offended that you did it without asking me first."

"I hope you're flattered. But right now, your time is mine. I wanted to get to know you a bit better before I made my final decision." He was interested in what made her tick.

She turned to face him, gripping her hands behind her back. Without knowing it, she had already given him her answer, leaving herself open to him. The art of Shibari had made him a master at reading body language.

"Possessive much? Here I thought you had already made your decision." She turned away without smiling.

He nodded. "Please, look around and tell me your thoughts." His hand swept across him.

She stood in front of one of his favorites. Her fingers were inches from the thick dried paint, but she stopped before touching it. "Is this what I think it is? No wonder you wanted me to sign a NDA."

"What do you think it is?" His hands gripped together.

She turned to him. "How is it possible? This was lost in an Allied attack during World War II. It's *Painter on His Way to Work,*" she said.

He stood next to her. "Bravo. You know your art history."

"I'm not just a pretty face." That had become abundantly clear.

"It was buried in ash due to a fire in Germany but has been restored. This van Gogh is a secret. No one knows it's here. That's my fa—the idea. I would like to share these paintings with the world. They deserve to be seen. But for now, they'll stay a secret." It was another bone of contention between him and his father.

She pivoted to take in the view of the rest of the room. "You have a lot of pieces here that were lost or went missing during the war. How did you acquire them?"

"The partners of the firm love art. How they got them, I don't have a clue. They didn't tell me." The Russians had taken many artifacts from Germany during the war. His father was the sole provider of them, bringing items in from Russia over the years. Their love of art seemed to be the only gene they shared from the family lineage. But the element of secrecy surrounding his father and the two other partners always made him uncomfortable.

She rushed across the room and gasped. "This is the Raphael, *Portrait of a Young Man*. It's still listed as missing. It's magnificent. I don't mean to second-guess your curator. But it's placed wrong. It shouldn't go next to the Courbet but next to the Bellini." She continued to walk toward the back of the room and stopped at the van Dyck. "Now, this is one of my favorites, mostly because it reminds me of the use of light you find in a Caravaggio." She spun toward him with a smile stretched from ear to ear. "I aspire to paint like him."

"You don't say. The use of light in your portraits is focused and refined and now I know why."

She stared at him for a bit. "You know your stuff when it comes to art."

He smiled while his heart broke. His first passion had

always been art history. His father had decided otherwise, leading them down a path into constant battle.

He watched with interest as she made her way around all three rooms, commenting along the way. She acted like a kid in a candy store, the same way he felt every time he came in here. He had purposely rearranged the paintings in the gallery to see what she would do with them.

She whirled around from room to room for an hour, making suggestions and commentary on every piece in the collection as to where it should be placed in the gallery given the light and location.

"You must be famished." He figured she had worked up an appetite.

"I'm always hungry." She looked at him sheepishly.

"God, that's refreshing. Most women deny that food even exists."

"I'm not a stick figure." Her cheeks pinked.

"Thank God for small favors. I like my women with a little meat on them."

"So first I'm kissing your ass and now I'm your woman. Are we speed dating?" She slid her arm through his and looked up at him. "Where to, Speed Racer?"

"Touché. I picked out a little place down the block. I hope you're up for a short walk in your stilts." His thoughts traveled to what she would look like in only her stilts.

"The stilts make my legs look fantastic, wouldn't you agree? They give my legs a good workout."

He hummed without giving her an answer.

She held onto his arm as they walked down the street. He stopped and looked at the dog coming toward them.

"Let's move to the other side of the street." He pulled her with him.

She looked at him with questioning eyes. "You don't like dogs?."

"Something like that." He didn't care to elaborate.

The small upscale restaurant was hidden down an alley to keep it anonymous for private guests. The maître d' showed them to a table tucked in the back corner. She sat down and opened her menu, blocking his view. After a few minutes of no talking, he used his finger to pull down her menu.

"Is everything okay? You're suddenly very quiet."

"Those pieces in your collection need to be viewed by the world and not kept hidden." The look in her eyes told him about her love for shared art.

"I agree. But this is the way it is for now." He could feel his temperature rise. This was another of his requests that his father had not acknowledged.

"Well, tell whoever is in charge why the world needs to see them." Her words stung.

He needed to change tack. This conversation would go nowhere fast. He didn't want to reveal the lack of power he had in his own life.

"You have an incredible eye for art. Where did you learn so much?" His eyes scanned the words on the menu without reading them. He knew what he wanted.

She sighed. "My father. He would take me to the Met every Sunday from the time I was very young. We would go to a different wing each time and discuss everything from lighting to brushstrokes." Tears formed in her eyes as she blew out a breath.

He put down his menu. "What's wrong?"

She took a sip of water. "I lost him recently. I hadn't thought of those wonderful memories in a long time."

"I heard he passed suddenly. It must have been awful. As

much as I go head to head with my father, I can't imagine losing him." His voice softened.

"To top it off, we learned he was poisoned, probably by someone close to him. My father was never home, so it had to be someone he traveled with on tour. I'm sorry. That was TMI you didn't need." She gave him a small glimpse behind the curtain of what made her so tough. Absentee fathers were another common denominator.

"It's fine. I don't remember those details being made public. I'm sorry for your loss." He had a great deal of respect for her father, along with everyone in the art community. The information about Antonio being poisoned surprised and shocked him. He wanted to ask if the police were involved but didn't want to pry or add to her agony.

She looked up at him. "I know you're only considering me for this project because my father was a world-renowned artist. But I'm not my father. I'm a talented artist in my own right and I want to be recognized for what I do, not who I'm related to." She swiped away tears with the back of her hand.

"I know who your father is—was, but that's not why I'm hiring you. Your work is unique. Anyone can see that. I think you're talented and deserve a shot."

"Wait. Did you just say *hiring*?" Her eyes widened.

"Yes, I did. Congratulations. I can't wait to see what you do with my face, so to speak." He took the extra security card from his pocket and slid it across the table. "This is your security card to use my private elevator. It's the only way to get in and out of CZR."

"Thank you. This means so much to me. Let's celebrate." Her face lit up from the inside. He wanted to seal her glow in a bottle so he could place it on his desk to bask in every day.

"My thoughts exactly. Will you be having the salad with

four pieces of lettuce instead of three?" He straightened the silverware.

"Hell no. I'm having the filet mignon, baked potato, and green beans. My workouts require protein. I need to load up."

He laughed out loud. His hardened heart was thawing. They talked for the next hour about everything from art to workout routines. She was a Tiger lily, a mix of tender and strong. The professional artist impressed him, but it was the hidden temptress in her that kept his curiosity stoked. As she spoke about his prized collection, he became distracted by his thoughts of wrapping the silken black rope around her voluptuous body.

He walked her back and they said their goodbyes.

He sank into his leather chair overlooking his monochromatic office. He was in the prime of his life, but nothing clicked for him. His attention was split between a needy mother and an overbearing father who thwarted his vision to propel his family's investment firm into a new era. His brothers were the smart ones, getting a top education and fleeing to the West Coast. Animosity lived just below the surface, but he was afraid to unleash the beast within.

"Hey, there's the king." Luc, his best friend from college, walked into his office unannounced, charming his way past Audrey no doubt. "Who's the hottie?"

"What?"

Luc gave him a puzzled look. "Your new hook-up I saw leaving here."

"She's not a new hook-up. Raquelle is the artist I hired to do my portrait for daddy dearest."

"Well, she's easy on the eyes, bro. I'm surprised you didn't hire someone well known." Luc held his stare. "You know, in all the years that I've known you, I've never met your father."

"You're not missing much. As far as Raquelle goes, I really like her work and wanted to support an up-and-coming artist. Believe me, talent runs in her genes. She can hold her own and then some. By the way, let's keep this between us. I don't want my father to get wind of this. It's a small world." He shuffled papers on his desk.

Luc smiled, "You always liked an enjoyable challenge. She's nothing like Victoria, I assume. Mums the word."

Raquelle had stood up to him plenty in the short time they had been together, unlike Victoria. He wasn't going to get away with much.

"Victoria was my mother's doing. She means well. As much as I tried, we weren't a match. She didn't have what I needed." His parents were pushing his limits and one day he was going to explode.

"Let's hope your mom doesn't catch onto your dark side, Shibari. She'd probably flip her shit." Luc laughed.

"Well, I need something in my life that is just for me and no one else. I want to find a partner who understands the beauty of the rope." His desire to find that connection drove his decisions when it came to women. Most were willing, but few kept his attention.

"You better keep Raquelle to doing her artwork. From the looks and sound of it, she'll never agree to being tied up."

Misha leaned back in his chair. "You'd be surprised. Sometimes the women who seem like they have it all together are the ones looking to hand it over to someone else. Then they can really let go."

"True. I've come across a few in my time. Speaking of which, how about we hit the club tonight? I could blow off a little steam. Pick you up around nine." Luc turned to leave.

"For a bank guy, you sure are bossy." Luc worked as an investment banker for one of the top banks in the world.

"That's what they tell me. Who do you think is carrying your ass? Banks call all the shots. See you later, sport."

Luc had a point. All of their portfolios relied on bank decisions, investments, and the market. Global markets demanded they all be intertwined without clear division. It reminded him of a dangerous game of roulette: any color, any number. His earlier conversation with his father rattled in his brain. CZR was in trouble, and his father hid more answers than he let on. Those answers needed to be unearthed before the ship went down.

Chapter Four

RAQUELLE STOOD in the middle of her studio, her sanctuary, and did a happy dance. Titus, her three-year-old pit bull, joined in barking and wagging his tail. This could be her breakthrough. In the highly competitive business of painting portraits, she hoped her unique style spoke for itself. She had made strides with some smaller gallery shows, but nothing at this level. People were looking for a unique artist, a way to stand out from the crowd with their acquisitions. She needed to get in front of the right people at the right time. Was this her moment? She could almost feel it in her bones.

Her Tribeca studio had a wall of windows overlooking the Hudson, giving her plenty of light. The back brick wall showed off the original exposed wood posts dating back to the building's factory days. A daybed tucked away in the corner was for her many late nights driven by her work. She couldn't stop once she started working, a genetic trait passed on from her father and the curse of being an artist. He had passed away only a few months ago, but his death still devastated her family. The cryptic message he had left for her sister Leigha was the beginning of the end of the sheltered life they had once known.

His last words were, "I tried to protect you from him the only way I knew how. He will come for you. Beware."

Her father's warning came to fruition. Alek Romanowksi, head of one of the most powerful Russian mobs, was Leigha's biological father. Their mama had an affair while Papa was away at one of his many international art shows. According to Mama, Alek and Papa had been the best of friends until Leigha's blond hair, light eyes, and fair skin marked the betrayal. Alek never saw his daughter again face to face. All three sisters had their own issues with Papa, but Leigha's topped them all. He had shunned her early on without explanation—until the truth came out.

However, Raquelle was Papa's shining star. She had showed a gift for painting portraits at a very young age. Paintbrushes seemed to be an extension of her being. She could easily become absorbed into a piece, finding that zone, mixing oil paints and strokes as everything fell into place. Papa doted on her, but he also put extreme pressure on her to perform many times to the breaking point, leaving her drained emotionally and psychologically.

Then there was Bernardo, Papa's right-hand man. Fear ran through her at the thought of him. She shook her head to rid her mind of the black memories. Her time with Bernardo sliced like a double edged-sword. He was her first love, and he was older, talented, and passionate. She had been young, but not so naïve. When her father had found out about the two of them, his words cut deep, shredding her self-confidence. Bernardo occupied a permanent residence in her head that cast a dark shadow on all the possible good in her life. After all these years, her choices still haunted her.

The sun appeared in the late afternoon sky. Rays streaked through the windows, spotlighting her oil portraits. The colors brightened, bringing the images to life. They were on the larger side, some taking up half a wall. She was working on three different ones: a wealthy woman in Greenwich, Connecticut, an accountant in Scarsdale, New York, and two children from Newport, Rhode Island.

Her favorite portraits were of children. Smoothing her finger across the wet oil, she blurred a line between the child's jawline and the background. She brought their innocence to life through dabs of paints, creating a sparkle in their eyes and a minor stroke for the mirth in their smiles. One stroke could make or break a piece.

A chill came over her as she pulled her sweater closer to her. Apprehension hung in the back of her mind as she thought of going to her father's studio to clean it out. The police had completed their investigation, and she and her sisters had put it off long enough. His warehouse stored more than his works, it stored their memories. Some good, some bad. Those memories had rocked her world on so many levels she couldn't keep up. But right now, she needed to celebrate.

She reached for her cell phone to call the two anchors she wouldn't live without.

"Hi, Lei, I'm going to get Mara on conference call." She pressed two buttons on her phone. "Hi Mar, Lei's here too. I have big news I want to share. Is everyone available for dinner tonight?"

"What news?" Leigha sounded weary.

"It's not bad news. It's good news for a change. Mara, can you make dinner, please? You know you're the best cook ever."

"Sure. Am I making your favorite?"

"Of course! Portobello ravioli for everyone. Thank you. I'll see you soon." She clicked off. They always let her be the diva.

Across the room sat her one of many stuffed animal versions of Babar. As a child she had read all the books about the orphan elephant. She remembered the roller coaster of emotions. Tears came when he lost his mother and happiness when he went back to the jungle to be crowned king. She held the elephant to her, burying her nose in his fur, hoping to smell the slight scent of baby shampoo. As time ticked on, the scent seemed to evaporate much like her childhood faded in the rearview mirror.

Elephants were mythical creatures with strong family bonds. The Luccenzo sisters were bonded through thick and thin, but they needed closure. Maybe their father's studio held some answers. Something told her there was more to come before they would find their ending.

She made it uptown to the west side of Central Park to Mara's apartment with Titus in tow. For the most part, Mara lived with her Scottish boyfriend Mac, even though she wouldn't admit it. Mac, an ex-MI6 spy, had saved her sister's life in Mexico when her not-so-dead husband, Brock, reappeared and kidnapped her. The Russian mob had taken care of Brock. The event shook them to their core, bringing them closer together than ever before. Mac had become part of the family, saving their asses on a few other occasions.

Dean opened the door to let her in. He was Leigha's Australian squeeze there for her through everything. For as tough as Leigha was, Dean had proved to be tougher, taking a bullet for her in a shoot-out with the Russians.

"Hey, BP, how are you?" It was short for Bulletproof, Raquelle's nickname for him.

"Hey, firecracker. I'm doing well. I hear you have some big news." He kissed her on the cheek.

Mara and Mac stood to greet her. Dean came up behind Leigha, hugging her to his chest.

Raquelle clenched her fists, buried in her pockets. Loneliness curled around her. She wasn't prepared for the emotions that came with being the fifth wheel in the room. It had never bothered her before. She couldn't pinpoint what had changed lately.

Her form of solace came from one-night stands. She had too much going on to be tied down to one man and commit to the difficulties of a relationship. Men saw her as an object to be worshipped, but she kept them at arm's length. Why did being in the company of everyone she loved make her feel so sad?

"I hope you've put heart and soul into that ravioli because I've been thinking about it all day." She shrugged her coat off and threw it onto a chair, making her way to the kitchen with a bottle of vodka in hand. Titus wrestled with Mac and Dean, who both adored him.

"Of course it has heart and soul. This takes awhile to make. I can't just whip it up. Homemade means from scratch." Mara said, leaning against the counter with her hand on her hip.

"I helped too, Leannan. I made tiramisu." Mac used the Gaelic name for sweetheart and wandered into the kitchen.

"But we all know that wasn't from scratch." Dean patted Mac on the back. Titus panted behind them, looking for his water dish. One bark let everyone know it was empty. Dean filled the bowl.

"Well, let's stop talking about it and eat." Leigha ended the conversation.

The table fell quiet as every bite was treated as a delicacy.

Moans and hums were the only sounds in the dining room. Mara's entrée should have been in a five-star restaurant. She had inherited Mama's flare for cooking. Raquelle could barely boil an egg and had all the local takeout places on speed dial. But she was choosy. A girl had to watch her figure. Only balanced organic meals for her.

She and Leigha cleared the table and made coffee.

"So, what's your big news?" Mara asked.

She sat on the couch as Titus curled up next to her with his head in her lap and fell asleep. "Well, I've landed a huge commission. The CEO of CZR Investments wants me to do his portrait. He requested I paint in his office, which is a little cray-cray. But hey, I'm up for it. This could really launch my career."

"I'm so excited for you, Raq." Leigha jumped up to give her a big hug. "Did you get a chance to tell mama?"

"Of course. She was my first call. She said she was busy otherwise she would have been here."

She looked over Leigha's shoulder to see Dean and Mac in a stare-off with some secret unspoken agenda. They were both ex-spies working for MBK Global Security and looking into Papa's death.

Mara came from the other side to give her a hug. Both Mac and Dean turned to look at her.

Dean got up first to give her a hug. "That's great, Raq."

"I'd say it's friggin' fantastic." Mac beamed.

"Do I even want to know what's going on between you two?"

Mara and Leigha frowned.

Mac spoke. "Well, you said CZR Investments, right?"

"Yeah, why?" She was afraid this was going to lead to no good.

"I think what he's trying to say is let's have dessert first and talk later." Dean gave Mac a hard stare and pulled him into the kitchen.

"What's going on?" Mara questioned.

"I don't know yet. But those two are up to something, and I know I'm not going to like it. I think it has something to do with your late husband's dealings at CZR." Raquelle was onto the boys.

Mara sighed. "Don't remind me of Brock or that place. It was always so cold. What's the CEO like, anyway? I never met him."

"Cold would be an appropriate description. He's stoic on the outside with a slight sense of humor. I'm not sure what's on the inside yet. He's definitely a man in control. His office has no color. I found it interesting he wanted to see me. My portrait of him would be a direct contrast to his office. Let's just say color is not his thing."

"I think we all know control can be an illusion. He sounds mysterious. Maybe you need a little challenge in your love life." Leigha grinned.

"What? Saving your asses isn't enough of a challenge?" Raquelle joked.

Mara replied, "Ha ha, you didn't save our asses."

"I helped. That counts."

"Not for nothing, but you could use a change up in the love department. You always pick those beta men for all the wrong reasons and then wonder why you're not satisfied." Mara's insight hit a little too close to home.

"Yeah, well, it makes things a lot easier." Raquelle nodded in the direction of the kitchen. "What do you think those two bird brains are up to?"

"Hey, watch it. That is my bird *with* a brain." Leigha crossed her arms over her chest. "I don't know. But it's never good." She admitted.

From the kitchen, their voices raised during an argument followed by hushed tones. Raquelle guessed they weren't arguing over the dessert.

Chapter Five

"ARE YOU KIDDING ME? I just got the commission that could thrust me into the spotlight and you want me to be a spy? No. Fucking. Way." Raquelle couldn't believe they would even suggest it.

"Listen to me. I'm not asking you to spy. I need you to get close to him. Every guy we send in there for an interview never gets the job. It's like the black hole for us. The FBI isn't faring much better. It's like CZR knows we're coming. I need you to listen to what's going on in his office. You may pick up on something." Mac's voice was tight.

"Obviously, he's not going to say anything in front of me. He's not stupid. Besides, my focus is going to be on sketching and painting." She had been on this wild ride with these two before. Once in Mexico and again with Leigha's mob boss father. She didn't want a third go at it.

Dean chimed in. "Hey, you can work your magic. Maybe he'll get comfortable and loosen up, forget that you're even there. It's worth a shot. We've got to find out what's going on in that company."

"First off, let me be clear. I'm there to work as a professional, not to get a date. Although, he is really easy on the eyes. Second, how could you even suggest that he would forget I'm there? I'm pretty sure that would be impossible." She gave him her one-cocked-eyebrow stare. She would not blow this chance at success. Her other clients weren't at Misha's level. Not in looks or stature. She needed to prove to herself that she could make it without sleeping with the customer. Her goal was to be accepted into the Auroto Gallery with her own work.

Mac stood with his hands on his hips, eyeing her. "Just think about it. We're not out of the woods yet. Alek is being monitored, but so far we haven't come up with anything. We need to find out where Brock put the money. I think the leads will trace back to the Russians."

"I'll think about it. I gotta go." She gave each of them a hug and a kiss. "Thanks for dinner, Mara. It was wonderful, as always."

She hooked Titus to his leash and made a beeline for the door, eager to get to her next location and escape the lovebirds. Pushing one button on her phone was all she needed to make her connection.

"Hi, Raq. What's up?" Her BFF, Briella, sounded bored.

They had known each other since kindergarten when Raquelle wiped finger paint on Brie's cheek. They had both giggled and had a paint war, forging a bond and a long history of getting into trouble together. Once Raquelle's popularity grew, she had hired Brie to be her right-hand woman to manage the business end of things while Raquelle created works of art.

"Hey, Brie. I got big news and I thought we could celebrate. I want to go high-end and party hard."

"Of course you want to go high-end, what else is new? If

you want to go to Club 24K, I have to get the pass from Logan."

Logan was the lead singer for the band YRN'TU and Brie's boyfriend for the last year. His band was making a big splash in the music industry and he had an in at all the hottest clubs in the city.

"Sounds good to me. I'm going back to my place to get dressed and then pick you up. I'll get us a car for tonight. Ciao!"

Sitting in the back of a cab to her Upper East Side apartment, she contemplated Mac and Dean's request. They had caught her and her sisters up in something out of International Spies 'R' Us. The drama was wearing on all of them, including Mac and Dean. She wanted to go back to leading a normal life. There were too many secrets, too many coverups, and too many lies.

The taxi pulled up to her building and the doorman opened her door to greet her. Titus jumped out, waiting for the treat the doorman always had for him. Of course there were tricks to be performed in order to get the treats, such as *sit* and *shake*. Out of the corner of her eye she noticed a man leaning against a mailbox, smoking a cigarette and staring at her. The hairs on her arm stood on end. She looked at him long enough to remember his face. Having a photographic memory had its benefits.

When Titus finished his tricks, she grabbed him, ran up the stairs, and slipped into the elevator. She clutched the front of her jacket and remembered to breathe. Was she being followed? If so, by whom and why? By the time she made it up to her floor, she had shaken it off as a fluke. The last couple of months of spy games had led to an overactive imagination. Besides, she had the ultimate weapon: Titus.

Titus was brown with a white stripe down his face, a

common coloring for pit bulls. The two of them had been inseparable ever since she rescued him as a puppy. He was always by her side as her muse. But tonight she needed to relax and unwind, and the perfect dress was waiting for her.

Her clothes fell to the floor and she wiggled into her bandage dress. The electric blue color made her eyes pop. The dress bound every curve of her body, leaving nothing to the imagination. Large pieces of Spandex material crossed in the front and back, leaving the sides partly open. Her Pilates classes had paid off. She hoped to catch herself a little something as a distraction from her over-caffeinated life.

She curled her hair and reapplied her makeup, wanting to be the center of the room. There was no stopping her unless Brie came to the rescue when she asked.

The car she'd ordered waited curbside. As she slid into the backseat, she noticed the same man leaning against the pole, smoking a cigarette. She watched him behind the reflective windows as he turned and hurried away in the opposite direction. A chill ran through her. Damn it. She didn't need this shit. Pressing the button for the partition to slide down, she rattled off Brie's address.

The partition went back up, and she laid her head back on the seat. The last year had been a mess for her and her sisters. She didn't know which way to turn. This wasn't the life normal people led. The hollow space inside her had a voice that wouldn't shut up. Leigha and Mara had found the loves of their lives, and she was alone. At this point, she wasn't sure she knew how to be in a relationship with anyone of the opposite sex.

Her one-night stands were convenient, but they were getting old. They came without remorse or emotion, just a release. She had spent her life watching her mother's loneliness wrap her like a shawl with thorns, dedicated to a man who married to his mistress: his artwork. No wonder her mama's attention had strayed to Alek.

But in the end, Raquelle had become as driven as her father, sometimes staying up for twenty-four hours straight, obsessed with a creative vision that made her blood flow. There were the moments at three a.m. when she popped out of bed with an idea for her next project. She understood her father because she lived his life. But she wasn't sure that's all she wanted for *her* life.

The car came to a slow stop and Brie threw open the door. "What's shakin', bacon?"

"Really? I don't think I've heard that since elementary school." Peace flowed over her when she was with Brie. They always had each other's backs.

"Hey, a blast from the past." Her friend giggled, pushing her ebony hair over the shoulder of her snug little black dress.

"What's around your neck? I noticed that you've been wearing it a lot lately."

Brie's fingers toyed with the diamond hanging from the end of the short graphite colored chain and bit her lower lip. "Logan gave it to me as a symbol of how we belong to one another."

Raquelle could have sworn Brie was holding her breath. "And? Because I know there's more to this story. It's me, remember?"

Brie cast her eyes to her lap. "I haven't told you because you'll think I've lost it." She raised her eyes. "Logan likes to do things a little . . . differently in the bedroom."

"Like what?" Curiosity baited her.

"He ties me up, among other things."

Silence dropped like a heavy curtain as the noise from the street faded away.

"Please tell me he's not hurting you. This sounds an awful lot like BDSM gone bad. Don't let him hurt you, not after everything you've been through." She tried to fight back her anger.

Brie grabbed her hands. "No! My God. No. It's just the opposite. It's empowering. He's an incredible man and takes care of me all the time."

Raquelle scanned Brie's face for any lies, but only found raw honesty.

The car stopped and the door opened before Raquelle heard the rest of the story. "Welcome to 24K." The bouncer, dressed like a secret service agent, offered his hand.

Brie took his hand and stepped out of the car.

"We're not done with this." Raquelle held Brie's elbow as they made their way to the door. The club was known for entertaining celebrities. A paparazzo jumped out to take their photo.

Brie put up her hand.

The man behind the camera said, "Are you Logan McGrady's girlfriend?"

"No." Brie dragged Raquelle through the doors.

"I guess you're not dealing with the whole celebrity girlfriend thing too well."

Brie gave her a sideways glance. "Everyone thinks it's so great. Honestly, it's a pain in the ass."

Briella's key card got them past security and through the door to the VIP lounge. An escalator took them upstairs to the exclusive rooms. Drinks were served in Waterford crystal and the decor was tastefully done in gold, with accents of silver, black, red, or blue for individual rooms. A window overlooked a smoky dance floor in the center. One touch of a button and the window turned to a privacy shield where guests could look out, but no one could look in.

"You called ahead and picked my favorite colors, red and gold. You know how to make a girl feel special." Raquelle gave her a playful smile and batted her eyes.

Briella moved to the bar. "I think we need a drink. What was that vodka you liked? Elite something."

"Elit Stolichnaya, my new favorite since my mama introduced it to me." She gazed out the window, searching for her next conquest.

"Is it good?"

She turned to see Briella pouring the clear poison of choice into two crystal tumblers. The LED lights above the bar lit the crystal, making them sparkle.

"Smooth doesn't even begin to describe it. Wait till you try it."

She took the glass from Brie and slugged it back, relishing the burn down her throat. She wanted it to scorch away the frustration of a dead father who had left behind a slew of crap for everyone. Loving thoughts were entangled with the hate. The combination proved to be toxic.

Coughing and gagging sounds came from the other side of the couch.

"Holy shit. This is like grain alcohol, only a lot smoother." Brie's features softened as she recovered from her drink. "You have that look. What's going on?"

"I got a commission today and not a little one either. Unfortunately, he's the CEO of Brock's finance group. He's incredibly handsome, witty, and smart but definitely has a cold, dark side. I have got to keep my shit together on this one. I'm not a kid anymore. It's time to play with the grown-ups. I have to force myself not to sleep with him. This needs to be completely professional. You may get odd phones calls to talk me down from ruining it all."

"Do you remember the time in fourth grade when you

made some portraits of some of your classmates and then charged them for it? You dressed in a skirt and blouse and stuffed the toes of your mom's heels with tissue to fit in them."

Raquelle had forgotten about how empowered she had felt, taking charge of the sale of her artwork.

Brie continued, "You were already practicing to be a professional. No one can take that away from you. Not your father and not Bernardo. You need to hold on to that. Handsome, sexy man be damned."

Briella got up and walked toward her. "Come here." Raquelle stood and walked into her arms. "You're going to do great. Maybe he has a tiny penis, that might help you resist." She laughed.

Raquelle laughed and swatted her on the shoulder. "Only you would think of that. I checked out his large hands, so no dice on that one. But it might help to imagine it small. Let's head downstairs, dance, and get drunk."

She grabbed Brie's hand and led them downstairs. A wave of bodies covered the floor and moved to the beat of the music. She closed her eyes, allowing herself the illusion of disappearing into the smoke filled room. Brie's words interrupted her escape.

"I'm taken, but thanks." Brie battled with a guy who had snaked his arms around her waist.

Raquelle moved in, curling her finger for him to come to her. Her arms wrapped around his neck and they danced, saving Brie from the struggle. Maybe the stranger would be her catch for the night. He wasn't Misha, but he'd do just fine. Wait. She shouldn't be thinking about Misha. God, she was in trouble if her mind was going in his direction.

The stranger leaned in closer and yelled over the music, "You want a drink?"

She nodded her head and the guy left.

Briella walked over and put her arms around her. "Thank you. I don't know what I would do without you sometimes."

"Probably be really bored." She smiled and pulled her childhood friend in for a warm hug. When her eyes fluttered open, she saw him. Perhaps her vision was playing tricks on her through the smoke. But there was no mistaking the mountain of a man standing at the bar. Misha's tie was undone. "I'll meet you up top."

She pushed her way through a sea of people to get to him, never losing eye contact. He locked on to her eyes as he lifted his drink to his lips. Her forward motion halted when someone grabbed her arm and swung her around.

"Hey, where are you off to? Thought we were going to get a drink?" His fingers dug into her arm.

She tried to pull herself free as he tightened his grip. "Let go of me!" Her voice caused attention and people stopped dancing.

His hand fell away from her arm. "I think the lady just told you to let her go."

Misha came up behind the man and pinched his shoulder, sending him to his knees. He waved his hand above his head and two security guards appeared. They pulled the guy off the floor and dragged him away. People on the dance floor encircled them, watching the show.

"I had it under control. I didn't need your help," she huffed.

"You're welcome." He smiled and put his hand on her lower back, pushing her toward the bar.

She smoothed down the front of her dress and looked up. He stood about a foot taller than her. "You don't strike me as the clubbing type." Her arms crossed in front of her.

"And I find it interesting that you would be at this

particular club." Misha winked. His fingers found a curl and twirled it around to the end. "You look stunning. You're catching the eye of every man in here tonight."

"Thank you. But what do you mean, *this particular club*?"

He held her gaze. "I'll save that for another time. Your dress is interesting. Almost like you're wrapped in bandages."

Curiosity flashed across his face as the corners of his mouth tweaked up. His fingers skimmed under the top bandage. His touch lit a wick in her veins.

"I like the way it hugs me in. It's comforting." She barely got out the words.

Thoughts ran through her head of him cutting her out of the dress, piece by piece, leaving her completely naked to him. Those imaginings were anything but clean and professional. Time to cut loose and save herself from disaster.

She looked up in time to see Brie waving from the lounge. "I have to get going. But next time, don't be a cock blocker." She backed away and his hand fell.

"God knows I wouldn't want to get in the way of your latest flavor. But I might want to be your favorite flavor. I'll see you soon, *malen'kiy*." His smile held something dark.

His words stung. She wasn't sure what he'd called her, but she had to get out of there. "Ciao." Turning into the throng of dancers, she made her escape.

She rushed into the lounge to find Briella in an argument with Logan.

"I wasn't with him. He came up behind me. Here. Ask Raquelle." Brie's face was red and irritation laced her voice.

"Logan, if you're asking about the guy on the dance floor, it wasn't her fault. I got him off of her."

Logan collapsed on the couch, holding his head in his hands. His arms were inked with intricate tattoos. "You must think I'm the over possessive boyfriend." He turned to Brie. "I love you so much. More than I've loved anyone. I feel like we're in sync."

Brie sat down next to him.

He played with the diamond on her choker. "I'm totally committed to you and I take it seriously. I will always protect you, no matter what. I'm sorry if I overreacted."

Brie hugged him. "I know. I love you too. And you can protect me anytime. You're right. We *are* in sync."

All the talk of love and protection made her head spin and her heart ache. Raquelle scanned the bar but couldn't find Misha. She would have to fight harder to stay away from him. She turned back to them and made a gagging sound. "Do you two wanna get a room?"

"We have a room right here. Wanna watch?" Logan challenged her.

Briella rolled her eyes.

"Okay, TMI on that one and I think I'll call it a night." She turned to leave.

"Hold up," Brie said. "What's going on with you? You haven't been here long enough to sample the treats. Who was the guy at the bar?"

"Mr. Dark and Dangerous. Believe it or not, I'm suddenly not in the mood. I've got to meet my sisters at Papa's warehouse tomorrow. Should be thrilling. God knows what we'll find. Ciao." She left without a second glance.

Chapter Six

THE CELEBRATION last night lacked fireworks except for the chance meeting with Misha. Raquelle struggled to keep her eyes off him as he screwed with her routine of distracting herself with casual sex. Instead, he had become the distraction.

The plan had been to find a one-nighter, release some tension, have fun, and leave undetected. But Mr. Dark and Dangerous had to show up and spoil her fun. She couldn't remember a time when everything had fallen apart when she was in party mode. Totally out of character for her.

The one vision she couldn't keep out of her head was Misha. She kept waiting for his leering eyes and grabby hands, but found neither. He seemed to enjoy baiting her with his words and touch. Without knowing it, he had saved her from herself. She would have easily gone home with a stranger to let off some steam. Misha was cut from a different cloth and his mysterious side intrigued her.

He made his interest in her clear. For the sake of her career, she was determined not to succumb to her hormones. It was what was underneath that caught her attention. She had failed this test in the past and didn't want history to repeat itself. If she succeeded, she would win the Mother Teresa award for celibacy. Keeping her hands off him would be a miracle. Pushing the distraction from her mind, she forced herself to focus on the day ahead.

She shuffled to her large window, looking down on the east side of the city. Snow blanketed the streets. Winter had come early and would not be kind. Cold crept over her body as she wrapped herself tighter in her oversize robe. Mac and the boys might think they were about to wrap things up, but she had a premonition this would only be the beginning.

Questions about her papa's death swirled in her head. In the end, she wasn't sure she wanted to know the answers. His studio might give them some insight. Mac and Dean were reluctant to let her and her sisters go to the studio by themselves, but gave in after they pointed out the police had already been there.

She wasn't looking forward to the visit. Papa's studio had so many memories for each of them. Some good and others, not so much. Their father's studio had always housed secrets. Chills skittered up her arms, leaving frost in their path. Over the last couple of months her sisters had brought their secrets into the light, but she had resisted showing her flaws. She had done what she needed to do in order to keep the peace. Fights with Papa were hellish. Not only did they fight over Bernardo, but as artists, they clashed over their artistic views. She was more like Papa than she cared to admit. But that's where it began and ended for her. Her wounds would stay locked in that studio and died with him.

After taking a hot a shower she thought the foreboding cold would go away but it clung to her with icy fingers. Trepidation gripped her as she took the elevator to the garage. Elevator rides were a constant battle. Her fear of confined spaces never seemed to go away. Breathing techniques were the only tool to get her through. As the doors opened, she peered out, looking for the guy with the cigarette, but there was no sign of him. Her high-heeled boots clicked on the concrete floor. Tucked away in the corner waited her Aston Martin DB 11. The engine started with a growl, sounding more like a purr in her ears.

She drove up the ramp that led to the street. As she stopped for traffic, she spotted the guy with a cigarette. They made eye contact as he opened his mouth and the cigarette fell to the ground. She hit the accelerator and sped off in the opposite direction. Her rearview mirror showed him running the down the street and talking on the phone. Beads of sweat broke out on her forehead and her hands shook. Next time, she would confront him and find out what was going on. Or she could ask Mac to look into it. The latter seemed like the better option.

The ride to New Jersey was seamless. Saturday traffic flowed without congestion. Papa had picked Kearny for his warehouses. He'd needed the space to build and store his enormous installations. During her childhood, it seemed like he'd spent most of his time there. There was even a studio apartment when his days and nights ran together. Aside from her artistic connection to him, the relationship between them had fallen apart long before his secrets surfaced in death. He was an absentee father. Happy memories of him were few and far between. The ones she had left a bitter aftertaste.

She pulled up to see Mara and Leigha doing the foot-to-foot dance to keep warm. Wind whipped around her as she left the warmth of her car to join them.

"Hey, you two look cold and I'm on time so you must be early." She laughed.

"Hilarious. Just open the door, please." Mara's face could barely be seen inside her fake-fur hood.

"I doubt it'll be much warmer in there. No one's been here for a while." This was their first opportunity to get into the warehouse since the police had sealed it off.

Her hand shook as she guided the key into the lock and pressed the code. The door opened to total darkness. They stood for a moment in silence, each hesitant to cross into their father's private world.

"Let's go." Leigha pushed through them and led the way, flipping the switch for the overhead halogen lights, which took a couple of seconds to light up.

Enormous silent figures confronted them. The sisters' footsteps echoed off the concrete walls. Harsh words from the past pressed down on Raquelle.

Mara laughed. "Remember how we used to hide in the bottom of some of these."

"And remember how Papa yelled at us that they weren't playground equipment." Leigha gazed up at an enormous elephant. "I remember Papa made this for you, Raq."

"Yeah." Raquelle had been overjoyed that Papa had made her an elephant just for her.

Years later the event was overshadowed when Bernardo, Papa's right-hand man, locked her inside it. Her claustrophobia and fear of dark places had become worse over time. After she broke up with him, he wore his jealously of her talent like a tattered suit, making her life miserable.

"Let's head to the studio so we can talk and decide what to do with all of this." She locked down her emotions to get through the day.

"You don't seem happy to be here." Mara never missed when something was wrong.

"I'm not. A lot happened for me here. And no, I don't want to talk about it." Raquelle bit out.

"You will one day. Take it from me, it's a tremendous relief. I never imagined that I would tell anyone about Ben. But I lived through it."

Leigha had been raped when she was a model by her photographer boyfriend, Ben. Her repressed memories came out in her dreams. Dean had helped her through it and stayed by her side.

Another reminder that Raquelle was incapable of any kind of serious relationship. She could never share what happened to her because of Bernardo.

Raquelle led the way to the studio and opened the door. They stopped in the doorway.

"Oh my God, what happened?" Mara stood next to Raquelle and grabbed her hand.

"I'd say someone beat us to it," Leigha said, stepping ahead of them. "Come in and close the door. Raquelle, lock it. Mara, turn off the lights to the warehouse. We don't want to draw any attention to ourselves. Someone could be watching. This must have happened after the cops were here." She stepped up and took charge.

Dumped drawers, scattered papers, and overturned lamps covered the floor. They had rifled the entire file cabinet. What were they looking for?

Papa's words on his deathbed had referred to someone coming after Leigha. But who had come after him? Raquelle wondered if Papa was in deep with the Russians.

"Well, CSI, what do you think is going on here? Papa was an artist. Why would someone be rummaging through his things? What could they be looking for?" Raquelle said.

"I don't know. But I think we should keep looking. Let's

head into the rest of the studio." Leigha led them into the room where Papa did his painting.

Raquelle hadn't been in his studio for years. After their blow-up, he wouldn't allow her access.

As they entered the cave their papa kept hidden away, Mara gave a pained gasp. Her hand covered her mouth as tears formed in her eyes.

A corkboard contained the history of each of them as artists: Marabella and Raquelle's first gallery show, Leigha's modeling and photos, and their teenage years showing promise of things to come.

Leigha walked over to a corkboard with the cover of a magazine that had launched her career as a model. "He cared about me and my modeling." Her finger ran down the cover and onto a photo she had taken of her sisters.

Portraits of their mother and each of them as children covered the walls, along with their childhood works of art. The three of them stood examining the board without a word. Confusion swirled around Raquelle. There was so much she didn't know about Papa.

A wall-size portrait of their mama hung on one wall, spotlighted with nothing else around it. The muted colors were in direct contrast to some of his more vibrant portraits. He paid homage to the love of his life, going back to his roots as a classically trained artist.

In the corner stood a large canvas on an easel covered by a tarp.

Raquelle hesitated to uncover it, afraid it would reveal another secret. Her sisters flanked her.

"Go ahead," Mara encouraged.

She whipped away the tarp to reveal a portrait of the three of them. This was by far the most stunning portrait she had ever seen by him, and not because she was in it. The women in the painting were smiling and even laughing. He had captured them the way he truly saw them. The light in their eyes spoke of joy, confidence, and intelligence. Tears crested in her eyes. Mara wove her arm around her waist.

"It's beautiful." Mara's words fell on a whisper.

Leigha wrapped her arm around Raquelle's shoulder. "It is. He really captured us."

Raquelle nodded to Leigha. "Help me take it over to the light. I want to see everything in it."

They each took a side and moved it to another easel under a light. Raquelle could feel something behind the canvas. Two envelopes were tucked between the canvas and the frame.

"Hey, guys, look at this."

He addressed one envelope to them, the other to Mama. Raquelle ripped open their letter and read.

Dear mia bellas,

If you are reading this, then I am no longer with you on earth. My life has ended at the hands of the Russians. It was not my choice to be involved with them. But it was my choice to protect you as much as possible, and hopefully I have done that.

My oldest and dearest friend, Alek, took something from me years ago, my beautiful Guilianna. But at this point you already know that because Alek came for Leigha like he said he would. I only blame myself for being married to my art, my obsession. I wasn't there for the love of my life when she needed me most.

When my beautiful Leigha was born, I took something from him, his daughter, and we struck a deal. I won't go into the details in order to protect you. You're better off not knowing.

In order to keep you safe, I had to stay away from you and put security on each of you. There was no other way. Your safety and happiness was all that mattered to me.

You must understand that you three beautiful souls are my world. I followed everything you did from wherever I was in the world. That had to be kept a secret. I needed to keep you away from me for your protection.

Raquelle, you are the most talented portrait artist I have ever seen. Your work will surpass mine. You are worth more than you know. My words were uncalled for. But what can I say, I'm the overprotective Italian father, especially when it came to Bernardo.

Marabella, I hope you leave Brock, because you are priceless. Trust me, he has nothing to offer. Beware of him. He's trouble. Keep sculpting, my tiny dancer. You have captured the essence of the soul in your work.

Leigha, my headstrong girl, I apologize to you most of all. I didn't know what to do with you. You are so beautiful but remind me so much of him. I loved you the best I could. You will go far with your photography. Your eye knows composition and light. Keep your head up.

You are all strong, independent, and talented women. Know that you are cherished and loved from where I am now as I look down on you. I am with you always.

Love forever and always,

Papa

P.S. Please give the other letter to your mama.

Colors in the kaleidoscope of Raquelle's life changed once again. Confusion covered them like burlap with too many holes to choose which one to look through. They had painted their lives one color, only to be changed one word at a time in his letter. Papa had spoken his truth, a truth they knew nothing about.

Mara's tears streaked her face. "It explains a lot and not

enough all at the same time. I want to know more about him. He kept himself hidden to protect us, the ultimate sacrifice."

"What harsh words is he talking about? What happened with Bernardo?" Leigha was quick to ask.

"Never mind that. I want to know what deal he struck with Alek." Raquelle's voice quivered.

"Shhh. I hear something." Leigha put her ear to the wall of the door. "Someone's here. Turn off the lights and get on the floor."

She peeked behind the curtain to the window that looked out over the warehouse floor. Men with flashlights were going into the installations of their papa's artwork.

"What are you doing? Get down here." Mara tugged on Leigha's coat.

Raquelle's blood slowed while her heart pounded in her ears.

Leigha slid to the floor.

Mara pushed one button on her phone.

Chapter Seven

"THEY'RE HERE. The Russians are in the warehouse and we're locked in the studio," Mara said. Her hand shook.

Raquelle could hear Mac swearing on the other end.

"They're going into each installation and back out again. It's almost as if they're looking for something. But what?" Leigha peered through the window and reported back to the group. "Shit! They're coming this way."

Raquelle grabbed the phone from Mara, pushed the *end* button, and set it on silent.

The three of them huddled on the floor without a sound. Mara grabbed Raquelle's hand and squeezed it so hard she lost feeling in her fingers. The door rattled and shook. Russian accents sounded muffled through the door. Footsteps rattled the metal stairs and doors slammed. Her heart pounded in her ears as quiet enveloped them.

"That was close." Leigha blew out a shaky breath.

"Yeah, too close. Here." Raquelle handed the phone to Mara as it vibrated in her sweaty palm. "You better answer this before he loses his shit."

Mara's finger missed the answer button several times before putting it on speaker.

"What the fuck is going on? Are you trying to give me a stroke? Why didn't you answer your phone?" Mac had hit the nuclear level.

"Calm down. They were at the door to the studio. But we're fine. They couldn't get in." Mara's voice quivered.

"Stay right the fuck there. Do. Not. Move. We're en route now. We'll be there soon." Dean blared through the speaker and then clicked off.

Leigha threw her hands up. "And welcome to the world of falling in love with the alpha male. Not just one but two." She held up two fingers.

Mara threw her head back as it thumped the wall. "I never thought I would see the day when I would be with a man who was so protective of me. After all of Brock's abuse, this feels normal and right." She grabbed Raquelle's hand. "Just wait till it happens to you."

She pulled her hand away and stood up. "Highly unlikely. I'm the one in charge of all my relationships. No man is going to call the shots for me." She pretended to smooth down the front of her coat. Her heart galloped in her chest. "Let's meet them downstairs."

She led the way to the entrance to the warehouse, putting on a brave face for her sisters. Underneath, she shook like a leaf. She opened the door for Mac and Dean, who were panting.

"You rang?" she said.

Mac pushed past her to get to Mara. "Leannan, are you okay?" He held her face as if it were porcelain and kissed her.

Mara wrapped her fingers around his wrists and closed her eyes. "I'm fine. I think. This was a little too close for me."

61

"I never should have let you girls come here alone." The muscle in his jaw twitched.

"Women, thank you. And yeah, it was too close for comfort." Leigha said.

Dean hugged her like his life depended on it, whispering her pet name, "Babe."

Sean and Beck, two of the owners from MBK Global Security, stood next to Raquelle. Mac and Dean worked for them.

"Raq. Raquelle? Did you hear me?" Mara said. "The letter. Where is it?"

"Right here." She pulled the letter from her pocket and handed it to Mac, keeping Mama's letter out of sight. She would make sure she gave it to her later.

Sean turned to her. "Are you okay?" His hand found her arm. He was the player of the group, and she didn't have time for his bullshit, even if his eyes seemed sincere.

"I'm fine." She pulled away from him as Mara frowned at her.

Beck smirked at Sean's play.

"I don't see where they broke in. They must have had the code. Your father had to have given it to them. They may be in here all the time." Mac said his thoughts out loud.

Dean started walking toward the installations. "Let's try to find out what they were looking for. Let's split up and do a search. You three stay here."

"Yeah, right. Like that's going to happen." Raquelle and Leigha followed Dean. Mara fell inline behind Mac, Sean, and Beck.

Using their phone flashlights, they searched the inside of each installation.

The words "nothing here" echoed several times as they reconvened back at the entrance to the warehouse.

"I don't get it. There's nothing in any of them. What the hell were they looking for?" Dean asked.

"What did your father do for the Russians? He was an artist, not a mobster. Or was he leading a double life no one knew about?" Mac's face grew concerned. "We need to find out what the deal was between Alek and your father." He turned to Raquelle. "We need you more than ever. All of this is tied together: Mexico, CZR Investments, and now your father's artwork. I need you to get close to Michael and report back. Please tell us you'll do it."

They were running out of options. "Yes, but on my terms. This is a big deal for me, my breakthrough. I'll get as much as I can but don't ask for anything else."

"Thank you. I promise to keep you safe." Relief didn't register on his face.

"That's not necessary. I can take care of myself. Besides, when would you have time when Mara's always getting into trouble?" She winked as Mara glowered at her.

"You have a point. I need you to change the code. They may have a key but without the code they can't get it. I'll have Sean check in with you." Mac's smile said gotcha. He turned to Mara. "Come on, Mrs. It's time to take you home."

"Mrs.? Really? I didn't see you put a ring on it." Mara huffed past him to the parking lot with Leigha in tow, followed by their men.

Sean smiled. "So I guess I'll be your contact."

"No, you won't. There are two men in this world I trust and they just walked out the door with my sisters. I'll be reporting to them. Ciao." Raquelle flew past him to the parking lot.

She could hear Beck's deep rumble of laughter in the background.

The ride home had her on edge. She didn't want to be

caught up in any espionage, but there didn't seem to be a choice. Knowing the Russians had killed her papa wasn't enough. She wanted to know why he was killed and how involved was he with them. The more she thought about it, the angrier she got.

She turned down her street, lost in thought, until she saw Butthead getting into his car. How many cigarettes did this guy go through in a day? A cord snapped in her.

She pulled her car in behind his SUV and got out. Second thoughts poured in as she realized this probably wasn't the smartest thing she'd ever done, but she was committed at this point. Standing outside the driver's side door, she waited for him to look at her. When he didn't, she banged on the window, making him jump.

"Don't act like you don't know who I am. You've been sitting outside my apartment watching me. Open the damn window." She said through gritted teeth with her arms crossed.

"Can I help you?" Butthead said with an accent.

"Oh, God. Do you have a Russian accent?" She took a small step back.

"No. Estonia."

"Why?" She gripped her coat around her.

"Because I'm Estonian," he said with a smile.

"No, I mean why is Alek having me followed?" Her hands were balled into fists.

"Who's Alek? I work for CZR Investments. Misha sent me to watch over you." He lit a cigarette.

She put her finger out. "Stay right there." She walked back to her car and tore through her bag to find Misha's card with his phone number. Digging her phone out of her pocket, she dialed the number and marched back to Butthead's car.

"Hello Raquelle." Misha's smooth voice came over the phone like syrup.

"Guess where I'm standing?" Forget the pleasantries.

"Outside my door?" he said smugly.

"You wish. I'm standing with your goon who stinks like cigarettes." Reaching down, she pulled the cigarette out of Butthead's mouth and threw it to the ground, crushing it with her toe. "Call him off. I don't need a security guard. I have enough going on in my life and I don't need another reason to look over my shoulder," she said, not bothering to hide the anger in her voice.

"Ah, I'm sorry. I just wanted to make sure you were safe. The city can be a dangerous place." He didn't sound sorry. He sounded like he wanted to know where she was at all times.

"Well, I've managed the city my entire life all on my own, thank you. I'll see you at our next appointment." She clicked off before he could reply.

"Did you hang up on the boss?" Butthead asked cautiously.

"Yes. He has no business having me followed." She blew out a breath. "Stop smoking. It's bad for your health. Now go home."

He smiled. "The boss doesn't like to be hung up on. You're too bossy. And now I'm going home but I won't quit smoking." The window closed before she replied.

* * *

"You did what?" Mac's voice blared over the phone.

"What can I say, I was angry but I thought you should know. He sounded Russian but when I asked him, he said he was Estonian." She had called him on her way to Misha's office the next morning.

He had demanded she paint in his office, and made it part

of the contract. As much as she tried to talk him out of it, she needed the commission. She was losing control of the situation with him, which really pissed her off. They would have to establish some ground rules.

"My God, you Luccenzo women are going to send me to an early grave. Next time, call one of us before you approach the car of a strange man who you think is following you. What you did was stupid and dangerous. Why did Michael say he was having you followed?"

"He wanted me to be safe. If you ask me, he's more than a little controlling. I'm on my way there now. I'll call you later." Raquelle's anxiety spiked. On the one hand, she was excited to see him. On the other hand, she needed to keep a hands-off approach.

"Be careful. Remember, we're only a phone call away." His voice softened.

Misha had sent his personal car to pick her up with all of her supplies. She hadn't included her easel because it wouldn't be needed for a while. She would wait to see if this arrangement was going to work. Titus would have to stay at home until she was more comfortable with the situation.

The car stopped in the underground garage, close to the elevator. The driver opened her door.

"You need to use your access card for the elevator. It will take you directly to the floor for CZR Investments." Jonas had introduced himself and offered his hand as she slid out of the car. "I'll take care of everything else."

"Thank you."

The ride in the elevator was so quick she didn't need to use her breathing exercises. The doors opened on the other side of the stark lobby. Head held high, she stepped forward as if she owned the place.

Her father's words came back to her. *Act like you're a premier artist.*

She nodded to the receptionist and kept walking, leaving the woman scrambling to put on her headset to forewarn of incoming. The leather straps on her Gucci bag were going to make marks in her fingers as her nerves got the better of her.

She breezed past Audrey on her way to his office. "Hi Audrey. Nice to see you again. I'll just let myself in."

"He doesn't want to be dis—" Audrey stepped from around her desk.

Raquelle opened the door. Misha looked up with wide eyes but waved her in while speaking to someone on his phone in what sounded like Russian. She stopped and stared at him. He frowned at her reaction and turned away.

"I gotta go," he said in English.

Her instincts kicked in. Remembering she was undercover, she closed the door behind her and carried on.

He had rearranged everything in the office to accommodate her work, including moving his desk in front of the blank wall across from the bookcase. A top-end H-framed art easel stood on a beige rug. There were shelves built in below the windows. She walked over to the easel and dropped her bag. The light was incredible. She would face him while painting.

He placed his cell phone in his pocket and walked around the desk. An abstract hand-painted tie accented his black suit and sage green shirt. The green made his hazel eyes blaze. He put his hands into his pockets and stepped closer. His body seemed to fill the room. "Do you like it? I wanted you to have as much natural light as possible."

"This must have been a stretch for you, having to rearrange your office for me. You seem to be a man who likes to have everything in its place." She smiled to herself.

His brows rose but his eyes remained steely.

"It's incredible. But I'm afraid the beautiful carpet is going to get ruined. I can get a little carried away sometimes." She took a small step back from the power that emanated from him.

"I had to make room. It's part of our contract, as I recall. I'm not worried about the carpet. I got a shag rug with extra padding underneath. You'll be on your feet a lot. I don't want them to be sore." The fact that he cared touched her.

Her fingers twisted in front of her. "That's very considerate of you. Were you speaking Russian when I walked in?"

His face darkened. "Yes. That was a private call. I need to remember that you never announce your arrival."

She turned her back to him, not wanting to get too nosy. "The view and light from these windows are amazing. I don't have this kind of light in my studio. I might have to bring all my pieces here to finish." A nervous laugh escaped her lips.

She didn't hear him approach, but she could feel the heat radiating from his body. She closed her eyes to steal the warmth of his proximity. "I want you here to see your creativity in action. I installed LED daylights above you for cloudy days. It can get gloomy up here." His finger pulled her hair over her shoulder and down the back of her arm.

She shivered. *Stay strong, girl*. If she made it through this, they should grant her sainthood.

"Oh, and Raquelle, never hang up on me. I find it rude and I don't play games." His breath ruffled her hair as goose bumps formed on her arms. She liked when he pushed back.

She turned around with hands on her hips. "I don't play games either. So let's be clear. I don't need your protection, and you won't be telling me what to do. I will work here until

I complete your portrait. This," her finger waved between them, "is strictly business."

He leaned in. "I'm sorry. I didn't realize you had a boyfriend." He smirked.

"From the looks of it, Mr. Dark and Dangerous, you already know I don't have a boyfriend. There are many reasons to keep this professional." A piece of her heart chipped off. She wished she could give into what she wanted.

"Dark and Dangerous? It suits me. I'm getting more interested in this dynamic by the minute and I understand your need to keep this professional. But you aren't the only one who will call the shots."

A knock at the door interrupted their exchange. A man peeked his head inside.

"Jonas, come in." Misha helped his driver roll in a cart of art supplies. "Looks like someone is moving in. So much for keeping it professional." He winked.

She gave him her hardest look.

They took several boxes off the cart and set them next to the shelves. He turned to Jonas. "Thank you for taking care of everything. I appreciate it."

"Anything else, sir?"

Misha replied, "No." His attention turned back to her. "We're good for right now." Jonas left.

"I should give you some time to–" He bent down to pick up her stuffed elephant, BB. "Who's this?"

"That's BB, short for Babar." She reached for her beloved childhood toy.

He looked at his elephant on the bookshelf. "He looks like he's been well loved."

She put the stuffed elephant on her easel. "This is where he belongs. It's a long story." BB was part of her past she couldn't let go. He was her muse, along with Titus. She would introduce Misha to Titus soon, whether or not he liked dogs. Titus was always with her when she painted.

"It's going to be an interesting ride. I have a meeting to go to. I'll let you settle in." Before he closed the door, he turned to her. "By the way, I think you might enjoy being controlled, *malen'kiy.*" He smiled before he left.

Chapter Eight

MISHA HAD NEVER USED the word *malen'kiy*, the Russian word for *little one*, for anyone, but it fit Raquelle. Her feistiness caught him off guard, but he welcomed their war of words. His title of CEO of a multinational company had no impact on her. She had drawn her line in the sand and challenged him to erase it.

He recognized the strength that came from wanting to step out from under the shadow of a parent. He was going to have to move with care. She was unpredictable and intriguing in any situation. One minute she was flirty, the next a jaguar. His weekly partners' meeting would serve as a needed distraction. He had been thinking about her since the day she walked into his office.

As he approached the conference room, he noted they had tinted the surrounding glass opaque, signifying the need for confidentiality.

Three families—Cavit, Zurich, and Raines—owned CZR Investments. They were the largest privately owned investment firm in the world. It involved the fathers of the other two families in some of the decision-making for business except for his father until recently. They kept their involvement top secret, but he wasn't sure why besides keeping up the appearance of being an American owned business. Today he, Zane, and Andre were taking a conference call from Dmitri, Zane's father.

"Where have you been?" Dmitri barked over the large screen in the front of the room.

"Does it matter? You can't start without the CEO." He bit back at Dmitri's overbearing ways.

"You have an ego like your father. Maybe the CEO should be on time." Dmitri baited Misha, no doubt waiting to reel him in before snapping his head off. He didn't take the bait.

He ignored the comment about his ego and unbuttoned his suit jacket, taking his time to find his seat at the head of the table. Then he turned his chair in the direction of the screen.

"Enough. Let's get down to business. Obviously, I'm not in the US." He rubbed his chin. "I had to come back to Russia to take care of some things that might affect our firm. I've spoken to the other two families and they agree. We are going to continue with the lockdown until further notice. No one goes in or out without proper ID, cross checks, and references."

Misha didn't like the tone of the meeting. "This lockdown seems a little much. We've paid back our investors in full and some have even stayed on as clients. We never got an exact answer on who's money was stolen. The accounts were very muddled. Don't you think my father should be part of this discussion?"

Dmitri's face darkened. "Your father has other things to take care of at this end. The less you know the better."

Unspoken fear blanketed the group with lingering nervous energy. His message was cryptic and didn't sit well.

Misha resented being left out of certain aspects of the business.

"You always leave us in the dark while the three of you call the shots from the other side of the goddamn world." His fist hit the table. Zane and Andre sucked up what little air was left in the room and jerked back. "We need full disclosure. What is going on? You need to tell us more so we can take care of business here." Misha was apparently the only one who had balls enough to make demands.

"No, there is nothing you need to know," Dmitri said through gritted teeth. "Business as usual. Carry on. We'll talk soon." Dmitri's face reddened, and the screen went black.

Misha pinched the bridge of his nose to regroup. He turned to the other two, who stared at him. "I'm tired of the charades with our fathers. Something's got to give."

Zane spoke up. "I've never seen you speak to any of our fathers like that. You need to get a grip."

"I will get a grip when I know what's going on." He fired back.

There was a knock at the door as the directors filed in to give their reports. Something niggled in the back of his mind. The head of the families were strung tighter than he had ever seen them. He made a mental note to ask his father later.

After hours of meetings, he made his way back to his office as thoughts of Raquelle took up space in his head. He needed to refocus his energy. Work had become more stressful than usual and riddled with uncertainties. The tense climate at CZR had him leaving the conference room on high alert as their fathers continued to bear down.

His end of the floor was quiet, the way he liked it. Opening the door to his office, he found Raquelle curled up on his couch. She looked up and smiled at him. The smell of hazelnut coffee permeated the air. A sense of peace came over him to see her there, but he couldn't explain why. She seemed to possess a calm that he was missing.

"I see you've made yourself comfortable. Good. Do you have everything you need?" He noted her rose-colored silk blouse that opened to give a peek of the top of her breast, tight black knit pants, and the sky-high stilettos placed neatly by the end of the couch. He sat down at his desk.

"Yes. Audrey ran out to get a French press, a coffee grinder, and some whole bean coffee for me." She looked at him over her cup.

"Just to be clear, Audrey is not your secretary. I won't have you ordering her around all day with errands." His throat tightened.

She placed her feet in her shoes, stood, and smoothed down her pants. As she moved toward him, it was the most graceful walk he had ever seen someone manage in heels that high. She leaned over his desk enough for him to get a hint of what was hidden beneath the blouse, skirting professionalism with a tease.

"I'm sorry. I didn't mean any harm. She was going out anyway, and I wanted to be set up for you. I'm a hellcat without my coffee. I need you to sit for me for an hour or two. There are preliminary sketches to do as well as photos that need to be taken," she said softly, using her blue eyes to appease him.

Her words wrapped around him. She knew her audience and how to work it, making it seem like she was doing it all for him. There was no doubt she was very familiar with the male species and what made them tick.

"You're very good at getting your way, aren't you? But rest assured I—"

His cell phone rang from his pocket. "Excuse me."

He walked to the far side of the office, away from

Raquelle. He exhaled in anticipation of a confrontation before greeting his father in Russian. Recently, his father had become paranoid and insisted they only speak in their native tongue for additional privacy. He watched the view as Raquelle made her way back to her easel.

"Hello, Father." His eyes never left Raquelle, watching her bend over to get her drawing pad and pencils. Her pants hugged her ass to perfection. Blood made its way to other areas of his body, leaving his brain.

"You heard Dmitri, we need to keep our guard up. Why do you have to give him such a hard time? Remember, don't ask, don't tell. Things have gotten off course and we need to get it under control again." His father's voice was strained.

"Would you like to fill me in on what the hell is going on? Everyone here is on edge and we have no information. I can't work like this. I need to do my job." He said in a hushed tone, watching Raquelle wrap her hair into a ponytail. He wanted to wrap her hair around his fist and pull as his lips made their way up her neck.

His father sighed heavily. "We've told no one else about this. The Russian government is involved."

"Involved in what?" His father's words caught his attention.

"That's what we are trying to find out. When Brock took that money, it affected many people. Some of them maybe top government officials." His father seemed to choose his words carefully. "For now, I need you to keep a close eye on everyone coming and going. I have to go. We'll talk soon." He clicked off.

He put the phone back in his pocket and cradled his head in his hands.

"Is everything all right?" she asked.

He needed to squelch his anger. "Yes. Everything will be fine."

Her eyes stayed focused on the pad. "Who were you talking to?"

"My father."

"Ah, yes. Fathers."

"I have a question for you. Your sister was married to Brock, the guy that stole our clients' money, as I recall. Do you have any insights?" He stood next to her as she continued to sketch on the couch.

Her body went stiff.

Interesting reaction.

"No, I don't. I never liked Brock. He was," She paused. "not a good husband to my sister. I'm kind of glad he's gone," she said without looking at him.

Not the answer he'd expected, but it was honest. "Well, he couldn't be a good husband if he was stealing other people's money. There's no room for dishonesty in any relationship, wouldn't you agree?"

"I agree but you seem upset." Her eyes lifted to meet his.

"There's a lot going on and my father can be . . . controlling. Overbearing might be another good word." His words came out in a bitter tone.

"What does he do?"

What doesn't he have his hands in would be a better question. He needed to shut it down.

"What is this, twenty questions? He's in imports and exports. Now, do you need me to sit here or somewhere else while you draw?"

Her face became pink. "No. You can sit at your desk and work if you want to. I can sketch you while you work." She curled into a tighter ball.

He regretted his harsh tone. "I'm sorry. It's been a rough morning."

"I see you've learned control from the best." She looked up and winked at him, diffusing his anger. He deserved that. To her it looked like he was trying to control her but he wasn't, was he? "You know there's a difference between wanting to control others and being a man in control," she said.

He sat down at his desk and clenched his fists in his lap. He wanted to sit behind her and weave his hands through her golden chestnut hair. His ropes called to him. He could picture them on her as she gave herself over to him, to them. The black silk artwork on her olive skin would be a perfect match.

"I'd like to think I'm a man in control." He waited for her response.

"The jury's still out on that and I haven't cast the deciding vote yet." She laughed.

Her face lit up like a child playing a prank on someone. He guessed his programmed childhood would pale in comparison to her creative spirit. She reminded him of his younger brother, Kiril, the prankster of the family.

He stood up and moved away from the barrier of his desk that kept him from engaging with the world around him. His father had groomed the prince to take over one day but the short tight leash was strangling him. She awakened something in him, the desire to cut the collar and run free. Creativity glimmered in her shiny blue eyes affecting him. He wanted a taste of what she offered.

As he walked across the room, she looked up at him, then averted her eyes back to her drawing. She had taken off her shoes and was resting her back against the arm of the couch, legs tucked up underneath her. He admired the level of comfort she'd found in her new surroundings. The view in his office had never been better.

He sat on the coffee table and leaned on his knees. "And what about you? Hmm? Are you in control? You're a spitfire one minute and then show me your soft feminine side— which I can appreciate." He pressed his thumb under her lower lip, and she gasped. "Are you committed to keeping this professional? Or is there room in there for me, for Misha, the man?" The tip of his thumb brushed her lower lip.

Her gazed stayed fixed on him as she grabbed his thumb. "I have to keep this professional." Her eyes pleaded with him.

"Why?" His curiosity ignited.

"Because I have something to prove . . . to myself." She pulled his thumb away with a look of surprise that she was still holding it. Her cheeks blushed.

"What could you possibly have to prove to yourself? You're an incredibly talented artist with beauty to match. I know this portrait will come out beyond my expectations. I'm attracted to you and I want to know who you are and what makes you tick."

Her eyes widened, and then the brightness darkened. "You wouldn't if you really knew me." She swung her legs to the floor and slipped her feet into her shoes.

He stood up with her as she put up her hands and bumped into his chest. She left them there, creating a spark. His heart skipped in his chest. Her sultry eyes had an undercurrent of sadness he couldn't ignore.

"Don't we all have demons? I doubt yours are any worse than mine." His finger twirled a tendril on her cheek. "You'll find that I speak my mind sometimes without a filter." The warmth of her hands fell away.

"Some demons are better left in the dark," she said, her words strangled.

She shook her ponytail out, leaving her curls to fall past her shoulders. His fingers itched to grab them.

He stuffed his hands into his pockets. "I have my charity event tonight, and I'd like it very much if you would attend it with me. We have artists auction off their works to support homeless men and women trying to enter the workforce. The money goes to help find them jobs and prepare for the interview process. A lot of these artists have been on the streets themselves so they understand what is means to donate from the other side of life."

She stared at him and blinked several times. "As much as I would love to support the cause, I don't think it would be appropriate for me to go as your date. But thank you for asking."

"I would introduce you as a new artist. Perhaps you'd like to donate a piece? We could consider it a work night instead of a date." His fingers curled in his pockets, willing her to say yes. He wanted to show her off in so many ways.

She crossed her arms in front of her. "Well, when you put it that way. It is short notice but I have a piece I could donate. I doubt it will hold a candle to some of your other artists' works. They've had time to prepare, but I always liked a good challenge." She pushed past him. "If I'm going to be ready, I need to leave now. I always strive to look my best." She batted her eyelashes. "I like to compliment my artwork."

What he wouldn't do to have her words ring true. If only she knew the challenges he had in store for her. He'd push her body to its limits and have her begging for more.

How could she ever doubt herself? She had talent oozing from her pores. "I'll pick you up at eight sharp. I'm sure your piece will be amazing. Be ready, Ms. Luccenzo."

"I was born ready," she stated.

"We'll see."

Chapter Nine

MISHA POURED himself a drink from the limo's bar. Alcohol was not his typical go-to but it might smooth over the jittery nerves. The disguise of a work night wasn't fooling either of them. He was drawn to her while she pushed him away. For once in his life, he needed to play it unsafe. He would wait it out with her and get her to see what they could have together.

He exited the car and walked into the lobby of her building. As the doorman called up to her apartment, Misha paced the marble floor. He didn't like to wait. When the ding of the elevator drew his attention and the doors opened and his jaw dropped. She walked out in a low-cut blue dress, a slit up the thigh, and sky-high stilettos. The outfit was wrapped up in a long fur coat. He remained glued in place.

"The fur's fake but everything else is original." She raised her chin, pushed out her chest, and walked past him. Without glancing back in his direction, she asked, "Well, are you coming? We don't want to be late."

He followed behind, taking in the view. Maybe he'd be trading his father's leash for her leash. She knew how to handle him, which wasn't in his favor. Jonas rounded the car and opened the door.

"Good evening, Ms. Luccenzo. You look incredible." He smiled.

Misha shot Jonas a look before he slid in next to her. "You look stunning. I know Versace when I see it. Your fur is a good knock-off."

Her hair was in a French twist, with tendrils hanging on each side. She looked up at him through a curl covering half her eye. "I would never think of wearing real fur. It turns my stomach. I'm an animal lover—especially pit bulls and elephants." She bit her lip. "Wait till you see what I donated tonight."

The words *pit bull* made his blood run cold. His experience with them had not gone well. He shook it off. "I have no doubt your piece will make a statement. I will have my work cut out for me fighting off suitors." He flashed her a glance.

"Oh, but this isn't a date, remember?" She tucked her smile away behind her hand.

He pulled her hand away and took her chin in his fingers, rubbing his thumb along her jaw. The steel in her eyes said she was ready for battle.

"If you think you're leaving with someone else tonight, you'd be sadly mistaken. I'll be the best cock blocker you've ever seen. You'll be leaving with me. I take care of the women who accompany me anywhere." He waited for her to refuse his demand.

Her eyes softened as she stuck her tongue out and pulled it back in just as fast, tasting his thumb. He held his breath. "I would expect nothing less from you," she whispered.

"Ms. Luccenzo, be careful not to blur the lines between business and pleasure." He wanted to devour her.

"From what I've observed, your life could stand to be a little more blurry and a lot less uptight." He let her chin go.

"And it would seem you could use a generous amount of control." He tugged one of her curls.

"I have control where and when I want it," she said, turning to look out the window.

Sexual tension cloaked the rest of the ride. She laced and unlaced her fingers. He wanted nothing more than to hold her to him. He hungered for warmth, but she would fight him all the way.

He entered the gala with the most beautiful woman in the room as heads turned in their direction. She commanded people's attention, nodding at everyone as if she were royalty, but knew each of them intimately.

People buzzed around the artwork as *oohs and aahs* could be heard throughout the room. Misha grabbed two glasses of champagne as she looped her arm in his and pulled him across the room. A crowd formed in front of one piece.

"Excuse me," she said, pushing through the crowd. "There. What do you think?"

Before him was a statement about wearing animal fur. People in the painting wore dogs and cats around their necks as mink, fox, and chinchillas roamed in the foreground in collars. Included in the work were pieces of material and animal fur. The brush strokes were subtle where needed, but powerful enough to carry the message. She had named the painting *Wear Your Pet*. The spectators mumbled not only about the power of the message but also about the quality of the work itself.

"You've executed this very well. The message is clear yet unexpected. Your technique is incredible. Well done." He stood behind her, focused on her work as the crowd faded into the background.

"This is an interesting piece. I'm not familiar with the artist," Ryan Thorpe said from behind him.

"Hey, Ryan, how are you? Missy, you look wonderful. Let me introduce you to the artist herself. Raquelle, I'd like you to meet, Ryan, an old college friend of mine, and his wife, Missy."

Everyone shook hands and exchanged greetings.

Ryan's eyes scanned the work. "This is really special. I love your use of color and materials. You command the brush strokes like you own them." Ryan had an eye for art.

"Thank you. I appreciate that. And yes, I do own them." Raquelle beamed. She turned to Missy. "When are you due?" she asked.

"Thank God, not until after Valentine's Day. February twenty-eighth." Missy looked happy and peaceful. A knot tightened in Misha's gut. He'd missed out on so much. Ryan and Missy had met in college and moved together as a team, connected and were in sync with one another.

"This is our second so he or she could come early—but not too early. We just bought a house in Connecticut and it needs some work. If everything goes according to plan and the stars align, we'll be in it before the baby comes. But we all know life doesn't always work that way." Missy's face was rosy and full.

Her words tore through him. Inside of a couple of sentences, Misha understood what he had been missing. So caught up in his job, following orders, and taking care of his mother, he hadn't lived life for himself. A slow ember burned. He needed to tamp it down before it raged beyond the safety zone. His sacrifice had garnered nothing but a full career absent of everything else. He looked at the woman standing next to him. Maybe it wasn't too late.

"I love babies. They smell so delicious. I could play with

them all day. I particularly love when they fall asleep on my shoulder." Raquelle swooned.

"Are you hoping to have a family soon?" Ryan asked Raquelle but he looked at Misha.

"Oh, no. That's a ways off. It's all about my career right now." She took a sip of champagne.

"Well, in case you're wondering, there's never a perfect time to have kids." He patted Misha on the shoulder. "It was good seeing you, Misha. Let's get together for drinks soon."

"Yeah, sounds good, and congratulations on everything." He swallowed down his jealousy of his dear friend.

He didn't dare look at Raquelle. He didn't want her to ask questions he didn't have answers to.

"Let's take a stroll around and see all the works." Raquelle didn't acknowledge the exchange. She acted like she tied her entire life plan up in a nice bow, waiting for her to unwrap it.

"Well, I see someone has already moved on." Victoria's words slurred from one too many drinks, not a usual occurrence for her.

"Victoria, how are you this evening?" Misha needed to make sure this encounter didn't go sideways.

"Better. I'm with Ben now. He knows how to treat me right." Her eyes were unfocused.

He took her by the elbow and pulled her close. "Since when do you drink? I told you to be careful with him."

She pulled her arm away. "What do you care?" Her eyes welled.

"I do care. We just weren't good for each other. Please watch out for yourself."

"Yeah, whatever." She turned to Raquelle. "Good luck, sweetheart." She turned away, weaving through the crowd.

"That was entertaining. What's she going to do for an

encore?" Raquelle sipped her champagne. "I take it she's an ex."

"Yes, it didn't go the way she wanted it to and I'm afraid she's headed in the wrong direction." He blew out a breath, frustrated with Victoria's lack of understanding.

"People need to take their own journeys, make their own decisions, right or wrong, to figure it all out." Her words pierced him.

He wanted to take his own journey, but how could he when his father undermined his ability to make decisions?

"I guess you need to have people accept your decisions in the first place." He stared at her, and recognition passed between them. Her struggles ran deep.

He wanted to get on with his life without parental control. His life, his decisions. The questions were when, where, and how. He had answers, but he needed to be strong enough to face the consequences of his decisions. The actions he took would upset a lot of apple carts. He needed to let his mother live her life, and she needed to let him go. His father needed to let go altogether, but with the company in jeopardy, that wasn't going to happen anytime soon. His loyalty was to his family and to the people who worked for the company. He didn't have it in him to leave them high and dry or put them in harm's way.

They floated around the gallery, viewing and commenting on all the artwork. He enjoyed the energy between them. He missed talking to someone about the finer nuances of art, the debate, and guessing the artist's message.

She stopped in front of a piece. "Look at his use of light. It reminds me of artists from the Renaissance era. It's very hard to master."

"Your insights never failed to amaze me. With every

comment, every move, I want to know more about you. Thank God I suggested you work in my office."

She stared at him with a slight smile. This would be a battle of wills, him wanting her and her wanting to keep it hands-off even as their attraction gained strength.

"I'm going to call it a night. We'll pick this up tomorrow," she said. Did her smile mask sadness or regret?

He walked her to the door and held her coat. She pushed her arms into the sleeves without looking at him. He held her long enough to smell the lavender in her hair. Closing his eyes, he took her in.

"Unfortunately, I have to stay. I want to make sure I thank all the artists personally tonight. Jonas will take you home. Your piece made quite a splash tonight. You have a gift. It should sell by the end of the evening."

She turned to him. "Thank you. I appreciate it since you have such an excellent eye for masterpieces. Oh, I'm bringing my muse with me tomorrow. He's very special to me. I can't wait for you to meet him. Ciao." She turned to go out the door without giving a clue to who *he* was.

Being possessive wasn't familiar to him, but he wouldn't be sharing her with anyone. One way or another, she would see that they were each other's muses.

She might even set him free.

Chapter Ten

RAQUELLE PUSHED her hands into her pockets to keep them from shaking. Misha had rattled her to her core. Where did he get off, peeking into her soul and wanting space in her heart? Damn it. She would battle hard to keep him at bay, proving she didn't need to have sex with every man she came across. But something flared in his hazel eyes. Respect. He wanted to know her, the woman inside the beautiful outside, and that scared her. Misha was a real man in control. She could easily fall under his spell. The portrait could take months, and she wasn't sure she could hold out that long.

She'd never really been in love before, except for high school crushes and timid boyfriends. But there was one man who almost destroyed her, Bernardo. Not because she was in love with him, but because he manipulated her and held her secret. When Papa found out about them, all bets were off. Papa painted her in scarlet and never let her forget she was worthless. Yet with every encounter, Misha made her feel special and worthy.

Breathing in and out, using Mara's technique, calmed her

down. She needed sleep tonight. Tomorrow would bring some tough decision-making on her part.

HER MORNING STARTED like any other day. She needed hazelnut coffee, protein shake, and oatmeal to keep her engine running. Titus lay at her feet after his breakfast. Once she was among the living, she had a call to make. She put Mac on speed dial.

"Hi, I thought you might want to talk," Mac said.

She didn't want to talk. She wanted this episode of *Mission Impossible* to end.

"We can't talk on the phone and don't come to MBK. You might be followed and we don't want them to connect the dots. Let's meet at Mara's. I'll have a burner phone for you and another little gift. See you soon." His words came out in a rush before he clicked off.

"Doesn't anyone say goodbye anymore?" she asked Titus.

Fifteen minutes later, Raquelle hailed a cab. Titus jumped up into the backseat.

The cabbie said, "No pit bulls allowed."

"Really? Look at him. Does he look like he's going to attack?" She parked herself next to Titus and shut the door. "There'll be a little extra in it for you." Titus put his head in her lap and looked up at her with sorry eyes. He had nothing to be sorry about. The world was misinformed when it came to pit bulls. Owners had everything to do with how pets turned out.

The cab took her across town through Central Park. Light filtered through the branches like fingers ready to grab her. The city had a split personality between day and night. Nighttime appealed to her wild side. The side that wanted to party, drink, and have sex with no strings attached. But her tides were changing and she wasn't sure she was ready for what they would bring. Misha's attention made her sit up and take notice. She wanted to itch her scratch. He had showed her a glimpse of the man he could be for her and what she meant to him. Even though he was still a stranger, he was laying the brickwork for the foundation.

She trudged down the hallway to Mara's apartment, not wanting to deal with any of what Mac offered.

Leigha opened the door. "Hey, you look down. What's going on?"

"Nothing. Can we just get this over with?" She pushed past Leigha and let Titus off his leash.

Mac stood up from the living room couch. "There you are. Come and sit down. Tell me what you discovered."

"First off, he knows Mara was married to Brock and asked me if I knew anything. I told him Brock sucked as a husband and left it at that. I don't want to do this anymore. This job is going to be hard enough without having to worry about spying on him." She brushed her hair back over her shoulder.

"I figured he'd make the connection, eventually. I'll be right back." Mac walked to the office.

Mara sat next to her, and Leigha sat on the other side. "You have to do this."

"Actually, I don't." She raised her voice.

"What's changed?" Leigha asked.

Mac walked back into the room. "Marabella and Leigha, I need you to give me some time with your sister, please. And take Titus with you."

Mara squeezed her hand before she left with Leigha.

Titus stood up from his bed as Mara tried to coax him with a treat. He waited for Raquelle's command with worried eyes. "Go on. I'll be fine. Swear to God, that dog's human," she muttered.

Mac threw down a three-inch-thick binder. "Do you know what this is?"

"No." She crossed her arms.

His eyes were cold and his face taut. "This is the dossier on Alek Romanowski and Brock. Go ahead, open it. I don't want to keep you in suspense."

She looked at the profiles of Alek and Brock. Page upon page contained photos of people Alek had killed over the years. She skimmed through the graphic details. The profile described him as dangerous and a sociopath. Brock's profile wasn't much brighter. The word *psychopath* glared from his pages.

"So what's your point?" she mumbled.

"My point is we need your help. We can't connect all the dots. There is a link between Brock, Alek, CZR Investments, and your father. You're the only one close enough to get the information we need to figure out what's going on." He clasped his hands together.

She sighed. "All I know at this point is that Misha took a call from his father and spoke in Russian. He wasn't happy about it, either. He was edgy afterward."

"Well, you could've started with that. Wait. Misha?" He looked confused.

"It's a nickname. Something about ice hockey." She blew it off.

"He spoke Russian? But he's not Russian at all. He's a born-and-bred American. We did background checks on the COO and CFO of the company, including him. None of them are Russian born. The company may have some ties to Russian families but no Russians actually work for the company. Did you get any information about his father?"

"Yeah, his father works in imports and exports. I didn't want to push it. I really don't have anything else." Her fingers twisted together.

"Don't."

"Don't what?" Her head popped up.

"Don't fall for him or get involved. I can only protect you so much and this is very interesting new information we need to look into. There are still a lot of questions where he's concerned." He unwound her fingers and held her hands. "Keep this all to yourself. The fewer people who know, the better, including Briella."

"I won't tell her, but this is some serious shit. Because if you didn't know he spoke Russian, what am I headed into? I'm scared." This added an extra layer of dirt they buried in her up to her neck.

He reached for something is his pocket. "I know you are, but we've got your back. Here." He handed her a phone identical to her own. "I need you to take this phone and turn it on when you get to his office. It has a device that will hack into their Wi-Fi and look around, so to speak. We need to see if they're hiding anything."

Between dealing with Misha, viewing the dossier, and Mac, she had become overwhelmed. "I gotta go. I need to process all this."

She attached her leash to Titus and said goodbye to her sisters' worried faces. Her place of refuge was her downtown studio. Artists seemed to seek solace in their place of creativity. When her emotions were at war, she would paint, becoming absorbed in color, shape, form, texture, and light. The escape was necessary, helping to balance her ship. Whatever she was going through often showed up in her work with all the peaks and valleys of happy to sad.

She came into the studio faced with several portraits to

choose from. The one that called to her was the portrait of the children. Their innocent eyes and smiles made her wish for her childhood before things became serious, challenging, and secretive. Stripping down, she laid her clothes out on the daybed. The feeling of air on her skin freed her and allowed nothing to come between her and her creative flow. Picking up her palette, she stroked the canvas with her brush. Using her finger, the lines blurred further, making it hard to see where one thing started and another ended. Any artist worth their salt would let the human eye make up for what the artist left out.

Deep into her flow, she didn't hear anyone come in until the woman spoke.

"I know I should be used to this, but maybe we use some kind of sign on the door to let me know you're naked?" Brie threw her bag on the couch and plopped down.

"Hard day at work?" Raquelle stayed focused on her work.

"Word is getting out that you're doing Mr. Dark and Dangerous's portrait. We have a list of new clients to consider." Her voice was even.

Raquelle's belly twisted at the mention of his name.

"I thought you'd be jumping for joy at the news. What gives?" Brie got up and moved toward her.

"Let's just say it was an interesting day and night. He's a fascinating man with many layers." She wanted Brie to take the bait. She needed to talk to someone.

"Oh? tell. Is he crazy in bed?" Brie rubbed her hands together.

"How about we go for a drink? I could use one right about now." She put her brushes in the glass jar with cleaner.

"How about you put some clothes on before we go out? I don't feel like getting arrested." Brie gave half a smile.

"Smartass." Raquelle put her blouse back on with a pair of designer jeans.

She leaned down to kiss Titus on the head. "I'll be back soon."

They walked down the street with their arms looped together, striding toward their favorite bar, The Stout.

"I couldn't ask for a better friend." She laid her head on Brie's shoulder.

She opened the door to the dark interior and led them to a booth in the back. The server came as soon as they sat down.

"Well, hello, ladies. I haven't seen you two in a while. Name your poison." He was tall, dark hair, gorgeous, and gay. Women came on to him all the time only to be disappointed.

Brie said, "The usual for both of us. Thanks." She looked sideways at Raquelle as the server turned away, taking his cue. "Okay, spill it."

"He's tall, dark, handsome, mysterious, debonair, straightforward, thoughtful, and kind. He's every woman's wet dream, and it's killing me." She rested her head on her forearms.

"And you haven't ridden this pony because. . .?"

"Do you know what he did? He rearranged his entire office to make sure I had a place to paint. Not just a place, but the perfect place. Right by the window with LED daylights for backup on a cloudy day. Who does that?"

The server came and put drinks on the table: raspberry vodka tonic and Brie's choice of a chocolate martini.

"Last night we went to a charity event and he asked for one of my paintings for the auction. He introduced me to everyone and stayed to thank all the artists. He respects me as an artist and he really knows what he's looking at." She twirled her straw around the ice.

"And the downside would be?" Brie was relentless.

"He's a control freak. We both know I do all the controlling in my relationships." Raquelle sipped her vodka through the straw.

Brie laughed. "What relationships?"

She ignored her. "He's different. I can feel it. You know how my sixth sense works. It's almost never wrong." That's the part that scared her.

"And again, you haven't hit this why?" Brie persisted, sipping her drink.

"I want this to be strictly professional. No funny business on the side. I don't need to bang every man I come across, especially clients." She played with her napkin, fraying the edges.

"So bang him after you've done his portrait."

Raquelle focused all her attention on the tiny pieces left of her napkin. "I don't know if I'll get the chance."

Brie stayed quiet for a moment. "There's something you're not telling me."

"Yes." She looked up and her stomach turned.

She and Brie were best friends who told each other everything—except the part where Raquelle was a part-time spy. "There are things going on I can't tell you about. When it's all over, I'll share it with you. It's called plausible deniability. You can't talk about what you don't know about." She searched Brie's face for disappointment, but found none.

"This has something to do with your father's death, doesn't it?" She never could get anything past her.

"Yes." She wished she could tell her more.

Brie reached over and covered her hands. "Please be careful. I don't have a good feeling about this."

She nodded, took out the straw, and threw back half her vodka tonic. "I plan on distracting him with my beautiful body." She winked.

"Well, that shouldn't be too hard." Brie laughed. "By the way, you've got one at three o'clock and he's closing in. This could be your boo for the night."

"Hi, can I buy you another drink?" Tall, Blond, and Athletic said. He wore a sports shirt and shorts as if he had just come off the field. Definitely her type.

Something poked at her from the shadows. Misha. He was the flavor she wanted. "No, thank you. We were getting ready to leave." She wasn't sure where those words came from.

"Hi, when you find Raq, could you send her back to me? What the hell was that about? When have you ever turned down a drink and sex?" Brie inquired.

She shrugged. "I feel out of sorts lately. I'm not sure what's going on." She pushed her half full drink to the side. "I have to go."

Brie stood up. "I'm always here for you, remember that."

She stood up and fell into Brie's waiting arms. "BFFs are always necessary."

Chapter Eleven

A HUGE TONGUE licked Raquelle's face and then came the nuzzling nose. Titus served as her alarm clock. He managed to get her up at exactly the same time every morning. She took him for a walk, fed him, and sometimes she went back to bed. Her love for him had no limits, even after he had chewed the frame around the door during an anxious moment. He didn't like to be away from her because he had spent too much time in the shelter. They completed each other in an odd way. He needed her for security and she had made him her only commitment.

Her meeting with Mac had her tossing and turning all night. She wasn't too perky without her beauty sleep. Being cranky meant she'd be hungry and eat things she shouldn't eat, get bloated, and be pouty. The day wasn't off to a great start. She swung her legs off the edge of the bed and put on some sweats.

"Go get your coat, Ty." He was smart too. "Good boy."

Titus trotted over with the gray-and-pink elephant fleece coat she had bought him from Snugpups. Only real pit bulls wore pink. He waited patiently while she strapped him up in it.

They hit the streets, waving to everyone they walked by and occasionally getting treats along the way. The wind whipped around them as she wrapped her coat tighter but Titus didn't care. He always stayed next to her and had guarded her in the past on more than one occasion. This morning, after he did some business, they ran back to the apartment.

She loved talking to him about everything from a good wine to bad men. He hadn't had the pleasure of meeting any of her boy toys because she never brought them home, but he was a great listener.

"You ready to go some place new today? It's a little different than what you're used to but I think you'll like it. I hope Misha likes you. I'm not sure if he's afraid of dogs or doesn't like them. I guess we'll find out. If he doesn't like you it's a deal-breaker because I can't paint without you." For that she got a big bark and a wagging tail. She swore he understood every word.

When they entered the lobby at CZR Investments, Titus held his head high as if he was in a dog show.

"Good morning, Audrey." She started to walk by her.

"Stop right there. How do you think you can walk on by with this beautiful boy without saying hello?"

Audrey stepped from behind her desk and came nose to nose with Titus. He licked her mercilessly and she returned the gesture with hugs and kisses. She never would have guessed Audrey was a dog lover.

"He's so friendly. What's his name?" she cooed.

"Titus. He's a rescue." She loved telling people about him. Dog rescue was one of her missions in life. "He's my muse. I try to take him wherever I go."

"I have a French Bulldog, Bella. I don't bring her to work." She pointed her thumb in the direction of Misha's office.

"Not a dog lover, eh? We'll see about that." She opened the door to his office and closed it behind her.

Misha was talking on the phone when they entered. His eyes grew to the size of saucers. "I've got to call you back. I have something that needs my immediate attention." He hung up the phone and stood. "Get him out of here now," he bellowed and pointed to the door.

"Nope." Titus sat at her feet.

"What do you mean, *no*? This is *my* office." His face paled.

"This is Titus, my muse and best friend. He stays." Misha's reaction was a little over the top. Then she remembered how he avoided the dog on the way to the restaurant.

Titus stood next to her and barked. Misha flinched and beads of sweat covered his forehead. He leaned on his desk, examining Titus.

"He's a pit bull isn't he?" His voice was laced with fear.

"Yes," she said in a quiet voice. "Did something happen to you?"

He broke his gaze to look up at her in surprise. He slumped in his chair and held his head in his hands.

In her pack leader voice she commanded, "Ty, down." He obeyed.

She walked over to Misha with the urge to touch and comfort him but retracted her hand. "Tell me. I might be able to help."

His head rested in the heel of his palms. "I was attacked by a pit bull when I was a boy. He almost ripped my shoulder off. Over the years I've grown afraid of all dogs." He sat back as the ghosts of the past floated in his eyes.

She leaned against his desk to face him blocking his view of Titus. "Things that happen in our childhood can be devastating and last for a long time." She looked down at her shoes. Those words held so much power as her mind grabbed onto a memory with Bernardo. She shook her head to get rid of the haunting thoughts and looked up to his worried hazel eyes. "I volunteer at a shelter that rescues pit bulls. I walk them a couple times a month. I can help you get over this if you want me to."

He gave a choked laugh. "Some impression I've made. A grown man afraid of a dog while you're half my size and deal with them all the time."

"It's not about the breed. It's about the people who own them. They used to be known as nanny dogs and took care of children. Then some people had other ideas on training them to fight. Titus is a mush. Do you want to try?" Her fingers dug into her arms. She wanted to hold his handsome face in her hands and take the fear away. He was uncomfortable losing his precious control. Maybe he would give it to her for a moment.

"Yes, I do want to try because I can't deal with this every time I come across a dog." Fear hadn't left his eyes.

"I want you to turn around in your chair away from him, and let your hand hang over the armrest. Are you okay with that?" Her heart broke for how much it was taking for him to do this. She was all too familiar with stories of pit bull attacks.

"Yes. Are you sure you have him under control?" he said with a shaky voice.

"Yes, I have everything under control. Titus, come. Come on, big guy." Titus came over to her and whimpered.

"Why is he crying?" he asked.

"He's very sensitive and tuned into people. He can feel your fear," she said calmly.

"Really?" His surprise made her smile.

"I need you to breathe in through your nose and out through your mouth three times."

"Are we doing yoga or meeting your dog?"

"You need to calm down first, smart-ass." She waited as he breathed in and out. "Feel calmer?"

"Yes. I could have used this years ago but I think it has more to do with the rescuer." He turned to her slightly and she could see the dimple from his smile.

"I see you haven't lost your sense of humor. Titus is going to sniff your hand and you're going to feel his nose. Okay?" She wanted to assess his comfort level.

"Okay." The air left his nose in a rush.

"Titus, come. Baby. Okay." She crouched down next to him and slipped her fingers through his. He curled them to grip her hand. She closed her eyes as heat, comfort, and peace came together in one touch.

"Baby," she said again.

"It's not doing anything for my ego that you're calling me a baby." He squeezed her hand.

"That's what he understands. He's trained to approach children differently, gentler. Baby is his word, not yours." She squeezed back.

Titus came over sniffed and then nudged his hand. Misha started to pull away but she held his hand in place.

"You're such a good boy. Right, big guy?" She kissed Ty's head.

"Why thank you," Misha replied dryly.

"Are you ready to turn around and face him? Titus, sit."

"Maybe." He lacked the confidence of the CEO she had

first met, the man who had taken up residence in her every thought. When he turned to face his imagined tormentor his hands gripped the armrests, and he pressed himself back into his chair.

"Breathe," she reminded in a whisper.

Titus put up his paw. "No, paw." He put his paw down and started panting as if he was as exhausted as Misha. Then he gave him his biggest pit smile.

Misha's body started to uncoil but he didn't touch Titus. He watched him in a stare-off. Titus gave another whimper and Misha's shoulders relaxed. "I like his eyes. They're golden."

Titus looked over to her like she was their interpreter.

"I think I'm good for today. Will he stay close to you?" His eyes never left Titus as sweat continued to form on his face.

"Yes. He sleeps a lot and curls up by my feet." She hoped this was only step one in Misha's pit bull rehab. The good news was she would be able to work in his office. The bad news, he was even more attractive, adding to her desire for him. His soft side must have been difficult to show her. Picking up his leash, she led Titus over to the shag carpet and gave him a bone.

"Excuse me while I go change my shirt. I seemed to have sweat through it." Without looking at her, he walked over to a concealed closet and grabbed a shirt.

The opportunity presented itself to set up her fake phone. Mac had instructed her to get the phone as close to Misha's computer as possible. When she came into his office she had put her bag on the floor near his desk. She pulled the phone from her bag. Her finger hovered over the power button. One press of a button and she would thrust herself into the dark side. She was resistant to join what had clearly become a web of deceit, but the need for answers fueled her courage. There was no turning back. She strategically placed her bag closer to his desk and activated the phone.

It was game on. She and her sisters needed to put an end to the questions about their papa's death.

Grabbing her drawing pad, she positioned herself on the couch, ready to draw. Her hand needed to stop shaking before the pencil touched the paper. She looked up at him standing in the bathroom, shirtless. He touched the deep scars on his well-cut shoulder. His arms and abs were defined, probably from hours at the gym. Her self-control was at its breaking point. The definition of handsome had his picture next to it. His exterior might be hard but he had shown her his vulnerable side. She wondered what other wounds came from his childhood and why the fact that he might be part Russian wasn't on anyone's radar.

He came out of the bathroom and smiled but it didn't reach his eyes. "So what else do you have in store for me today?"

"I need you to sit for me so I can continue to sketch. You can work while I draw. Go on. You can do your thing." With her nerves calmed down, she started to get into her zone.

"Why thank you, your highness." He shuffled papers around his desk.

"It's Princess Raq." She stayed glued to her drawing.

He laughed under his breath. "Really?"

She didn't respond, watching her sketch begin to unfold. He concentrated on his computer and stroked his ear. When his hair fell onto his forehead, he brushed it off with his thumb. He took a phone call and rolled his eyes at something said on the other end. She captured all of his nuances with strokes of her charcoal, as she did with all her clients. Whenever she sketched a client, she saw him or her in fine detail, creating an intimacy she hoped came through in her drawings and paintings.

Maybe the ability to see into someone's soul was what always got her into so much trouble.

Her bubble of concentration broke as he spoke, "I get the feeling you're going to know all my secrets by the time you're done. You see everything from there, don't you? All the little things that make me tick. But while you're drawing, you give yourself away. I see you as well." He got up and walked toward her and sat at the other end of the couch.

She wore a black velvet shirt. With knees bent, the back of her skirt was tucked up behind her thighs. He reached out and stroked the back of her calf with the lightness of a feather. His touch sent a current of warmth up her leg. She released a gasp that visibly pleased him.

He continued to graze her calf, testing her strength, "Your skin's so sensitive, yet your will to deny me is so strong." His eyes were locked on her.

She hummed in the back of her throat. "I thought we agreed to keep this professional."

"I didn't see that in the contract. Let's see—"

The door flew open as an older woman barged in with bags dangling from each arm. "Misha–" She stopped abruptly to take in the scene, not failing to notice Misha's hand draw back as he slipped it into his pocket and stood. "I see you've already moved on from Victoria." Ice clung to her every word.

Chapter Twelve

MISHA'S DAY had just taken a turn for the worse. First the pit bull, and now his mother with tentacles of bags. His nerves were shot. Titus lifted his head to see who had entered the office.

Raquelle gave her command. "Titus, stay."

"Mother, let me introduce you to Raquelle. Raquelle, this is my mother, Yvonne." He prayed his mother's mouth would behave.

Raquelle placed her feet into her high heels and stood up to greet her.

Yvonne put down her bags and extended her hand like a queen waiting to have it kissed. "It's nice to meet you. Are you my son's new girlfriend?" Her inquiry was still covered in frost.

"I really hate to disappoint you but no, I'm not his girlfriend." Raquelle gave half a smile, sizing up his mother.

"She's the artist I hired to paint my portrait." He shoved his hands in his pockets and held his breath.

"I didn't know you were having your portrait done."

Yvonne's eyes scanned Raquelle from head to toe. "Well, I would know a Chanel outfit and Louboutins anywhere. You have excellent taste. I can appreciate that in a woman."

"You also have excellent taste. The latest Gucci looks stunning on you. You pull off this season's bright colors nicely." Raquelle clasped her hands in front of her.

He dared to step between the battle of the designer outfits. "Yes. I'm having my portrait done, but please don't say anything to father. He's hounded me for years. I want it to be a surprise."

His mother plopped herself down on the couch. "Well, what are your credentials, Raquelle? I want only the best for my son." She looked at her nude-colored fingernails.

Misha craned his head back and looked up to the ceiling. She hadn't lasted more than five minutes until she was sizing up whom she perceived to be Victoria's replacement. Raquelle searched her canvas bag of art supplies. She sat down at the other end of the couch and handed his mother her card.

"My website is on the card with a gallery page of all of my works. I have references if you need them. I would love to do your portrait. You have beautiful skin." She gave her a flirty smile and had managed to turn a grilling into a sales pitch. Score one for *malen'kiy.*

His mother blushed at the compliment. "Oh, thank you. I do try to keep my skin out of the sun. It can be so damaging."

"If I didn't know you were Misha's mother, I would have guessed you to be much younger." Raquelle poured it on. His mother had just had the tables turned on her and didn't even know it.

He stood next to Raquelle. "Mother, is there something you needed today?"

"I wanted to know if you would have dinner with me tonight. I haven't spent any time with you lately. I miss you." She folded her hands in her lap and her eyes pleaded with him.

He flashed back to a memory of her holding him in her lap. At four years old, he didn't understand how the world worked yet. His father had left them again for a trip to Russia. She whispered, "I know you will never leave me, *moy malen'kiy knolik*." She always called him her *little bunny*. Her tear had landed on his forehead. Her words were heavy in his chest and he still carried them with him. In the end, she was the parent who was there for him, not his father. The battle between loyalty and escape raged on.

"Of course I'll have dinner with you. Why don't you make reservations at your favorite place and text me the time? But you have to promise, no more talk about Victoria. I've moved on." He put his hand on her shoulder.

She nodded. "I'll make reservations at The Supper." She turned to look at Titus. "Is that a pit bull?"

"Yes, that's Titus," Raquelle said.

His mother turned to him. "Since when do you allow dogs, especially pit bulls, in your office? You're deathly afraid of dogs."

"Since I found someone who's going to help me through my fear. Besides, she can't paint without him." He shrugged.

She nodded. "Oh, I see." He knew she had no idea.

He helped her off the couch. "Do you want Jonas to bring your bags down to the car?"

"No, no. I'm fine." She kissed him on the cheeks three times. "I'll see you later. Raquelle, it was nice to meet you." She picked up her bags and was out the door.

"I'm sorry about—"

"Don't worry about it. She's only looking out for you. Believe me, I know about overprotective mothers. Mine is Italian." She smiled up at him. "Do you mind me asking about Victoria? Your mother doesn't look happy."

"She's the ex-girlfriend you met last night. Emphasis on the word *ex*. My mother was instrumental in getting me together with Victoria in hopes we would be getting married. She wants grandchildren. But it wasn't meant to be. Victoria and I are . . . different. I couldn't continue in the relationship knowing that we weren't good for each other. I didn't want to hurt her."

He sat beside her on the couch and couldn't resist pulling one of her stray curls. "You handled my mother very well. Better than most. If I didn't know better, I would say you were trying to make a sale."

"There's never a bad time to make a sale." She smiled.

He stared at her still playing with her curl. "I have a meeting to go to. I'm hoping to pick this up later. Besides, I started a calf massage I need to finish." His orbit had begun to sync with hers, and he wondered if she sensed it too.

He left for his marketing meeting. His specialty was numbers on the stock market, not advertising. His place at the head of the table left no doubt who was making the decisions for everything. The director of marketing droned on about where, when, how, and why they should be on social media as well as other platforms to drum up business, business they very much needed.

The door to the conference room burst open as the head of IT and Security rushed in wearing his signature head set, holding his tablet.

"I need to speak with you immediately." Marco's face was sheet white.

Misha addressed the group at the table. "Carry on."

He led Marco to the secure conference room that included walls impenetrable against any kind of electronic device and sound.

"There's been a breach. Someone tried to hack into our Wi-Fi and they're still in the building." Sweat was starting to form on his brow.

"Did you narrow it down to who?" Misha said in a calm voice.

"No. I ran the search but whoever it is turned off their device."

"How is that possible? We have state-of-the art security." Misha's nerves were on edge. He didn't need this on top of everything else. His father would continue to perceive him as weak.

Marco gripped his tablet in front of him with white knuckles. "We have a lot of employees and they all have phones that use the system. They're on them all the time. The system has to search each device in order figure out which one is doing the hacking."

"You only report to me. Understand? I don't want this to get out. Contact me immediately if anything comes up. Thank you. You can go." His stomach knotted. His father would have a complete meltdown if he found out about this. Something poked at him from the back of his brain. There was a lot more going on than an ex-employee diverting funds. Maybe he was being kept in the dark on purpose.

On his way back to the office, he overheard some of the traders talking. "I hear Cavit and Zurich are the real ones in control. Misha is just a pawn." Misha's shoulders curled inward. He turned in the other direction and headed for the roof. Up there he could clear his head and try to come up with a plan. He braced himself on the edge and looked down at the people on the street below, who looked like ants.

He had always been his father's pawn. From birth, he was groomed to be good, dress well, and take orders. The gears turned in his head. He didn't want to be disrespectful or disloyal but what he had in mind would look the same no matter what he did.

During times of uncertainty, the silk rope called to him. He needed to get lost in the feel of the rope as his hand tied knots on the curves of a beautiful woman. He would control how tight or how loose, the pattern, and where to place the rope. The times between sessions had grown longer, weakening him. He fought a losing battle with his father on a daily basis, stripping him of his power. His private life afforded him the opportunity to bring joy to his companion, allowing him the feeling of being in control.

Raquelle. He looked down at the hand that had held her calf, memorizing her soft skin. He remembered her moans. His cock tented his pants, reminding him his libido needed attention. He used his breathing technique to calm himself. As great as the distraction would be, other things required his attention now.

He returned to his office and stopped at the doorway to see Raquelle looking at his portfolio in front of the bookcase. She brought calming energy into the space she occupied. Looking up, she made eye contact and held his stare.

"You look like you've been in a wind storm," she said.

"Oh, I think I might be now." He stared at the binder in her hands.

"I'm sorry. I needed a break and thought I would look at your book collection. I came across this." Her words came out in a rush but she didn't close the book.

He clicked the door closed. "See anything you like?" He

stood behind her, looking down at photos of his rope creations. Nerves snaked under his skin waiting for her judgment. The circles he traveled in didn't judge him. He craved the freedom to be himself but wanted her approval.

"It's beautiful. I've never seen anything like it." She turned to look up at him. "What is it?"

Time ticked by as he tried to figure out what to say. His throat dried. Honesty. "It's called Shibari. It comes from the Japanese style of bondage called Kinbaku. Kinbaku means 'the beauty of tight binding.' Shibari is the Western term for the Japanese word that literally means 'to decoratively tie.'" He waited for her disgust and disapproval. This was a piece of himself he never shared with anyone outside the club.

"Did you tie up these women?" Her finger traced over the rope pattern in the photo.

"Yes. I also took the photographs. I left most of their faces out of it to protect their privacy." His hands curled into fists.

"From the little bit I can see of their faces, they seem at peace, as though they're enjoying it." She looked up at him with curiosity.

"They are at peace. This is all consensual. Some women enjoy being tied up and submitting to the rope. What else do you see?" His fingers began to unfurl.

"The black rope against their skin is beautiful. Some of them are wearing red lingerie, which is a great contrast. The knots are exquisite and intricate." She paused. "What's most beautiful is their surrender. They seem truly free." She continued to run her finger along the curves in the photos.

He gasped. "Really?" He couldn't believe what she had seen in those photos. He went out on a limb. "Is it something that interests you?"

She hesitated and looked away. "I don't know."

He closed the binder and put it back on the shelf. Reaching around her, he opened a drawer and pulled out a black silk rope. "Hold out your hands." He placed the rope in her hands. "Feel it. Run it through your fingers and over your wrists. Tell me what you feel," he whispered.

She pulled the rope through her fingers and over and under her wrists. He pushed her hair behind her shoulder and kissed her neck. She gasped and leaned her head away, giving him permission to continue. He took the rope and slid it between each finger then bound her wrists making a knot underneath. He covered her soft strong hands.

"Talk to me, little one. What do you feel?" He kissed up her neck to behind her ear, biting the lobe.

She sucked in a breath. "It's tender and soft. It feels good." Her eyes became hooded.

As if she remembered something, she said suddenly, "We need to stop and take this off, please."

He removed the rope from her wrists and she checked them for marks. Of course there were none. His years of expertise had trained him to accommodate different levels of restraint.

"Is there something wrong?" he asked.

She turned and pushed past him toward her purse. "I have to get going." Her cheeks flushed a beautiful shade of rose. "I have to put some time in at the studio. Titus, come," she said without looking at him.

The dog lumbered to her as she made several attempts to attach his leash with shaky hands. When she final hooked it on, she looked up at him and smiled. "I'll see you tomorrow."

"Raquelle." She turned to him. "Don't forget to breathe." And she was gone.

He couldn't figure out what had just happened but he had rattled her cage. Had she had a bad experience with someone who tied her up? Did she feel guilty because she enjoyed the feel of the rope? That woman had more mysteries than answers, which was what intrigued him. But how was he going to get her where he wanted her?

Within his rope.

Chapter Thirteen

JONAS APPROACHED Raquelle on the street. "Madam Raquelle, Mr. Raines instructed me to take you home."

"No, thank you," she said, flustered. "I'm going to walk. I need the fresh air."

The late afternoon sun sank behind the skyscrapers casting blocks of shadow on the streets. There used to be a sense of safety in between the tall, elegant buildings. The events of 9/11 had raised the curtain on the illusion. Her emotions vacillated between the darkness and light.

The feel of the rope had opened up a dark side. She imagined what the rope would feel like on her skin, tied up at Misha's mercy. Those thoughts had never crossed her mind before. She wasn't into the pain that came with bondage but the idea of surrendering to him and the rope made her flutter inside. The new sensation excited her.

Her thoughts were doused in red like a big blinking warning sign. Her attraction to him made her weak, wanting to succumb to her desires. He wore his power like a wetsuit making it clear he wanted her in his rope. The woman she was, who lay down with men at the glint of a sweet smile, was fading away. But the pit bull in her would fight him because her artwork was worth it.

Titus looked up at her as if he could read her thoughts. He was more than a pet; the bond they shared flowed both ways unconditionally. Titus filled a space in her she didn't even know was empty. Humans should take their cues from dogs.

She exited Central Park and left Titus on the curb. She stepped off and placed her fingers in her mouth to whistle for a yellow cab. A black limo stopped in front of her. Jonas got out.

"Can I assist you?" He stood in front of her in his black uniform and hat with hands folded.

"Were you following me?" she asked, startled.

"Yes. I was instructed to make sure you were taken care of. I didn't think you would walk all the way back to your apartment." He remained in place next to the car.

Misha's rope reached out and wrapped around her chest. He wasn't trying to control her; he was protecting her, taking care of her. No one ever took care of the defiant one. She was like a baby eating peaches for the first time, sampling a different but delicious food.

I guess he wins this round.

Jonas opened the door for her and Titus went right to him. He bent down, grabbed the dog's jowls and rubbed them–Titus's favorite kind of love. "In you go."

She lay back in the seat and petted Titus's head for comfort. Misha was the alpha male she usually avoided at all cost. She didn't want to be taken care of or told what to do. But he had showed her his soft side. The side that also needed comfort, love, and understanding. The last man to show her love had betrayed her on every level. He was her last attempt at love. Sex was sex. No feelings involved. But that train of thought was dripping away.

The car pulled up to her Upper East Side apartment and Jonas opened the door for them.

"Please thank Misha for me and Titus." She winked at him.

"Very well, madam." He smiled.

"I have a feeling we're going to be seeing a lot of each other. Just call me Raquelle."

The ride on the elevator took forever making her anxiety spike but the comfort of her apartment beckoned. She opened the door, took off Titus's leash, and plopped onto the couch. The lush fabric hugged her in and formed to her body. Her taste in decor was contemporary with rich details of burgundy, navy blue, and creams. Everything was round and soft. No hard edges or leather. Her furniture was designed to cuddle and squeeze her.

Titus came back into the room carrying his favorite Babar elephant. She had a collection of them in her bedroom, but he was particular with his favorite.

She pulled out her phone and pressed one button. "Hi, you comin' over?" She needed to talk to someone.

"Sure. You got the champagne chilled?" Brie said.

"You know I do. Always. See you in a bit." She threw the phone down and covered her eyes with her arm.

Later, the knock at the door startled Titus and he started barking. His tail was already wagging, waiting for their guest. She opened the door to Brie, who leaned against the doorframe.

She came in carrying a brown paper bag filled with wonderful smells. "You two must have been out cold. I knocked twice."

"God, you know me so well. Chinese food is exactly what I need." She closed the door.

Raquelle followed Brie to the kitchen. "It always cracks

me up that the only things you have on your counter are a French press and a pasta maker." She laughed.

"Well, you know I love my hazelnut coffee and homemade pasta. I may not be able to boil water but every Italian woman knows how to make pasta. Although Mara inherited the real cooking talent. I notice you never turn me down when I attempt to make it."

She reached for the dishes in the cupboard as Brie arranged the cardboard boxes and opened the flaps. They each dug into their favorites. This was their once-a-week cheat meal. Music played in the background as her phone shuffled through songs ranging from R&B to hard rock.

Brie got two flutes and popped the champagne bottle. "You want to talk about it?" Brie's keen insight was on full alert.

"I do want to talk. I'm just not sure where to start. It was a bizarre day, kind of." She spun her Lo Mein with a fork. "By the way, who has champagne with Chinese?"

"Don't change the subject. Why don't you start at the beginning? I have a feeling this has something to do with your mystery man."

She proceeded to tell Brie blow-by-blow about what had happened in Misha's office, rope and all. "He is different than any man I've ever met—and I've met a lot of men." This got a chuckle out of Brie.

"Does he want to tie you up and inflict pain?"

She put her fork down, giving up on eating. "I don't think so, but we didn't get that far. I got spooked and scared myself."

"I have something I want to tell you. I need you to have an open mind." Brie's eyes begged for understanding.

"Okay," Raquelle said with trepidation.

"Logan and I are in an exclusive relationship and we like to play."

"Play?"

"He likes to do things to me like tie me up and we play with . . . toys. He introduced me to a different way of relating to each other that requires a lot of trust." Brie pushed her plate away and folded her hands on the counter.

Raquelle was glued to Brie's words. "And how does it make you feel?"

"I feel empowered. I love everything we do together. But you have to understand that we talk about everything. There are rules and safe words. We're not hardcore. But sex is definitely more interesting. I trust him with my life. I surrender to him when we play. Giving up control comes naturally because my life requires me to be in control all the time. Don't get me wrong. I love my job but it's exhausting. He gives me a chance to hand it over to him. I'm free in those moments and those are the moments he craves. We're like ying and yang. Am I making any sense?" Worry crossed her face.

"Yes. Actually you are making sense. It sounds intense. You trust him with your life? And are you trying to say working for me is exhausting?" She had never trusted anyone but herself.

Brie laughed. "Well, I am managing your entire career and it's growing by the minute." She rubbed the diamond on the end of her chain. "This is a symbol of our commitment to one another. But we didn't do any kind of ceremony. It's just our thing. There is a wide range of people who play at various levels. I've seen Shibari done and it's quite beautiful. Maybe for once in your life you feel like you can trust someone."

"Let's not get carried away. When were you going to tell

me about all of this? I had no idea," she said, even as she kept another secret from Brie.

Brie shrugged. "I don't know. It never seemed to be the right time. Besides, how do you really bring that up?" She stood up and put her arms around Raquelle's shoulders. "We had to grow up sometime."

Raquelle held onto her forearms. "Yeah, I know. It sucks sometimes."

The phone rang on the wall.

"Hello?" She couldn't imagine who would be coming to see her at this hour.

The doorman said, "I have Leigha and Dean here to see you. Should I send them up?"

"Yes. Thank you." She put the phone back. "Leigha and Dean are on their way up. They usually don't come without calling first." She left the kitchen to let them in.

"Hey, what are you two up to?" She gave each a hug and a kiss, Italian style.

Dean shook hands with Brie and introduced himself then looked at Leigha. "We have something to talk to you about."

"Ah, sounds personal. Brie, do you mind calling it a night? We can talk more later." Her hands clasped together.

"Sure. Logan would love leftover Chinese for whenever he gets home." She sighed, grabbed the bags, and headed for the door.

"Let's go sit." Raquelle led the way to the living room.

Dean sat next to Leigha. "We can't thank you enough for today. Peter got past their Wi-Fi and into their system. It's pretty sophisticated. He's going to nose around a little bit and see what's going on. Did you turn off your phone when you got the text?" Peter Bryan was ex-military and one of the partners for MBK Global Security working as their top IT guy.

"Yes. Right away. He wasn't even in the office." She sat with her legs tucked in under her, running her fingers over her skirt.

Dean continued, "We may need you do some other things for us but we'll let you know. In the meantime, keep your eyes peeled and look around a little bit. You may see something we can use."

The soft velvet under her fingers soothed her. "Sure." She had found something, just not anything Dean would be interested in.

"Dean, can you excuse us for a minute?" Leigha said.

Here it comes.

"I'll go look for a drink." He got up to go in search of his favorite scotch.

Leigha sat back on the couch and crossed her legs. "So, what's up? I know you well enough to know when something's not right."

"I don't know what you mean." Raquelle kept looking at her skirt.

"Something's going on, because your smart mouth is taking a holiday." Her expression didn't change.

"Ha, ha, CSI. Maybe you should work at the security firm with the boys." She crossed her arms over her chest.

Leigha's face softened. "Is everything okay? Is all this spy crap getting to you?"

She looked up and met her eyes. "Yes and no. Misha is a good man. I would hate for us to be wrong about this. He's kind and generous. You know I'm the first one to see the bad in people, but not this time. My radar is usually never wrong."

"You're right, but maybe you're too close to this one. You read people like no one else I know. Maybe they're wrong about all of this or maybe there's a connection within the company Misha doesn't even know about." She held her hands. "Please be careful. This spy stuff can be rough. Talk to me when you need to. Please." Leigha had experience in being an operative. Her Russian father had made her part of his world when he took a photo of hers and placed a security chip on it.

"Thank you. I will." She hugged her.

"Are you kidding me? You only have champagne in this house? Where the hell is the Macallan? I'll be bringing my own stash with me next time." Dean's loud voice came from the kitchen and then he appeared with a flute of champagne.

He leaned against the chair. "How the hell do you drink this stuff? It goes right to your nose."

They started laughing. He took some sips and made faces of disgust.

"Champagne doesn't look good on you and that's saying a lot. Everything looks good on you." Leigha smiled seductively.

"Get a room already." Raquelle's heaviness clung to her heart.

Dean handed Raquelle the flute of champagne and held his hand out to Leigha. She took it and cuddled into his arms. He mumbled, "Someone's getting a spanking when we get home."

Leigha smiled and blushed. She turned to Raquelle. "We'll see you later."

After they left, Raquelle sat in her apartment alone surrounded by memories of a day full of surprises. Her head was jumbled with thoughts of Misha, the rope, Brie and Logan, and Leigha and Dean. She wrestled with her role as a spy. Espionage was not her thing. She wanted, no *needed* things to go back to normal. But that would only happen when they found out how deeply her papa had been involved with the Russians. She hoped it didn't include Misha. He piqued her curiosity in a whole other way. She wanted to explore him and his rope but needed to hold back. Brie's question about trust rattled around in her head.

Her phone dinged.

Misha: I hope you're okay. You left the office flustered. I apologize if I upset you.

Raquelle: You didn't upset me, just got me curious. I'm fine. Thank you. See you tomorrow.

Misha: Good night, *malen'kiy*.

She was treading water in the deep end with him.

Chapter Fourteen

MISHA CAME into his office riled up. The morning run and boxing session hadn't released any pent-up energy. For a brief moment, he'd felt that connection to Raquelle when she let him bind her wrists. He had sensed that she felt the power of the rope when her body became lax. Maybe it was his imagination playing tricks on him. He had spent years searching for the strength two people had to have to truly trust one another. He worried he had pushed her too far, causing her to bolt. Then he remembered her rule about staying professional. He was pretty sure he was about to break that rule. His pull toward her outstripped anything else he had ever felt for another woman. At thirty-six, he was experienced in the field of love and sex and wouldn't accept an imitation.

As the morning dragged on, the numbers on his screen blurred. He couldn't focus. His mind wandered between his father's demands, a company in crisis, and everything Raquelle. With every minute that ticked by, he waited for her to make an entrance.

He pressed the button for Audrey's desk. "I'm in the middle of something. Can you please make me a cappuccino? It's that time. Thank you." He began to lose steam in the early afternoons.

The door opened and Raquelle walked in with Titus on his leash. His amped-up energy turned to relaxation—until he saw Titus.

"Are you ready for him?"

He nodded and stared.

She walked over saying, "Baby," close to Titus's ear.

"You can stop saying that. You're starting to give me a complex." His heart pounded in his chest.

"Remember to breathe," she said. "Titus, sit."

Misha consciously breathed in through his nose and out through his mouth.

"I would like you to try and pet him today. First, you're going to put the top of your hand out to him. He needs to sniff it. Ready." Her voice was calm.

"Yes." He stretched out his hand as Titus sniffed it and then gave him a gentle lick. He pulled his hand back as Titus continued to wag his tail.

"That wasn't so bad. Now, put your hand out and touch his head."

His heart rate started to come down from its peak position. His hand lightly brushed Titus' head. The dog never moved, as if he sensed his tension.

"That's enough for today. You must be feeling brave." She winked, taking Titus off his leash, and ordered him to go lay down. He went over and plopped himself on the rug under her easel. She threw him his favorite bone, which kept his attention.

She dropped her bag on the floor and took off her coat.

Without looking at him, she said, "I'm going to paint today," and walked over to the easel. "Damn it, I forgot my paint shirt."

No doubt her designer outfit wouldn't tolerate oil paint. He went to his closet and got one of his many dress shirts. "Put this on." He held it out for her to put her arms in. She kept her back to him, so he turned her around and began to button up the shirt. His fingers itched to touch her skin again.

After the last button was put in place, he ran his fingers along her jaw. She caught his hand.

"We need to talk, Raquelle."

"I don't think there's anything to talk about." She moved to turn back to the canvas.

He held her by the shoulders to stop her. "I think you got spooked yesterday. You probably have questions for me. So, fire away." His hands dropped away from her. He needed to give her space.

She held the hem of the shirt. "I talked to a friend last night who's into all this. Then I looked it up online. I don't think we're a match."

"Why not?" He needed to push her to open up to him.

"Because I'm not into that pain and pleasure thing. In other words, you're not going to tie me up and then beat the crap out of me and think I enjoy it."

He laughed. "Have I given you any indication that I'm into dishing out pain?"

"No." Her mouth turned down.

"It's not about bondage and pain for everyone. I'm not into that. I'd love nothing more than for you to be in my rope, but it would be all pleasure, no pain." He ran his thumb down her neck.

"Why?" she asked.

"Why, what?"

"Why do you do it?" There was no judgment in her face, only curiosity.

"My life has been mapped out for me since the day I was born. Every decision has been made for me. I needed to make some decisions of my own. I fell into this through a friend at college and it spoke to me. When I have a woman, who trusts me and completely surrenders to what I'm doing, there's an energy and peace that comes over both partners. There is nothing more powerful than seeing the pleasure you can give a woman. The sex is amazing. I would never do anything that a woman doesn't want to happen. There's a lot of communication that goes on before you ever get to that point. Yesterday, when you held the rope, you felt something. I felt it too. Tell me I'm wrong." His thumb registered the uptick in her pulse.

Her lips tightened for a moment. "Yes. But I can't describe it. I liked having my wrists tied together. At the same time, it felt wrong, dark."

"That's a normal initial reaction. Some things that are dark are very right." He nodded his head in the direction of the stuffed elephant hanging on her easel. "I made you something."

He took the black rope bracelet off BB's neck. The bracelet had been made from the strands of one of his silk ropes and tied in intricate knots. Gold clasps were attached at both ends.

"This is beautiful. I've never seen anything like it. Are you sure you're in the right business? Maybe you should design jewelry." She held out her wrist for him.

"You add to the beauty of this bracelet. Not the other way around. Nothing could add to your beauty. You're wonderful just the way you are, inside and out."

"Thank you."

He leaned down to kiss her but was interrupted by Marco barged in his office.

"We've got a lead on yesterday's breach." He looked at Raquelle, questioning whether he should say any more. "Who are you?" Marco demanded.

"She's my portrait artist and that's all you need to know. Go on." He cleared his throat.

"Ah, well, I don't know how to tell you this, but the last trace on the breach before it went dead came from your office." Marco swallowed. "I need to check all your equipment."

"Go ahead. I doubt you'll find anything. I have nothing to hide." He remembered leaving Raquelle in his office alone the day before. He watched her reaction to the news.

"Were you here yesterday?" Marco glared at Raquelle.

"Yes." She looked at Misha for help.

"Then I need to see your phone," he ordered.

She nodded and got it out of her bag. He took it from her and turned it on.

"Did you have it on or off yesterday?" Marco asked, looking down at his tablet.

"Off."

"Why?" His face turned hard. Misha was curious on how she would handle Marco's Spanish Inquisition.

"I don't like to be bothered when I'm working. Why does it matter to you?" She put her hands on her hips.

"Because I need to find where the breach came from." Marco's voice hardened.

She turned to Misha. "What was breached?"

He waved a dismissive hand.

Marco pressed a couple of buttons on her phone. "Well, it's not your phone. I'm going to check all phones in-house and keep searching." His face stared down at his device as he left the office.

"I'm sorry about that. It's pins and needles around here lately." His father's obsession with security was at an all-time high.

She turned off her phone and dropped it in her bag. "Should I even ask why?"

"When you have someone leave the firm with other people's money and then turn up dead in Mexico, it raises a red flag. We had to pay out our clients and reassure them. Everyone is scrambling for answers."

She nodded. "Tell me more about your father. You seem close to him." She continued to work on her canvas.

"My father likes to give his advice when it comes to running the company but mostly runs his business in Rus— internationally." He stopped himself before he gave her more information. His father had always told him to keep his business quiet as well as the fact that he was Russian. His comfort level with her allowed him to open up and want to share his life with her, or lack of it. He was so tired of being ashamed to be Russian and keeping secrets.

He stepped behind her and began twirling her curls. Her hair, with its golden strands and big loose curls, mesmerized him. His fingers worked their way up to the base of her skull. She stopped drawing and fell back into his touch. "I have an idea. I say we have dinner at my place where there are less distractions."

She turned around as he held the back of her neck in his hands. He reached for her bracelet and slipped his finger underneath. "I made this for you, to wear on your wrist at all times as a reminder of what you're denying us to be. Imagine what it feels like to be bound, to be mine. I want that. I want you and I'll have you, but tonight comes with nothing but dinner and conversation." He kissed her forehead.

The sun had been playing hide and seek with the clouds all day, casting the office in shadow and light. A ray of sun peeked out from behind the opaque mist and shined on her face. Tears shimmered at the edges of her eyes. One fell as he caught it with his thumb.

"You don't know who I am or what I'm about. I've slept with a lot of men for many different reasons. I'm trying so hard to keep this professional and you are making it so damn difficult." Shame spread across her face.

"I just confessed my love for tying women up. Most women would have run for the hills. You came back and asked questions. I want to know why you didn't run. You helped me with my fear of pit bulls without judgment." He touched his forehead to hers. "Let me teach you about the art of Shibari. You can't deny there's something here. I don't care about your past. Just let me in. Let me decide." His heart tightened with fear. Having tasted her warmth, he wanted to be burned by the sun. He would peel away her layers and find out more about her, from the sorrow and hardship to the newly discovered dark side she hid from him.

She smiled. "You had me at pit bull. But what does *malen'kiy* mean?"

"Little one. It's a term of endearment in Russian." He turned over her wrist and kissed the inside.

She sighed. "You're so gentle."

"Sometimes." He wiggled his brows. "I have a meeting to attend. I'll leave you to paint."

The afternoon dragged on, but he couldn't stay focused on anything but the thought of dinner with Raquelle. There was much to explore: her body, her mind, and the chemistry that sparked between them.

When he made it back to the office at the end of the day, she had completed a preliminary sketch of him on canvas.

He stood behind her. "Amazing."

She spoke to him over her shoulder. "It's a very complex piece," she said dryly.

"I can't wait to see you give it life." He held her wrists with his fingers. "So, can I expect you at eight tonight?"

"Yes, for dinner and conversation. I'll expect that you will be cooking and not ordering out." She gave him a sly grin.

"Do you doubt that I can cook?" He acted offended.

She put her hands on his chest and looked up at him. "I don't doubt that you can do anything you set your mind to." She pushed away. "I have to get going. I have to put myself together for dinner with a handsome man who says he can cook. We'll see."

Her words rang in his ears. She believed he could do anything and yet his father second-guessed his every move. He needed her on his team.

She grabbed Titus's leash and he followed her to the door. Lucky dog.

"I'll call Jonas to give you a ride home. I'll see you tonight." His heart ballooned. He hadn't felt like this since he was in high school going to the prom. *People move, things change, and you lose track of each other. But you never forget your first love*. Raquelle might be his first love all over again. Lucky him.

He stood by his office window and called Raquelle. The clouds had dissipated enough for him to see to the street below. "Jonas said he'll meet you by the curb. Do you know you're like one more piece of chocolate for me? I can't seem to get enough." He thought he could see her talking on her phone with Titus sitting next to her.

The boom came, first rattling the windows followed by a

plume of white steam. The explosion tore a hole in the street the size of a city bus. He couldn't see her through the smoke as debris filled the air.

"Raquelle!"

Chapter Fifteen

MISHA RAN through the office and shouted to Audrey, "Call 911. There's been an explosion!" He pounded the elevator button several times in frustration.

The urgency grew heavier with every passing minute. Sweat covered his body. He loosened his tie and unbuttoned his shirt. He needed to get to her. She had only just begun to breathe happiness into his life. He prayed that in a single moment she hadn't been taken from him. Everything in his life had been controlled, so precise, and yet in the beat of a sparrow's wing he might have lost what he had been searching for his entire life. Fate would be in someone else's hands once again.

The elevator opened to a packed lobby as he pushed screaming people out of his way. He powered through the doors onto the street and into chaos. Floating pieces of debris rained down as the smoky fumes surrounded him, filling his nose. Before he had a chance to scan the street, he heard a dog barking and whining. Titus stood over Raquelle on the sidewalk closest to the building. He whimpered, licking her face and nudging her with his nose. He growled and bared his teeth at anyone who tried to approach. No one dared to cross him.

Misha understood his bark. Fear clawed at him. What he saw before him ripped him open. Her words came back to him. Breathe in through his nose and out through his mouth. Raquelle wasn't moving and he had to get past Titus to get to her. He would use every trick he knew but it would require all his courage.

"Titus, come. It's okay." She called him 'big guy.' "Come on, big guy." He reached for the leash. "Baby, right? I'm going to help her."

Titus whimpered and growled a warning then moved away from his mistress in understanding. Misha kneeled beside Raquelle and Titus flanked her. His heart pounded in his ears as he bounced between anxiety and fear. He checked for her pulse and breathing. Both were strong. Blood gushed from her forehead. He took out his handkerchief and applied pressure to her head.

"Raquelle, come on, little one. It's time for you to wake up. Please," he begged.

Titus licked the side of her face and laid his head on her shoulder. Misha thought about propping her up but didn't want to cause more harm if she had a neck injury. Blood soaked through the handkerchief. Her eyes weren't opening. Sirens blared in the distance, finally coming to a stop at the curb. The paramedics approached and Titus barked and lunged.

"Whoa. You want to control your dog so we can get to her?" one of the paramedics said.

"Titus, no." He gave it a shot. "Come." He tried his authoritative voice, which seemed to work.

He held Titus away from Raquelle. "She's breathing and has a pulse." He heard his own voice but wasn't sure where the words were coming from.

"Those are good signs. We'll load her up and take her to Presbyterian for evaluation. It looks like a concussion but they'll want to run some tests."

"Her name is Raquelle Luccenzo." He choked out.

The young paramedic took a closer look, "Hey, I know her. Let's get her to the hospital." He didn't know or care how the handsome paramedic knew his woman, he only hoped his diagnosis of just a concussion was true. *His woman*. His heart dropped to his stomach.

They loaded her up and sped away as Titus barked and whined, struggling to follow, only to be stopped by the end of his leash. Out of the corner of his eye he saw her bag and phone flung by the windows. He picked up her phone, stuffed it into his jacket pocket, and slung her bag over his shoulder.

His phone rang. "Boss, I can see you but I can't get to you. They've closed off the street. Can you walk down this way? Where's Raquelle?" Jonas sounded panicked.

"She got hurt in the blast. They already took her to Presbyterian. Can you get us there?" He started walking with Titus by his side.

"Is that really a question?" He paused. "Titus?"

"He's with me but only has superficial cuts. He'll be fine. We're on our way."

Jonas waited outside the car and opened the door letting them in. Titus jumped in beside him as he sunk in the seat. His five-thousand-dollar suit was covered in soot and ash. He could get another suit, but he couldn't get another Raquelle.

Titus lay down and put his head on Misha's thigh. His hand hovered over the dog's head and then slowly lowered to pet him. What amazed him wasn't how he comforted Titus, but how petting Titus comforted him. He left his hand on his back and closed his eyes. They breathed in sync, getting ready for what lay ahead.

The car stopped and Jonas opened the car door. "We're at the ER, sir."

"Thank you," he said wearily.

He hesitated getting out of the car. Hospitals weren't his favorite place, not since the attack that sent him there many years ago. They had wanted to amputate his arm and he had lost a lot of blood. Death had knocked on his door but he never answered. He had too much to live for—and she was waiting for him.

Without thinking, he took the leash with him and walked into the ER with Titus.

"I'm here for Raquelle Luccenzo. She was in the explosion."

"Sorry, no dogs allowed." The nurse peered over her glasses.

"What?" he said, confused.

"The dog. He can't be in here."

He looked down to register he still had Titus with him. "Oh, right."

Jonas walked in with a hand held out. "I'll take him and clean up his cuts. You have other things to focus on. Come buddy, let's go." Titus followed him reluctantly.

The nurse was still looking at him over her glasses. "Now, are you family?"

"Yes, I'm her fiancé." He flashed her his charming smile.

She looked at him suspiciously. "She's back in room twenty-two."

Twenty-two was his lucky number. That had to be a good sign. He made his way through chaos as the ER came alive trying to save other victims of the blast. Crying and screaming could be heard at various decibels in the waiting room. He left the noise in search of her room as the voices receded and quiet took over. He wished he could hear her scream or cry, just to know she was alive. He pulled back the curtain to see her lying in bed, eyes closed. Cuts and bruises covered her arms and face. A temporary bandage covered the gash on her head and her left wrist was wrapped. He sat next to her and held her right hand.

He struggled for words. "You're going to be all right. I'm going to make sure you have the best of everything. I'll take care of you. You've sparked something in me I can't let go of. Stay with me, *malen'kiy*." He pushed the hair off her forehead. A lump formed in his throat.

He noticed her bracelet was gone. On the floor was a plastic bag full of clothes and other items. He searched through it until he found the bracelet and put it back on her wrist. "This will remind you that I'm always with you. When you wake up, you will see it." He could have sworn she squeezed his hand.

"Hello, I'm Dr. Strauss. I understand you're her fiancé." He offered his hand.

His throat went dry. "Yes. How is she?"

"She has a pretty good concussion. We did a CT scan and there is no internal bleeding. She broke her wrist, which we are going to be casting shortly. She's also going to need stitches on her head. I assume she's going home with you because she's going to need aftercare."

He answered, "Yes," without hesitation. "But why isn't she awake yet?" His heartbeat kicked up a notch.

"Her body is protecting her brain. It's shut down everything so her brain can heal. She'll wake up when she's ready. When she goes home, she'll need to wear dark sunglasses in the light. Otherwise she should stay in a dark room until she's cleared. There can't be any electronic devices like cell phones or tablets. It's crucial for her recovery that she follows the guidelines." He tapped on his tablet.

"Understood. However, I have a plastic surgeon I would like to handle the stitches in her head. I'll put in a call and see if he's available. Thank you."

"I'll leave you with full instructions before she's released." The doctor left, wearing a faint smile.

He had the number he wanted on speed dial. "Mother, I need you to call your plastic surgeon. I have an emergency."

"What? Oh my God, what's happened?" His mother went into panic mode.

He choked on his words. "It's Raquelle. She was standing on the sidewalk when the explosion went off in the street. Can you call? She needs him right away."

"Yes, of course. Is she going to be all right?"

"I hope so." He knew his feelings were apparent. "She's going home with me when she wakes up."

He was met with silence. "She's turned into more than your portrait artist," his mother said reluctantly.

"Not yet. But I need to see where it goes."

His mother was always on his side. "She'll be fine, Misha. I know you'll take good care of her. I'll bring dinner to your place tonight. It sounds like you could use some company."

He knew how to take care of everyone but himself. "That sounds good. Thank you. I'll see you later." He clicked off without her response.

Raquelle had already shown him she was a fighter. Guilt crashed down on him. He should have had her picked up in the garage. She wouldn't be in the hospital if he had.

He bent down and kissed her cheek. "I'll be back for you, little one. You need to fight and come back to me. We've only just begun to explore each other." He needed to prepare for her arrival to his home.

He walked through the ER oblivious to the chaos around him. Jonas would pick him up at the entrance, and then he could go through his checklist of things to do for her stay with him. As he slipped into the back seat, Raquelle's ringer went off with Adele's song *Rumor Has It*.

"Hello?"

"Who is this?" The voice on the other end questioned.

"This is Michael Raines. Who am I speaking with?" He hoped it was one of her sisters.

"This is Marabella Luccenzo. Do you want to tell me why you're answering Raquelle's phone?" Her angry voice was cut with fear.

He held his head in his hand. "She was in an explosion and I'm at the hospital."

"Oh my God, which hospital?"

He proceeded to fill her in on all the details. What he failed to mention was how Raquelle would be coming home with him. He threw the phone on the seat as a to-do list ran through his head.

Chapter Sixteen

RAQUELLE'S HEAD swam in deep murky water. She grabbed for anything to get out of it. The memories of almost drowning at the hands of Bernardo crashed over her. He had laughed as he held her underwater, watching her struggle to come up for air. Panic set in as her head pounded. She could hear herself scream from a distance. Someone was calling her name. They must be here to save her.

"Raquelle, it's me, Mara." Mara held her arm.

She took in a huge breath. "What? What's going on? Where am I?" Her anxiety turned to panic.

Leigha put her hand on her arm. "Calm down. You're in the hospital. We're here. Everything is going to be all right."

Mara wiped her face with a tissue. "One of the pipes under the street exploded and you were right next to it. You have a serious concussion and are lucky to be alive."

Whenever she had a migraine, nausea always came with it. "Bucket."

Leigha reached for the pink bucket and held it in front of her.

"Lights off, please." Her voice sounded like sandpaper on metal.

The room went dark and Mara got her some water. She took a few sips to find out if her stomach agreed. She lay back down and calmed herself using her breathing technique. Her sisters sat on either side of her without a word.

A nurse came in the room. "Time for your pain meds. Looks like you could use them," she said in a soothing voice.

She pushed something into her IV to dull the pain.

"Thank you," she managed.

"Push the call button if you need anything." The nurse left, and the sound of the closing curtain was the last thing she heard before she went under again.

When she woke up, her head was clearer but still painful. Her sisters were still there.

"How are you feeling?" Mara asked.

"A little better. How long have I been out?" She had no concept of time.

Leigha leaned over the bed. "Most of the day. Do you remember anything?"

"I remember the explosion and that's it. Oh my God, where's Titus?" Her mind fought the fogginess of the pain meds.

"Titus is fine. He's with Misha. He found you lying on the ground and got you to the hospital." Mara placed a towel with ice against Raquelle's head.

"Wait. Rewind the tape. Misha has Titus? You're kidding, right?"

"No. I called your phone and he answered, giving me the details. Is there a problem?" Mara looked confused.

She tried to laugh but her head hurt too much. "He's terrified of Titus. He was mauled by a pit bull when he was little. He had a panic attack when I brought Titus to the office with me. I had to peel him off the ceiling. I taught him how to calm down so he could be around him." She looked up at the ceiling, noticing the glow-in-the-dark stars. "It must have taken a lot for him to get near Titus."

"He sounds like a good guy." Leigha squeezed her hand.

Mac and Dean crowded into the room, interrupting the quiet moment.

Mac's worried face came into view. "How are you feeling?"

"Oh, I don't know. I only got hit in the head with a boulder. By the way, could you reach up in the cabinet and see if you can find a pillow?"

"Sure."

He reached up to grab a pillow and handed it to her. As soon as she took it, she hit him with it.

"Hey, whadda doin'?" He put his arms in front of his face.

She fell back in the bed. "Oh, crap, now I feel dizzy. But it was worth it."

Mara stood in the corner covering her giggle. Mac stood out of reach with hands on his hips, waiting for a response.

The dizziness left and she said, "That's for putting me in danger. The tech guy came into Misha's office looking for the device that hacked the Wi-Fi. He grilled me on what I had done with the phone yesterday. I can't do this anymore." She didn't want to be spying on Misha and his company anymore. He had saved her life. She couldn't see that there was anything malicious about him.

"It sounds like they have a sophisticated security system. Good to know. I wouldn't expect anything less. I hate to be the bearer of bad news, but you're not done. We found out that there are two operating systems. One works behind another one. Peter's working on the breaking the firewall and developing software to get in. We need to see what's in the second operating system." His body took up half the room. The king had spoken.

"Can't you go in and do that? Isn't that your job?"

Mac folded himself into the chair. "We can't get anywhere near the place without causing suspicion. Raquelle, we need to get to the bottom of this. Something is going on at that firm and it may tie everything together. You'll finally find out who poisoned your father." He hit her soft spot.

Tiredness came over her. "We'll talk more later. I need to get some sleep." Damn it. Her injury would delay the completion of the portrait for a submission to Aurtoro Gallery.

"Besides, you're deadly with a pillow. I don't know what you're worried about." He smiled.

"Very funny, Highlander." She held out her hand and he squeezed it.

The nurse came back in and announced she was moving Raquelle to a room for an overnight stay. Her sisters made an exit and kissed her on their way out.

Dean leaned over. "In case he didn't tell you, you're doing a great job. We wouldn't have gotten this far without you. Thank you. Sometimes he's a little bit of a meathead."

"I can hear you," Mac said from the door.

Dean squeezed her hand and left.

When her visitors had gone, the room became silent as the "what ifs" settled into her rattled brain. The braided rope on her wrist grabbed her attention. *Misha.* The thought of him delivered a welcome distraction. A wave of peace washed over her as she twirled the silken band between her fingers until the comforting motion put her to sleep.

.   .   .

MISHA CREPT into her room and watched her chest move up and down. He wouldn't leave her side now. Guilt caged him. If he had made the right decision none of this would have happened. Her injuries fell squarely on his shoulders. His father never would have put his sons or his mother in harm's way. He was always in control of every damn decision he made. Misha would make this right with her and make sure she was never harmed again.

He sat down in the lounger next to her bed. She looked like an angel. Blue light from the monitor glowed on her as she lay curled up. She looked even smaller, like a child in need of a good night's sleep. He reached out to move the hair off her cheek. She stirred and rolled onto her back.

She rubbed her eyes. "Hey, what are you doing here?" she said with surprise.

"Where else would I be?" He required no answer.

She tilted her head and stared at him. "You have my fur baby, so I'm told."

"Yes. Titus is fine. But I couldn't do it without Jonas's help. I don't know anything about pets. I never had any growing up. I remembered his stuffed elephant and bones. That seemed to calm him down." The events of the day were starting to catch up with him too.

"This is a big deal for you. You should feel proud. Tell me what happened after the explosion." Her eyes got droopy.

"Maybe tomorrow, *malen'kiy*. You need your sleep. I'll be right here if you need anything." He kissed her forehead.

"What? You're staying here? In my room?" She sounded alarmed.

"This chair becomes a lounger so I'm all set." He patted the armrests.

She curled onto her side and tucked her hands under her head. She reached out to him. "Thank you," she whispered.

He took her hand and kissed it. "Go to sleep. I'll see you in the morning."

He pulled his shoes off and sat back in the recliner. His thoughts traveled back to the reason he'd never had a pet: his father wouldn't be able to handle it. God forbid he and his brothers had something to look after, something they could love and care for. He had ended up taking care of his mother. He wasn't sure that counted but he did his best. His life revolved around numbers, education, and discipline. There was very little room for play and fun.

He looked at the beautiful creature next to him. She seemed to have cornered the market on fun, his exact opposite. There would be a trade. She would teach him how to have fun and take care of a pet and he could teach her discipline. Under his control, he could take care of her. His hand would test each knot, sliding under the silk to make sure it wasn't too tight. But tonight he needed to get rid of those thoughts or he would never get any sleep.

Tomorrow he would take her home and care for her until she got better. And then what? He didn't want to get ahead of himself thinking about their next chapter.

Chapter Seventeen

RAQUELLE'S HEADACHE subsided to a dull throb. The nausea came and went, much to her relief. She had despised vomiting since she was a child. It made her feel weak like she didn't have control over her body. The only light in the room streamed in around the sides of the shades, highlighting Misha's light beard and tousled hair.

She pulled the sheets up to her neck as a chill brushed her skin. He had stayed by her side through the night. Titus was the only other male who had ever stayed with her all night. Her breathing picked up as her papa's words assaulted her.

You're nothing but a whore. How could my own flesh and blood give it away so easily? Get out of my sight. She had run out of the studio and hidden.

His words were forever seared her soul. She had never forgotten them and then she lived them. He was the reason she had never let any man get too close. Her papa had been the center of her world. She had admired him for his talent and teachings. He used to stand behind her, guiding her hand, trying to make her feel the strokes. But in a few short sentences, he had destroyed her. Hate ran through her veins and she kept her distance from him. When he died, the emotions collided as hate slammed into love and loss.

The mind worked in mysterious ways. Of all the memories that could have been triggered, the nasty one of her father came to the forefront. She lay back in bed, counting the holes in the ceiling to see if they compared to the number of men she had slept with over the years out of spite. Most of them were faceless, one-night stands she had pursued after a night of drinking to scratch an itch. She never got a number or a last name. Sometimes no first name either. But lately her heart yearned for more of a connection. Taking cabs home in the wee hours of the morning was depressing and lonely.

"Raquelle, what's wrong? Are you in pain?" Misha sat up in the recliner and wiped the tears from her cheek.

"I'm fine. Just taking a trip down memory lane." Her heart broke. Misha was the opposite of her papa and every other man in her life. She needed to get away from this beautiful caring man. He deserved better than the likes of her.

He stroked her cheek. "Must not have been a very good one."

"Thank you for staying with me last night, but you need to go. I'll be fine. My sisters will take care of me." She pulled his hand away from her cheek.

He leaned his elbows on the bed and propped his head in his hands. "When I came out of the building after the explosion, I saw Titus standing over your body. He cried and then growled at anyone who got close to you. His love and protection for you is unconditional. It was the most beautifully heartbreaking thing I've ever seen. But I had to get to you, despite my fears. I remembered your cue words for him and he let me get close to you. I was elated you were alive and thankful that I could get near Titus. *You* did that for me. You gave me the courage to be near Titus so I could help you. So, sweetheart, I'm not going anywhere. Get used to it."

She swiped at the tears running down her face. "That damn dog is going to be the end of me. I love him so much it hurts. I rescued him when the owner tossed him aside." She paused. "By the way, last time I checked only family gets to spend the night. Would you like to explain that to me?"

"I might have told them a little white lie—like I'm your fiancé." He smiled as his brows arched up.

"More like a big fat lie." The smile on his face was serene and sincere. She couldn't say no to him staying. He was starting to sneak under her skin.

The doctor knocked and then came in. "How are you this morning?" He focused on his tablet.

"Good. A headache but that's it." She failed to mention her exhaustion.

"Excellent news. We're going to do one more CT scan to look for any bleeding, soft cast your wrist for a small fracture, and then send you home. You'll need to rest with limited activity for at least five days. We'll have you follow up with your doctor. The nurse will give you information on what to watch for. Have a good day and take care of yourself."

"I have it all under control. Thank you, doctor." Misha held Raquelle's hand, stroking his thumb across the top.

"Hello, Mr. Control. What are you talking about?" Her hackles were up and ready for a fight.

"I thought I was dark and dangerous. Is Mr. Control an upgrade? You're coming home with me. I have everything ready for you." He smiled.

"Right now, you're being a tad on the controlling side and no, it's not an upgrade. I won't be going home with you. I'm quite capable of taking care of myself." She snatched her hand away from his.

"Actually, no. You can't take care of yourself. I researched the recovery from a concussion. There are many symptoms from a headache to nausea, dizziness, vertigo, and memory loss. You need a blacked-out room with no electronic devices. I have it all set. My staff will be there around the clock. I'm not leaving you alone. What if you fall and knock yourself out?" His face was set in stone.

She whipped the covers back and swung her legs over the edge. "Watch and behold. I don't have any vertigo."

She stood up as dizziness hit her full force. He caught her under her arms as she almost passed out. She sat back down on the bed and started breathing through her mouth to get rid of the nausea. When it passed, she said, "Okay, so you may be right. I didn't realize how bad this was going to be. Besides, you owe me dinner."

He laughed, a sound that was hardy and heartfelt, like a drug of happiness.

A nurse came in the room. "Time for your CT scan and then we'll have you right back."

She wheeled her out into the hallway as she heard him say, "*Ciao, bella.*"

Smart-ass.

When she came back to the room, he had everything ready to go.

"Now, we're going to go slow so you don't get too dizzy," he said softly.

"Why?" she asked.

"Why what, *malen'kiy*?" He didn't look up as he guided her legs into her pants.

"Why are you doing this for me? You don't even know me." Her voice was so small she wasn't sure he could hear her.

He sat next to her on the bed and held her hand. "Partly, I

147

feel guilty. I should've had you picked up in the garage, then you wouldn't be hurt."

"You had no control over any of that. Don't blame yourself." She squeezed his hand.

"Well, there's also the fact that you're really hot and might need me to give you a sponge bath." His lips twitched.

"Now the truth comes out." She laughed. "Ow. Don't make me laugh. It hurts my head."

"Let's get you out of here." He kissed her hand.

Jonas picked them up and drove them straight to his brownstone. "I need clothes and other stuff. We need to swing by my place."

"You can give Jonas a list of things and he can get them for you."

"You know, I'm not really cool with people giving me orders." He frowned at her. "It would have been nice if you asked me what I wanted to do, that's all."

"Ah, yes. You're right. I'm so used to giving orders in my business and having other people rely on me, I tend to forget. I'll try to remember next time."

She stayed tucked into his shoulder on the drive to his place. He buried his nose in her hair.

"Lavender."

She turned to him. "What?"

"You smell like lavender. It brings back memories of my summer in the south of France near Marseille."

She smiled. "And what was her name?"

"No name, just memories. There are fields of lavender that go on forever. I always associate the smell of lavender with a total sense of freedom. That summer, I was away from everyone and everything." A flash of pain came across his eyes. "It was wonderful. I would love to take you there someday." His finger skimmed her face.

"Lavender helps me relax. Sometimes, I'm in overdrive."

"I noticed. I guess we have that in common."

Jonas double-parked outside a three-story brownstone on the Upper West Side.

"God, I hope you're on the first floor. I'm still tired." She felt exhausted thinking about walking up the stairs.

"I own the whole building and there's an elevator." He looked out the window. "If you can't walk, I'll carry you." His eyes penetrated hers.

She looked away and pushed the car door open. He followed as they made their way up the stairs and into the foyer. The decor consisted of warm tones and different kinds of plush fabric-and-wood furniture, a complete one-eighty to his office.

"Here's the elevator. I'll take you up to your room." He held her elbow to support her.

She walked slowly to avoid the headache from getting worse. Using her breathing technique would help with her anxiety in the elevator and stop the return of nausea.

When the elevator doors opened, he said, "This is my room. Your room is right across the hall. If there's a problem, there's an intercom in each room to get hold of me or my staff."

Raquelle opened the door to her room. Titus jumped off the bed and pushed into her legs, whining and barking.

"Hey, you. Are you being a good boy?" She looked up to see the remains of a throw pillow flung everywhere. "Oh, no. I think someone had some anxiety." She turned to Misha. "I'm sorry. I'll pay for any damages."

"No worries. I got him a bed, which he didn't want to sleep in. I left my door open and let's just say he's a bed hog. The snoring was delightful." He shrugged.

"He usually sleeps with me. He's Mr. Needy, most pit

bulls are. I nicknamed him the Snuggly Pack dog. If he could be in a one all day with me, he would. I appreciate you taking care of him." She put her hand on Misha's arm. He had a warmth that made her want to curl up next to him and go to sleep, just like Titus. "I'm exhausted. I think I'm going to lie down for a while."

A cell phone rang inside his jacket. "Oh, here you go. I've been carrying your phone around with me. It's how I got hold of your sisters." He handed her the phone and turned to leave.

She knew who was on the other end. "Hello, Lei."

"Where the hell are you?" Leigha's irritated voice came through loud and clear.

"Misha made arrangements for me to be at his place. It was easier for everyone."

"You could have let us know. We were on our way."

Silence on the other end meant Leigha's wheels were spinning.

"Can we come over? We want to see how you're doing." Leigha's tone did a turnaround.

"Yeah, but later, okay? I'm really tired. I'll call you." She said goodbye and shut off her phone.

She looked around the huge room. Babar, her stuffed elephant, sat on top of a tall dresser facing the bed. There were blackout curtains, sunglasses, and an iPod. Under the iPod was a note.

Classical music helps the brain heal. Enjoy.

Misha xxx

He'd thought of everything so she could heal. Her resistance was wearing down.

Chapter Eighteen

RAQUELLE OPENED the curtains accosted by blinding light. Covering her eyes with her arm, she reached for the sunglasses. She sat down and took some deep breaths, hoping the headache would subside. The curtains would need to stay closed.

She had slept most of the previous day, not giving her sisters a chance to see her, which she was sure drove them batty, but she had texted Leigha this morning to come over for lunch.

Jonas took care of Titus, taking him out during the day but returned him to her for naps and nighttime sleeping. Her wrist was still sore and her head throbbed as a reminder of her concussion.

Titus nudged her leg, wanting to go out. His tail wagged and his eyes were bright. He was so attentive. Somehow he knew she was getting better. She didn't want to stay here longer than necessary. Misha was getting in where he didn't belong.

She opened the door and Titus led the way down the hall

to the stairs leading to the kitchen. Misha was on the phone, yelling in Russian and then English.

"I know, I know. You've told me many times. For once, just let me handle it. I've been groomed my whole goddamn life for this. You would think you could let me run things." Silence. "I'm at home because I don't feel well. *Da, da. Poka.*" He sighed heavily.

"Good morning?" She came around the corner, noticing that all the curtains had been drawn in the house. Titus left her grip and ran up to Misha. His jeans fit his tight ass perfectly and his casual shirt clung to his cut frame.

He turned around, and she could see his eyes were bloodshot. "Good morning. How do you feel?"

"Apparently better than you. Is everything okay?"

"Yeah, my father is just being himself. He found out about some things at work and lost his mind. He's the ultimate control freak." He let Titus out the sliding glass door into a beautiful garden.

"Control freak? You wouldn't know anything about that now, would you?"

"Touché" He gave her a weak smile.

"Your home is beautiful. I wouldn't know I was sitting in the middle of New York City. And why aren't you at work? Because I don't think you're sick."

"As long as you're here, I want to make sure you're okay. My father doesn't need to know everything that goes on in my life. He's suffocating me." Misha's eyes were weary. She understood the sadness she saw there.

"Let me get you some breakfast and then we'll take a tour so you know your way around."

"I usually just have coffee in the morning." She sat on the stool at the counter.

"Nope. You need to get your strength back. Your body

and brain have been through a trauma. I made you bone broth soup with vegetables and chunks of filet. I know it's not the usual breakfast but it will help get you better faster."

The soup simmered on the stove and he served a bowl up for each of them.

"This is incredible." She moaned, wanting to eat until she exploded.

"You should probably have this for the rest of the day. You'll heal up in no time.".

"Can't wait to get rid of me?" She smiled.

He looked up. "No. I just can't stand to see you in pain."

She wondered if he was talking about her or something else. His words seem to come from a place deep within him. Her hand covered his.

"Thank you. You've gone out of your way for me and I greatly appreciate it." He squeezed her hand. "I hope you don't mind, but my family is coming over later." She rolled her eyes. "They need to make sure I'm okay. It's an Italian thing."

He laughed. "It's fine. I'd like to meet them. It must be nice to be so close to your family." He looked away from her.

"It has its pluses and minuses. But I wouldn't trade my sisters for the world. How about you? Any brothers or sisters?"

"I have two brothers and . . ." He looked down at his coffee cup.

"And?"

"Nothing." His eyes told the story of a secret he wouldn't reveal. Good. Now they both had one.

They ate in silence as he shut down. Glancing up at one another every now and then. He had remembered her favorite hazelnut coffee. *Tick-tock*. It was only a matter of time before she succumbed to his caring ways. She felt the pull between falling for him and wanting to keep her integrity. Heart versus head. Her head usually prevailed but her heart was making its point.

He took her on a tour of the house. "This goes to the wine cellar. Feel free to take anything you want." He opened the door to let her downstairs.

She stalled at the top stair. Memories strangled her. That bastard Bernardo had locked her in one of papa's installations for hours while he worked, ignoring her pleas to be let out. Confined places were an anxiety attack waiting to happen. She couldn't even go into an MRI without Valium. But she needed to fight through this. She wanted him to view her as a strong woman. Taking the first step, she put one foot in front of the other until she was at the bottom. Thank God, the lights were bright enough to keep her panic attack at bay in a wide-open space.

"Are you okay?" Misha asked.

"I'm good." She smiled even as she started to sweat.

He gave her the tour of everything from red to white, Australian to French. His hand never left her body, roaming from her lower back to her shoulder as if he sensed her continued discomfort. She was in awe of his collection of her favorite wines. Her palate preferred a dry red with a hint of fruit. His collection was impressive but her unease in the cellar made it hard for her to focus. She concentrated on keeping her anxiety under control with her breathing.

Once they were upstairs, her body relaxed. She went back to bed for a short nap.

When the doorbell rang an hour later, Titus raced down the stairs to greet the guests, barking as if he owned the place. Misha followed behind and flung open the door to her two sisters and their significant others, the four amigos.

Misha introduced himself to each of them, "Please come

in. I hope you brought your appetites. I have lunch ready for you."

Raquelle made it to the door and received kisses and a hugs from them while Titus wagged his tail a mile a minute.

"That would be great. Lately, I've been wanting to eat all the time," Mara commented.

Raquelle gave her the evil eye. As much as she loved them, she wanted them out as soon as possible. There was nothing like being in the nest of the perceived enemy. Mac and Dean would no doubt have a good look around.

Misha led them to the den with oversize leather couches and chairs, large-screen TV and sound system. He called Flora on the intercom to get drinks.

Mara was the first to break the ice. "We can't thank you enough for all you're doing for Raquelle. We're very close and we want to make sure she's cared for."

"It's my pleasure. I wouldn't have it any other way. She's a gifted artist who has more to share with the world." He sat with his hands steepled in front of him.

"Oh, my God. Who took those photographs?" Leigha stood up to take a look at one of the many photographs on the walls.

Misha got up to join her. "I took that one on my trip to Bora Bora."

The two of them huddled together talking about aperture, lens, shutter speed, and other photographer jargon. They seemed giddy with delight at having found someone with the same interest, love, and language.

Mac turned to Raquelle and lowered his voice. "I have something to tell you but I want you to just listen and smile every now and then. Got it?"

She plastered huge grin on her face. "You mean like this?"

"That's a little over the top, dial it back a notch," he said without humor.

"This whole spying thing is a little over the top. This man has invited me into his home and is caring for me. I know we need to find answers but this doesn't make me feel good." She countered.

"I never said this was going to be easy. It never is. But it's necessary." His eyes pinned her. "I'm going to give you another phone before we leave. I need you to turn it on and wait for my text to turn it off. It's going to hack the Wi-Fi in his house, which should be easier than the office and take less time."

She smiled as she said, "What do you hope to find?"

"Not sure. But some interesting things have popped up from the office hack." Mac returned his attention to Misha and Leigha who rejoined the group.

Masks were slid into place as the charade continued. She hated every minute of the game. Misha was making sure she healed. In return, she spied on him. Guilt poured over her. She understood the reason but it didn't sit right. To top it all off, she was madly attracted to him. The lines blurred between personal and professional. Her resolve weakened with every smile and touch.

Misha started the conversation at lunch. "What do you two do for a living?" he questioned Mac and Dean.

Oh, God, no.

Mac glanced at Dean. "We both work for MBK Global Security."

"Sean Knight is a friend of mine. What kind of security do you do for them?" he said and sipped white wine from his collection.

"Anything anybody wants from extractions to security at

a gala event," Dean said as he stuffed Chicken Marsala in his mouth.

"How did you get into that?" Misha asked.

Mac leaned back in his chair. "We're both ex-military intelligence. I worked for Scotland Yard and Dean is ex-ASIS in Australia." His eyes were hard.

"Ah, so no connection to any Federal agencies?" Misha probed.

Dean sat up. Tension vibrated in the room. "We're a private company. Most of our assignments are for hire. By the way, the chicken is excellent. My compliments to your cook. They'll have to give Leigha the recipe. I've got to have this again." He always knew how to alleviate any tense situation.

Misha smiled. "Yes, I have a superb cook. Thank you."

The rest of the lunch was more relaxed with an undercurrent of suspicion.

The Luccenzo crew finally left and the house was quiet again. Misha lay back on the couch and held out his hand. "Come sit with me." He patted the space between his legs.

She couldn't think of a better place to park her weary body, but she knew the invitation would lead to more. "My head hurts. I need to take a nap." She would try to hold him off as long as possible.

He smiled, "Come, *malen'kiy*. You need a shoulder massage. Your family is a lot to take all at once. They're an interesting group." *He had no idea.* She didn't have the energy to resist the comfort of being enveloped in his arms.

She sat between his legs and allowed his magic fingers to massage the knots out of her shoulders and neck. Relaxation took over and her headache began to lessen. She lay on his chest with her head on his shoulder.

"Wow. Your fingers are amazing. Where did you learn to do that?" She closed her eyes as her body molded into his.

157

"Years of practice. How do you feel?" He wrapped his arms around her waist, cradling her broken wrist.

"Very relaxed." She felt herself slip into sleep.

He kissed her head, traveling down to her ear and sucking on the lobe. Her blood heated at the touch of his lips. His fingers ran down her arm.

"I see you're still wearing the bracelet." His warm breath caressed her ear.

"It's funny, but I hardly notice it." She slipped her finger under the rope bracelet and he slipped his under too.

"You're ready for your first lesson," he whispered and kissed her temple.

"Lesson?" she asked.

"Are you still interested in being tied up in my rope?" His fingers tensed.

"Maybe. I can tell you're trying to break me." She didn't want to commit to it just yet.

"Turn around," he ordered. There was more to this than his need to control her. "You could become a fascination for me. When I'm around you, I always want to touch you. Do you feel well enough for me to really touch you?" he asked.

Holy crap. Was he actually asking permission? The men she had been with never asked before they touched. So dumbfounded, she only nodded. Her stomach fluttered, a new sensation for her.

She turned around to face him.

"Wrap your legs around my waist."

They sat chest to chest. He held her face. "I will never do anything that you don't want or ask for. Understood?"

She nodded.

He leaned in to kiss her, his lips like the wings of a butterfly, soft, gentle, cautious, and new. She followed his lead, which wasn't typical, letting him deepen the kiss. He nibbled on her lips and then played with her tongue. The heat from his kiss was like pure octane but held honesty, tenderness, and escape. She wanted to dive into all his layers.

"Do you trust me, *malen'kiy*?" he whispered.

"With my life, apparently," she replied.

He opened a drawer in the table and pulled out a black rope. "Feel it."

"Good God, you have these everywhere."

He chuckled. "I like to be ready at all times."

"Silk?" She held it in her hand, letting it slip through her fingers.

"Of course. Put your hands behind your back, arms together." He kissed her neck while he tied her upper arms together. "I've tied it so you can break out of it at any time and I avoided your wrist." His thumb caressed her jawline. "I want you to close your eyes."

She complied without resistance. Everything fell away as she gave over a little of her control to him. It wasn't a stretch. He had taken care of all her needs. What was one more? She found relief in this new place full of unfamiliar sensations. She was exhausted always being the seductress in her encounters. Being seduced for once was a welcome change and she looked forward to lessening the grip on her hands-off policy.

He kissed, licked, and bit her neck and shoulders while unbuttoning her shirt. The light material slid off her shoulders, stopping at the ropes, leaving her in only a black lace bra. His thumbs swiped across her nipples as her chest pushed out for more attention.

"Someone is greedy. You only get what I give you. It's part of the game. Close your eyes." He gently pushed her away from him and pulled down her bra, lifting her breasts out.

He continued his assault, using his thumbs to brush and tweak her nipples. Her mind was lost to his touch. All she could do was feel what he was doing. With her eyes closed, her senses focused inward.

"God, you are beautiful. You're being very good, keeping your eyes closed. Your cheeks are flushed and if I slip my finger in your pussy, you'll be very wet. I'm going to make you come. But it'll be my way."

"Okay, let's see what you got." She wiggled her hips in his lap.

He grabbed her waist to stop her from moving. "Not so fast. I set the pace, not you." His growled in demand and, oddly, it turned her on.

His thumbs went back to her very sensitive nipples. He rubbed and played as arousal poured over her. His mouth latched onto one of her nipples while he played with the other one between his fingers. He went back and forth between them as she struggled to sit still. Her orgasm started to build and she wanted to reach out to touch him and grind on his erection.

"Focus on what I'm doing, not what you think you need." She tried to focus only on what he was doing to her.

He seemed to sense her inner struggle with the push and pull of desire. "Let go." He sucked hard on one nipple and bit it while pinching the other one. Her orgasm ripped free as her body shook from head to toe. She fell forward with her head on his shoulder. His fingers untied the rope making it fall from her arms.

She panted as peace came over her despite her beating heart.

"That was incredible. I've never had an orgasm with only nipple play." She brought her head up to look into his eyes. "Where'd you learn to do that?"

He was breathing heavily, but laughed. "There's so much I want to do with you." He pushed her hair away from her face. His eyes sparkled. Now she understood something of the joy and strength in the art of Shibari.

"It's your turn."

"No. You gave me more than you can imagine today. This was for you. You look exhausted." He sat back and pushed her into a seated position.

His arms came under her legs and shoulders as he carried her upstairs to her room. He undressed her and put a T-shirt over her head. Laying her in bed, he tucked her in and kissed her on the forehead. She was too weak to move.

"Thank you," she whispered. "I guess I've crossed that line between professional and personal."

"This is only the first line to cross. Have a good nap, *malen'kiy*." He kissed her forehead.

She watched as he took Titus out for his a break. This man would be her undoing.

Chapter Nineteen

RAQUELLE SLIPPED OUT OF BED, stretched, and headed for the shower. On her way, she passed a tented note on a tray with coffee and a ceramic mug with a hand-painted elephant on it. The card was in the most beautiful handwriting she had ever seen.

Malen'kiy,

You were exquisite last night and beyond my expectations. I think you enjoyed my rope and you're a natural at it. I only want you to feel when you're with me.

There is an old Russian game called I know five.

I know five things about Raquelle:

Beautiful

Talented

Gracious

Loved

Fierce

I had to go to the office today and get some work done. Jonas is on call for you should you need to go anywhere. The windows on the car are blacked out so you should be safe from headaches.

I'm only a push of a button away. Please don't hesitate to call. If you need your art supplies, they are still here.

Don't overdo it today. That's an order ;)

Misha

XX-one for each cheek, X-for your forehead

It was as if this man had fallen out of the sky to take care of all her needs. She needed to remember to tread carefully while she was spying on him. It would be so easy to get caught up in everything he had to offer. She had allowed him to take a peek inside her, and she'd given in to his seduction. He had taken control from her and it felt good. Her feelings were more conflicted than ever but she couldn't build the bridge between sex and deceit. Those tools weren't in her arsenal. As she placed the note into her purse, her phone rang.

"Hey, Mac."

"How are you feeling?" he asked.

"A lot better. He takes really good care of me." Anger boiled up.

Mac's sigh was audible. "I know this is hard. Please hang in there until we get this resolved. I actually like the guy too. But looks can be deceiving. I need you to turn on the phone I gave you for a couple of hours. I'll let you know when to turn it off."

"Yeah, Yeah. I need this to be over with. *Capisci?*" Spying had its ups and downs, like being at the top of the highest hill on a roller coaster, anticipating the fall.

"Understood. And thank you. According to Dean, I don't say that enough. I'll be in touch." He clicked off.

She reached for the other phone in her bag and turned it on, placing it on the nightstand. The phone was identical to her own except for a small black mark by the headset hole. Despite an achy head and wrist, her body felt great. A Misha-induced orgasm was the cure to what ailed her.

She needed go to her studio. Painting was her soul food. A week had past since she put paint to canvas. Creativity was the life force running through her veins. She imagined it was the same with any artist: passion took over your life as you pursued the ultimate piece.

Jonas was double-parked outside, waiting for her and Titus. The sun shone bright without a cloud in the sky but the cold air had a bite. She slid her wrap-around sunglasses in place and attempted to dash for the car. Her body was stiff from sitting around healing and her dash turned into a hobble. Jonas jumped into action.

"Good afternoon. Let me help you." He supported her by the elbow and opened the door.

"Much better, thank you. Your boss knows how to take care of a lady." The heated seats warmed her back as Titus laid his head on her lap. She inhaled Misha's clean scent lingering in the air. The windows were designed so she could see out but no one could see in.

"That he does. He's a good guy and treats everyone well. Are we off to your studio?" He made eye contact with her in the rearview mirror.

"How did you know?" she inquired.

"My sister is an installation artist. I know how creativity runs an artist's life. She admired your father a great deal and was devastated by his death. She hoped to work with him someday."

Quiet fell over the car. She formed her words carefully. "He was very dedicated to his art. Sometimes to the detriment of those around him."

The rest of the ride remained quiet. She hadn't meant to reveal her father's underbelly but she had unresolved issues with him. Her father had never been available and only showed interest when he saw one of his daughters had a gift for painting. Raquelle had become his pride and joy until she wanted to be her own woman.

She had been young and foolish, enjoying the attention of an older man. Bernardo had led to her greatest downfall. As she reflected back on her relationship with him, she realized he had had an anger that he'd taken out on her. He had tended to laugh things off as if he was joking, but she knew he meant to hurt her. All these years later there remained a darkness surrounding her memory of him that unsettled her deep in her core.

She snapped out of her train of thought as Jonas stopped to drop her off. "Call if you need anything." He got out and held the door for her.

"Thanks."

She climbed the stairs and Titus led the way with his elephant in his mouth. Light bombarded her as she drew the curtains across the windows. Her eyes were still so sensitive to light, the sun brought on a headache in an instant. Titus went to his basket, dropped the elephant, and found his favorite bone. The studio was as much his home as hers.

She tossed her large bag onto the bed, then stripped out of her clothes. The smell of oil paint filled her senses, igniting all of them. The scent brought back happy memories of her childhood when she and her sisters used to run around Papa's studio and he would shoo them out. Her fingers itched to hold a paintbrush as an extension of her being. Thank God her left wrist had broken instead of the right one. Even one day without painting seemed too long.

Her studio surrounded her like a security blanket. She felt safe and free in her world of creativity. Things inside her were changing, mostly due to Misha. He had softened her tough exterior. In the space of a week, he made sure every one of her needs were met. She had never allowed anyone to take care of her, always relying on herself. The distance she created from people protected her from being hurt again. Her father had taught her to always be strong, never vulnerable.

Now vulnerability seemed like the key ingredient to satisfaction. Sex for his own satisfaction seemed to be the last thing on Misha's mind; he hadn't pushed her for more. His rope extended beyond its reach and wrapped around her heart. She was slipping under his spell, wearing her down with every kind gesture. Still, he had granted her permission to submit willingly.

Across the small space, she stared at the portrait of smiling children. The air felt cool against her skin but, once she got painting, her energy would heat her from the inside out.

She turned off her ringer and tapped her phone, turning on Mozart in the background. Music poured into her head and through her fingers. For hours she blended and blurred lines, creating an illusion of realism, tricking the human eye. Her fingers knew instinctively which of several small brushes to choose as she secured them in her mouth.

A knock came from the door. "Who is it?" she said around the brushes.

"Are you all right? It's Misha." His voice was alarmed.

She took them out of her mouth and said, "Come in," never turning around.

She heard the door open, a small gasp, and then the door clicked shut.

"*Malen'kiy*, you've caught me off guard."

She looked over her shoulder and realized her situation. "Oh, God." She reached for her clothes lying in a heap on the floor. He placed his hands on top of hers to stop her.

"You're beautiful like this, comfortable in your own skin. I didn't mean to disturb you. But your phone kept going to voice mail." He got rid of his jacket and tie, rolling up his sleeves and exposing his corded arms. He looked over her shoulder at her current project. "That's a gorgeous portrait. You've really captured the joy in their eyes." His hands were on his hips and a bulge was in his pants. "The housekeeper called to tell me you had left your phone at home. I didn't want you to be without it in case you needed something. That, and it gave me an excuse to see your studio." He reached into his pocket to give her the phone. Her real phone sat on a small table by her bed. He looked at the phone and then at her.

With her foggy thoughts had forgotten about the phone at his place.

"You have two phones?" he questioned.

"One for business," she said succinctly.

He nodded his approval and moved toward her other works.

She looked at her phone and noticed a missed text from Mac telling her to turn off the other phone.

"Thanks for bringing it by." Her eyes roamed to the tent in his pants. "Someone's happy to see me."

"How could I not be? You're standing naked in front of me . . ."

"At your request, I might add," she quipped.

He smiled. "Yes, although my requests don't always get met. Any man would get a hard-on looking at your gorgeous body. I'm only human." He didn't move toward her but his eyes commanded that she go to him. She took the steps necessary to be within inches of him. His hands caressed her face.

"How are you feeling? How's your wrist?" He didn't grope her, touch her, or try to seduce her. His focus was on her healing.

"I get stronger every day. Thank you for all you've done for me. I've never had someone show so much concern for my well-being." She kissed his palm.

Her hands skimmed the front of his shirt, revealing a firm chest from a man who worked out. She went to unbutton his shirt and he held her hands. A pained look crossed his face.

"What's wrong?"

"I call the shots, remember?"

He pulled her closer to him and devoured her with his kiss, running his hands down her back, grabbing her ass. "You Italian women and your great asses," he mumbled on her lips. His erection bumped into her belly.

"How many Italian women have you had?"

"Just one, and I haven't even had her yet." His lips curled.

"What? No comment about the great rack?" She stood back from him.

"Baby, that's not a rack. That's a work of art and very responsive as I recall." His finger skimmed her nipple making her body jolt. "Sensitive. You're incredible."

"You're talented."

"We make a good team." He kissed her deeply as his hand roamed between her legs and his fingers slid into her folds. "You're already wet for me."

She panted, "Please, tie me up."

His body stilled and he stopped to look at her. "What did you say?"

"I have a bed with a metal frame. I want you to tie me up when you fuck me."

He stared at her without blinking. "I have no intention of fucking you. It's not how I want you, not with the way I feel. And you're not strong enough yet. Lie on your bed." Something changed in his face and body as he gave his command. "Hold onto the bars above your head."

She lay on the bed with arms above her head, gripping the bars in the headboard. His eyes took a tour of her body from head to toe. He spread her legs and tied one with his tie and the other with one of her scarves.

"I'm going to tie one arm but not the other. I don't want to hurt your wrist. Do what feels comfortable."

His chest moved in and out with his breath as he stood back taking in the curves of her body. "Your body should be worshipped. Don't ever give it away, Raquelle. Based on your comments at the club, your flings with men make you weaker, not stronger. You flaunt yourself in front of them but never really give them a piece of yourself." He climbed over her body on hands and knees. "I want all of you, not just the outside, the inside too."

Tears trickled out of her eyes. The hard outside she used for protection cracked only to have him expose her soft center. Her reaction made him untie her arm and legs. Climbing in behind her, he sat her between his legs and covered her with a blanket. She huddled into his warm hard body.

"Talk to me. Tell me why you don't have a man who completely adores you?" He kissed her forehead, burying his nose in her hair.

Her laugh came out on a sob. "My papa, the great Antonio Luccenzo, had an ego, mouth, and attitude that could destroy people in their paths." She took a moment. "When I was a teenager, my papa's right-hand man, Bernardo, convinced me to pose nude for him. I posed in the middle of the studio as Bernardo sketched me. I felt comfortable, free, and grown up. My father walked in on the scene. He yelled at me that I was nothing but a"—she could barely get out the next word—"whore, and how could I be naked in front of Bernardo. My papa had many nude women model in the studio, just not his daughter. He made me feel cheap and stupid and I believed the lie after a while. After that, I fucked Bernardo out of spite and it was my undoing. Bernardo turned out to be jealous of my talent. Everything he did to me was in an effort to hurt me, even as he brushed it off as a joke." Memories burned a raw piece in her heart. "I thought I was in love with him. I was so wrong. I made an effort never to fall in love again." She looked up at him. "It was working really well until you came along."

He kissed her.

"It's amazing how much of our childhood stays with us as adults. I have my own axe to grind with my father and I'm getting damn tired of it. I have plans to break free. You can break this cycle too." His voice sounded far away.

She sat up and reached for his face. "Thank you."

"For what?" He frowned.

"For not taking advantage of me, not expecting me to put out, and listening, really hearing me."

"I would never think of taking advantage of you, *malen'kiy*. I have other plans for you," he said with a gleam in his eye.

Chapter Twenty

AFTER BEING SUMMONED BY MAC, Raquelle decided to walk through Central Park to Mara's apartment to clear her head. She had her protector by her side, which gave her a great deal of comfort. Her unexpected confession to Misha had thrown her off. She wasn't in the habit of baring her soul to anyone, let alone a man. He read her so well and knew she wasn't ready to surrender to being tied up, giving herself over to him completely. Maybe a clean break would be her best bet. She could get the portrait done and leave without getting any more entangled with him.

She arrived at Mara's without remembering how she had ended up there. Mara opened the door and must have read something in her face, because she wrapped her in a mama bear hug.

"Come on in. Everyone's here and I have dinner ready," Mara said as she rubbed her arm. Titus ran to the guys for his usual round of affection.

"Of course everyone's here. Can't you people ever do anything alone?" Her words were meant to bite. Suddenly she wanted to be at her apartment wrapped in a big cozy blanket, away from the world next to her fur baby. A cup of hot chocolate wouldn't hurt either.

Leigha heard her from the other room. "Someone's in a pissy mood."

"Oh, Miss Prim and Proper knows how to use the word *pissy*? Congrats." Raquelle let her fangs show and didn't care.

"What's going on with you two?" Mara stepped in.

Leigha folded first. "I'm sorry, but this whole case has me on edge. I don't like Raquelle being in this position. It's getting scary."

"I *hate* being in this position. I want it over as soon as possible." Raquelle threw her purse on the couch.

Mac and Dean came around the corner. They looked at each other and Mac said, "Well, we've hacked the Wi-Fi in his house and accessed his computer. There's nothing incriminating on it, but . . . Mara has something to tell you." He and Dean ducked away into the living room.

Mara rolled her eyes. "Chickenshit."

"What is going on now?" Raquelle let her irritation show.

"There are some photographs on there—" Mara started.

Leigha interrupted. "That are very well done, I might add. I think they're beautiful."

Mara glared at Leigha. "They are pictures of woman who have been tied up with a lot of knots."

"Yeah, I know. I came across a binder of photos in his office. He explained everything. I, for one, think it's beautiful artwork," Raquelle said defensively.

"Oh," Mara responded.

"Well, I'm so glad we're over that hump." Dean peeked around the corner. "We need you to get into his computer at the office and download all the files from behind the firewall."

"What?" Raquelle exclaimed.

"We have a drive for you that will get past the firewall. It'll give you access with a password. You'll only have five minutes to download any files before you trip the internal alarm," Dean said.

"Are you kidding me right now? I. Am not. A spy. I can't do this shit." Raquelle's nerves were frayed.

Mac spoke, "Yes, you can. We're so close. Getting behind this firewall and getting the files may give us the clues we need to solve the case, including your father's death. We have no other way of getting the information. You're our only hope." His eyes pleaded with her.

Her head began to pound. She wasn't up for this but knew they were too close to stop now.

"Give me the damn drive. I'll see if I have an opportunity," she said reluctantly. "I've been thinking about Papa's studio. There's something not sitting right with me. We need to get back there and look around some more. Also, the one person who keeps popping up in my mind is Bernardo. Can you do a search on him? I don't trust him."

"You're starting to sound like me," Leigha said with a grin.

"How about we go after dinner?" Mac offered.

Leigha and Mara tried several times to make conversation during the meal but were met with grunts and mumbles. Raquelle wanted closure to this whole situation, fast, so she could get on with her life. The loose ends were everywhere: her feelings for Misha, who killed her papa and, more importantly, why? She sounded selfish in her own head but, truth be told, they *all* needed to get on with their lives.

Mara let out a yawn. "God, I've been so tired lately. I think I'll stay here while you guys go check things out."

"Are you okay?" Mac voiced concern.

"Yeah, I'll be fine." She gave him a kiss before leaving for the bedroom.

"Okay, let's roll. I want to get in there and see what's going on." Dean stood up to lead the group out.

On the car ride over to the warehouse, she tried to connect the dots and picture where this all would lead. The pieces to this mystery were few and scattered. What was Papa's connection to the Russians besides Alek?

The Suburban pulled up to Papa's studio and everyone piled out. Raquelle punched in the new code and the door opened. A shiver ran down her spine. Her senses were heightened. They were missing something, she just couldn't put her finger on it.

"Let's start by looking over those big things again," Dean said.

"Installations," Leigha corrected.

"Yeah, those." Dean moved toward the first one.

Leigha and Raquelle paired up as she let Titus off his leash. Dean and Mac went in a separate direction.

On a hunch, Raquelle began knocking on the walls and noticed different pitches. Other knocks echoed around the warehouse. She knew how the walls were constructed. The knocks should have sounded the same.

Titus's bark, followed by growling, caught her attention. Something was about to go down. She grabbed Leigha and ran toward him, stopping short.

Bernardo.

"What are you doing here?" Raquelle demanded.

"Call off your beast, *bella*." Sweat formed on Bernardo's forehead. Titus had never liked Bernardo. His sense of a person's character was spot-on.

"Titus, come." He backed away and stood in front of her

in a protective stance. "How did you get in here? I changed the code."

"No shit. I rigged a window so I could always get in and out in case—" He swallowed his words.

"In case what?" Leigha narrowed her eyes at him.

Mac and Dean had joined them. "Answer her question," Mac said.

Bernardo stood before them, looking worn out and ragged, older than his thirty-eight years. His eyes traveled between them. "In case I forgot my key." His jaw tightened. She knew his tell when he lied. "I have to go." He took her hands in his, pain etched in his eyes. "Be safe, *bella*." Then he turned and jogged out of the warehouse but not before something floated out of his pocket. Titus ran toward it and picked it up with his mouth.

"Come here, big guy." She lifted the paper from his mouth. "It looks like a two-thousand-ruble banknote." She handed it to Mac. He examined it for the markings of authentication.

"It's real. But where did he get it?"

"He's lying and his expression scared me. What do you think he knows?" Raquelle asked.

"I don't know. But I think we need to start taking some of these pieces apart. The walls make different sounds, as if there's something behind some of them," Dean said.

"I noticed that too. Let's start with this one. It's one of his smaller works." Dismantling her papa's work tore at Raquelle's heart. She worried they would find out something about him that was better left hidden.

They all stayed together with Titus in tow. Mac and Dean knocked on the inside walls until they found a different pitch. "Let's start with this panel."

Equipment lay everywhere as Mac and Dean picked their

tools of choice to dismantle the structure. They unscrewed the bolts one by one and supported the section as it fell forward.

"What the hell?" Leigha said the words on everyone's mind.

Dean reached down and grabbed stacks of wrapped hundred-dollar-bills, gold bars, and rubles. "It looks like your father was using the installation for smuggling international currencies around the world."

"No, it can't be. He didn't need the money. He made plenty selling his artwork." Raquelle stared at the evidence.

"I'm going to guess he was working for the Russians, maybe laundering money, but the question is why and how," Dean said. Leigha stood stock-still in shock. He pulled her close and kissed her temple.

"I'm going to have to call this in." Mac turned away.

"How about I drive you two home and you call it a night?" Dean offered. "Mac and I have a long night ahead of us."

Leigha snapped out of it and said, "Do you think Alek has something to do with this?"

"I don't know. But this is the biggest break we've had so far." Dean seemed hopeful.

Mac's eyes gleamed, excited to be on the verge of a new discovery. "Police are on their way. You can meet me back here after you drop them off."

Raquelle didn't want to believe any of it. She sat in the back seat, stunned by the new revelation about her papa. How could he judge her when it looked like he had been in business with the Russians, moving money for them? The man she knew as her papa was fading away. In its place was someone she didn't recognize.

The streetlights flew by her in a blur. Emptiness and vulnerability didn't make for great company. She knew the cure. He could tie her up and let her float away. "Dean, can you drop me off at Misha's brownstone?"

Dean pulled up to the curb. "Are you going to be okay? I know tonight was quite a blow to all of you," he said.

She nodded her head. "I'll be fine . . . eventually."

"Be careful. We don't know everything about Misha yet. He might be wrapped up in this somehow," Leigha said.

"What difference does it make? All the men in my life have turned out to be fakes and frauds. What's one more?" She broke from the inside out.

Leigha reached out to grab her arm. "Call me if you need anything. I've already had my meltdown over papa. I want to be there for you."

Raquelle covered Leigha's hand and squeezed. "I know. Thank you."

She and Titus jumped out to the curb as the skies opened up with sheets of rain. She didn't even try to hurry to the door, letting the rain soak her, washing away her sorrow. Titus didn't run ahead, instead choosing to stay next to her. Rustling could be heard on the other side of the door. Misha grabbed her right arm as she flew into the foyer. Titus pushed past them, making his way upstairs.

"What are you doing? You're going to get sick, little one. Flora, get some towels please," he yelled to the back of the house.

"All is not as it seems." She cringed at her choice of words.

"What do you mean?" He held her chin in his fingers.

"My papa was a fake, a fraud, and not the man he wanted us to believe he was. He may have been into some illegal shit." Her chin trembled, the dam about to burst.

He folded her in his arms as she let loose.

MISHA SPOKE to her softly in Russian with words his mother used to say to comfort him. He couldn't imagine how it must feel to find out the parent you looked upto turned out to be something different, let alone a criminal.

He led her up to bed, stripping off her clothes as she told him about her evening. Tears intermingled with words painted in anger, regret, sorrow, and suspicion.

"Please stay. You have a calming effect on me," Raquelle begged. "I'm not used to asking for what I want or need but I need you tonight."

"I'll be right back."

He usually slept naked but he wasn't ready for her to see all his scars. He threw on a shirt and boxers and made his way back to her room.

She crawled into bed and lay on his shoulder. Tears streamed down her cheeks, wetting his T-shirt.

"This too shall pass. You'll come to terms with it in your own time." He wasn't sure if his words were for her or himself. His father needed to be set straight on couple of things between them. Maybe he would be taking fewer of his father's calls from now on and start making decisions for the company without fatherly input. And his mother needed to stop relying on him and make her own life. He would be having a heart-to-heart conversation with her.

Raquelle fell asleep in his arms as he watched her. The moment of distress was gone, replaced by her youthful glow. She had latched onto his soul in a very short time. He wanted more of her. He wasn't sure how to get there without scaring the crap out of her. One step at a time seemed to be the best course of action. Her life was in turmoil and she needed some reprieve.

He closed his eyes as Raquelle's phone dinged with a text message. He peered over her shoulder at the message.

Bernardo: Bella, stop looking into your papa's death and stay away from the warehouse. It's going to bring you big trouble even you're not prepared for. Don't say I didn't warn you.

The wheels turned in his head. He wasn't normally a jealous man but after she had told him about Bernardo, he couldn't imagine why she would still have contact with him. And better yet, what had she been doing at the warehouse with him.

Chapter Twenty-One

RAQUELLE ROLLED over with her arm flung over her eyes, knowing the space next to her was vacant. Misha had slipped out and started his day. Time alone would give her a chance to reflect. Each day brought with it more strength spiritually and physically but it also brought more questions about her feelings for Misha and her papa. As much as she didn't want to, she had to come to terms with the fact her papa wasn't the man she thought she knew. For whatever reason, he had been mixed up with Russians. Alek and Papa must have been in it together. There was no other explanation.

More than ever, she wanted to dive into her artwork and finish Misha's portrait. He touched something in her she couldn't put into words. Painting him had brought her artistry to a new level, and his portrait was her best piece to date. The goal of being accepted by the Auroto Gallery was still in her sights. Her artwork served as a great distraction from the things she didn't want to face in her life.

She swung her legs over the edge of the bed in time to see the text message from Bernardo. Mac would be very interested in this new piece of news. After forwarding him the message, she went about getting ready for the day. She couldn't wait to see Misha and get busy on his portrait, the portrait that would get her what she wanted: acceptance.

As she walked through the office door with Titus, Misha looked up from a phone call and waved to her. His eyes held a cold glare that unsettled her. Dressed in comfy pants and an oversize paint shirt, she whipped off her shoes; if she couldn't be naked, she'd be bare foot. The sun shone through the window at the right angle to spotlight the portrait.

"Good morning." Misha addressed her without looking up from his desk.

"Good morning," she chirped even as a nervous motor ran inside her.

"Everything good with you? Anything going on I should know about?" He folded his hands on the desk and the air turned frosty.

"I'm good. I'm ready to work and get your portrait done. I still want to submit it to the Auroto Gallery." She watched as he rearranged papers on his desk without looking at her.

"Of course," he said.

She hadn't seen this side of him and didn't much care for it. Something was wrong but she didn't have time to pursue it. Let him have his hissy fit on his own. His portrait had to get done and it took priority over everything else.

As she began to paint, she could feel herself melt into the zone. Colors mixed and blended perfectly as her strokes flowed with the music. She wanted to stay in her blissful state and never come back. Reality held too many disappointments.

Engrossed deeply in her work with her earbuds in, she looked up and realized it was well past noon. Misha hadn't spoken to her for the rest of the morning, leaving the office several times and coming back.

Titus nudged her knee, letting her know it was time to go outside. She slid into her Louboutins and headed for the door. "Oh, hey, we were going to lunch. Do you want to join us?"

"No, thank you." He dismissed her with his eyes.

That was the last straw. "Okay, spill it. I've had enough of Mr. Cold and Distant." She turned, holding Titus's leash tightly.

"So now I am the one that's cold and distant. How distant could I be if I'm sitting right here?" He gave her a slight smile.

"I'm waiting." She crossed her arms in front of her trying to protect herself from the possible onslaught of questions regarding her spying.

"So am I."

He was going to make it really easy for her to walk away by being an asshole. But she wasn't sure she wanted to walk away.

He frowned. "What the hell is going on in that head of yours?"

She released her hands to her sides. "Nothing . . . everything."

He leaned back in his chair. "I saw the text from Bernardo."

"And?" she shrugged. Relief washed over her as she realized he didn't know about her espionage activity.

"I don't know. Why don't you tell me?" His lips drew a tight line.

"There are things about my papa's death that don't add up and my sisters and I are looking into it."

He pinched the bridge of his nose. "That's not what I'm talking about. Bernardo. I didn't realize you're still in contact with him, let alone seeing him."

"Whether I'm in contact with him or not is none of your

business. You and I are not dating. By the way, I'm moving back to my apartment. I need my life back. You're a little too possessive for me. I'll see you later." She spun on her heels and walked out.

This might be the clean break she was looking for. How dare he think he could ask who she was or wasn't in contact with? She didn't need to explain herself to anyone, let alone him. The only option was to cut him loose. It was only a matter of time before he found out she was spying on him. He read her too well. He wouldn't want anything to do with her after that.

Every minute with him, though, made her want to cave to her desires. So as much as it pained her, leaving was for the best.

MISHA RESTED his head in his hands. The conversation hadn't gone the way he wanted it to and if she thought she was going to walk out on him, she had another thing coming. She was a woman he was willing to fight for.

He picked up the phone to contact his IT guy. "Marco, I need a favor."

His next call was to Jonas to drive him to Little Italy. His impatience grew as they moved at a snail's pace through lunch-hour traffic.

The car came to a stop in front of Benito One, one of the best Italian restaurants in Little Italy. He hopped out of the car and leaned down to the driver's side window. "Thanks, go get yourself some fresh Italian food." He handed him a wad of cash. "I have a feeling I'm going to be here a while. I have an Italian temper to calm down."

"Go get her, Boss." Jonas smiled.

His black cashmere coat protected him from the sunny yet cold day. He made his way inside, his eyes adjusting to the dark interior. The walls were brick and the tables were covered in red-and-white checkered tablecloths. Near the back, he saw Titus lying at her feet. Titus walked toward him wagging his tail. He bent down to nuzzle his head. This guy was growing on him and so was his owner. He never thought he would feel this comfortable with a dog, let alone a pit bull.

"How is Titus here? Aren't there health codes to consider?"

"Not when you know the owner."

"May I join you?" Asking might be the best approach.

"Sure." She didn't look up as she read her romantic suspense novel.

The main course had already arrived, complete with linguini and red sauce and fresh bread for dipping.

"I see you're carb loading. Getting ready for a big workout?"

She looked up at him with unreadable eyes. "Italian comfort food," she said simply. "How did you find me?"

"I had help from Marco. Don't blame him though. I had him track your phone."

She responded, "Uh huh."

The waiter came to the table. "I'll have what she's having and your best bottle of red wine, please."

He could tell she wasn't reading the book so he reached over and slid it out from between her fingers. "It looks pretty steamy. Are you sure you're old enough to read this?" He smiled.

"The two main characters are amateurs compared to my sexual appetite." Her eyes softened.

"I'm sure." He held her hand in his. "I'm also sure that I'm not used to feeling jealous, especially of a man who hurt you in the past." He focused on his thumb rubbing across her fingers. "I know you want to keep this professional, but it's a losing battle."

"Why do you have to be so damn wonderful? By the way, there's nothing to be jealous of. Trust me. It takes everything I have not to be with you, but I have to do this for me. I want to earn my way to the top, not sleep my way there." She pulled her hand away and stared at him.

Honesty was his best approach. "By the way, I'm not as wonderful as you think I am."

She turned her linguini around her fork, holding it in a spoon. "What do you mean?"

"Ten years ago I almost drove the firm into the ground. I partied a lot and came into work lit from the night before, all in the name of rebellion. My father rules with an iron fist and threatened to take everything away from me. That's when I woke up. I've spent the last ten years proving my worth but I'm tired of being second-guessed at every turn. This time I won't go down without a fight." He leaned forward and waited for her reaction.

"Whoa." She stared at him in awe.

"I'm fighting for us too. Because it's what I want and I know you want it too. So here's what I propose. I'll put your fee in a trust and then I wouldn't be your client." He threw out his reckless suggestion to see where it would land.

She hadn't moved a muscle. "Fine."

He was caught off guard. "Fine?"

"I agree to your terms as long as you stick to the contract." She blinked.

He sat back, contemplating his options. "I had no intention of not sticking to the contract." He grabbed his napkin and dabbed the corner of her mouth. "I want you to come home with me tonight. I have some things I want to show you. Then you can decide if you want to leave and go back to your place, *malen'kiy*. I need to see this through. If I don't, I'll never forgive myself." He felt a pain in his chest that had never been there before.

Her eyes were heated, the windows to her wild imagination. "It sounds like you have something specific in mind."

"Oh, I do. But I think I'm going to keep you guessing." He sipped his wine. His eyes scanned her face.

He spent the rest of the lunch listening to her talk about her childhood and her love of her sisters, art, elephants, and pit bulls. She hooked her arm in his as they walked back to his office with Titus in tow. She leaned her head on his shoulder and let the sun warm her face. It was so comfortable and felt as if they had always done this together.

Back at the office, she took off her shoes, put on her oversize shirt, pulled up her hair, and began to paint.

"Audrey, please make sure I'm not interrupted for the rest of the afternoon. Thank you."

He leaned back in his chair and watched her paint, the way her wrist turned to the side for a broad stroke or straight on for a slim stroke. She shifted from side to side and smudged lines with her fingers. For her, painting was a full-contact sport. He thought he could make it a bit more interesting.

Quietly, he made his way to the windows where she worked in the sunlight. His fingers started up her thighs and under her shirt. She jumped but then continued pretending he wasn't a distraction. Her skin was warm to his touch as he placed his hands around her waist. He kissed her exposed neck, applying enough pressure to get her attention. Her hand fell away from the painting and her body went lax.

His hands cupped her breasts through her lace bra,

rubbing her nipples. He didn't spend long there, as his hands traveled south to remove her pants. She complied and pushed his hands away to strip them quickly, baring her long, beautiful, toned legs.

He stepped away from her. "There. That's much better. Please continue. I don't want anything to distract you."

She looked over her shoulder at him with rosy cheeks. "You're a pussy tease."

"And you're a cock tease without even touching me."

His pants were tented, making for an awkward move back to his desk. The afternoon dragged on with his focus on her legs and his imagination running wild. The image only served to whet his appetite for later.

She lifted her shirt and tied it at her waist, revealing her lace-covered ass, paying him back in spades.

Two could play at this game. He took off his jacket and tie as he walked toward Titus lying at her feet. Titus welcomed his attention with a big slobbery kiss. Kneeling behind her, his fingers made a path from her ankle, past her calves, behind her knee, and to her hips. His body was flush against hers as one finger brushed against her sex and she moaned with want. She was ready for him as she put down her brushes and turned to him, grabbing his hair and kissing him deeply.

Their tongues played with each other in a battle for control. But once she was in his ropes, she would have to relinquish her control. Her fingers unbuttoned his shirt and he held them in place.

"There is an art to wanting. You need to be patient, little one. I will make it worth the wait."

"Now that you're not my client, I don't want to wait. You've been teasing me all afternoon." She pouted. "Five things."

"What?"

"There are five things I know about you. You're kind, sensitive, bold, smart, and bossy."

He laughed out loud. "You're very observant. I think I need to take you home and spoil you with my bossiness."

Her impatience was rubbing off on him. Grabbing her pants off the floor, he mustered all his restraint and helped her back into them. "Patience," he whispered again into her neck before he lavished her sucks and nips, leaving her breathless.

The fight was worth it. This was the beginning of something beautiful.

Chapter Twenty-Two

HE HAD ASSAULTED every one of Raquelle's senses, from his touch, kiss, smell, and words. She was done for in every way. She couldn't pretend she wasn't attracted to him down to her cells. His suits were always impeccable, made of the finest fabric and tailored with no room for error. All his ties were hand printed with intricate designs. In a way, he lived art too. She might have found her match in the fashion department.

Then there was who he was as a man. He had done everything right through his respect and care for her. He rattled her and there was no more fight left in her. She wanted him. Client be damned. She didn't need money or fame. She needed him.

His fingers trailed a path of fire down her skin with tenderness and dominance. He whispered words of encouragement and directions, bringing her to the edge and then backing off, all in preparation for her release.

"I see you've already taken off your shoes. Does this mean I have to carry you inside?" His fingers feathered down her chest following the curve of her breast. Her frustration built, fingers curled, and breaths shortened.

"We'll see if all the working out you do pays off." She felt her cheeks warm.

With their fingers entwined, he helped her out of the car and swooped her up into his arms, carrying her up the stairs to his brownstone. He closed the door behind them and set her down. Quiet surrounded them. He stared into her eyes with wonder.

"Let me slip into something worth looking at." She turned to leave. He grabbed her hand.

"Your father may have made you think you're not worthy, but you are. I want you just like this. I want your smart mouth, sassy attitude, and creativity and I want you to stop running away from someone who really cares about you. It doesn't make you more in control." He pulled her to him by the back of her neck. "I want you to trust me enough to surrender to me, completely."

The heat in his eyes confirmed his belief in her. He saw through her mask as it evaporated, exposing her insecurities.

He kissed the inside of her uninjured wrist. "Follow me." He led her to his bedroom, the one room in the house she hadn't visited. The bed frame was hand carved from walnut with small loops and hooks. Warm cream walls served as a backdrop to the gray bedspread and black accent pillows.

He took his jacket off, loosened his tie, and sat on the end of the bed. "Take your clothes off." He demanded.

A shiver ran through her. Her past boyfriends never would have ordered her to take off her clothes. He held her at his command using only his voice. She could have denied him but she had a strange need to please him.

She tugged off her pants and panties. Her fingers shook, unbuttoning her shirt, letting it fall to the floor. A new sensation of uncertainty ran through her. His eyes roamed her body like he was mapping something out.

"You have beautiful skin. My black rope will look exquisite on it. I'll go easy. This time." His eyes darkened. "I need you all to myself, nothing between us. Come here."

He held her face in his hands and started to kiss her gently. She didn't want gentle. She wanted animal. Her tongue dove into his mouth, making demands.

He broke the kiss. "*Malen'kiy*, you have to be patient. Good things come to those who wait." The swat on her ass made her jump.

He pulled off his shoes and socks, unzipped his pants and let them drop to the floor. She stepped up. "Let me," as she reached for his shirt.

She took her time unbuttoning each button and pulling his shirt off his shoulders. Shock came over her but she didn't move away from him. Her fingers traced the scar that ran from his sternum to his abdomen and other ones that ran around his shoulder. Other smaller scars were in various spots on his torso.

She had a hard time finding her voice. "How bad was the attack?" she whispered.

"I was five years old and we were out for a walk. A dog jumped the fence and pinned me to the ground, tearing at my chest and biting down on my shoulder. The pain was like nothing I've ever experienced. I lost a lot of blood and almost didn't make it but I fought for my life." He took her hand and put it over his heart. "I don't share my story with many people. I don't want their pity or sadness. It drains me too much. I usually don't take off my shirt even during sex but if I'm going to ask you to bare yourself then I have to give you some of me as well."

He wiped the single tear making its way down her cheek. "No tears, Raquelle, not for me. I've been given a second chance." He said her name and her heart stilled for a beat. He brushed her lips and made his way inside her mouth, swirling his tongue around hers. With her eyes closed all she could do was feel him, want him, and need him.

There was nothing between them except the secret of her being a spy, which she could live with for the time being, but not forever. Her lie would come back to bite her. But this was about here and now. Besides, she had been bitten many times before. She couldn't deny the pull that overrode everything else, including rational thought. For a split second, she worried what would happen when he found out. But she would deal with all of it later.

"Lie down on the bed. I'm going to tie up your forearms and ankles. You'll be able to break it with one pull if you want to. Are you ready?" His eyes flashed dark and wild.

"Yes." She climbed up on the bed, held her arms above her head, and closed her eyes.

His weight dipped the bed on either side of her body as his cock lay on her belly. She wouldn't be disappointed with what he had to offer. He spent time tying her up with his silk rope, avoiding her wrist, and teasing her body with strokes, kisses, nips, and rubs.

Once the ropes were secured, he started playing with her nipples, heightening her awareness, making her hips buck.

"No moving," he ordered. His tongue licked down to her belly button, reaching the target between her legs.

"Of course you have a beautiful pussy to match the rest of your beauty." He took his time with her clit, bringing her almost to climax and stopping. Her arms and ankles pulled at the ropes but not enough to break them. She didn't want out. His two fingers sought her sweet spot. He worked her until she couldn't hold back.

"Now," he said with a husky voice.

She yelled his name as she came. Sweat broke out across

her chest as she tried to catch her breath. "How do you do that?"

"Stay with me. I'm not done with you yet." He released her ankles, pushing her thighs up, holding her by the backs of her knees. He reached for a condom in the top drawer of the nightstand and ripped it open, putting it on in one move.

He slid inside her pushing past her tightness, deliciously filling her up.

"Open your eyes, *malen'kiy*. I want to see everything you're feeling."

His eyes turned to an intense green, fierce yet gentle, determined to deepen the connection weaving them together. His pace slowed down.

He pushed her legs further back, picking up the pace. Sweat formed on his forehead but he didn't let up as his eyes seared into hers. His body folded over her and his hands clasped hers over the rope.

"I want you to come with me. I'm almost there," he panted.

Her breathing picked up and her hips ground in time with his thrusts. Her pussy began to tighten and she let loose, shouting his name again.

"Yes." He grunted out and bellowed her name.

He braced himself on his forearms not to crush her. His eyes had something in them she'd never seen before: respect and kindness. None of her previous romps had even came close to what she had just experienced with him. He wanted to make it good for her and connect with her. She could have sworn he saw into her soul.

The men in her life had damaged her years ago. Forgiveness was a wicked tormentor. Rolling in the hay with faceless men over the years had taken its toll. She had given them her body but missed out on giving them her heart. Feelings of completeness, fullness, warmth, and acceptance washed over her. She wanted and needed Misha in her life.

He untied her and rubbed her arms. His finger traced her face. "What are you thinking about?"

She swallowed, debating whether she should really voice what was going through her mind. "You're different for me."

"This is different, you're different, we're different. You hit back when you need to, surrender when necessary, and are crazy talented among other things." His eyes shone.

"You know how to take from me, give me space, and have a smart mouth. We seem to be a match," she said.

He started tickling her and she laughed with abandon trying to fight him off without much effort.

"*Malen'kiy*, we could have something very special together, but you can't hold back." He held her down.

"And what about you? Are you holding back?" She didn't know if he knew what the words meant.

He jerked back as if she'd slapped him and frowned. "Not in the bedroom." His jaw ticked and he moved to the side of her.

"So where *are* you holding back?"

He was clearly wrestling with telling her the truth. "At work. My whole life is my job but it's the one place I can't gain any traction, especially with my father. He makes all the decisions with or without me and yet I'm the CEO. It infuriates me."

She couldn't believe her ears. He never seemed to hold back at work. "Make some decisions. Rattle his cage a little. From what I can tell, you're well respected and people listen to you."

"I have a plan that will do just that. I can only be pushed so far." He attempted a smile.

She snugged into his arm, laying her head on his chest. "You'll get your chance."

"Ummm." He kissed the top of her head. "Why don't we get some sleep?"

Her breath fell in rhythm with his and she fell asleep right away.

The morning brought a nudge from behind her and she couldn't help but laugh at his small pokes in her directions.

"What are you laughing at?" he growled in her ear.

"I don't think you're doing it right." She giggled.

"Are you sure?" He chuckled.

He bent her knees forward and she realized her ankles and legs were tied. The herringbone weave on her legs was intricate and delicate. A warm rush ran through her at the thought of being at his mercy. She welcomed having someone else to hold the reins, at least for a little while. He must have tied her while she was asleep. Damn, he was good.

His fingers ran up and down the back of her thighs, starting at her knees. She felt the warmth of his lips down her back to her ass. Without warning, he slid into her.

"Condom," she said.

"Already on," he fired back.

"God, you feel so good." She gripped the sheets.

"I'll be a God when I've made you come to exhaustion." He laughed.

Her laugh came out short as his rhythm increased and she began to climax. He knew her signals and came with her. She'd never come that fast with any other man. This was some kind of record.

"You certainly know your way around a woman's body," she murmured.

He untied her and rubbed her down. "Your pleasure is my pleasure."

"I'm going to get in the shower and then pack up my things." She looked at him over her shoulder.

"I'll join you shortly. Jonas will pack for you and get it to your place." Sadness covered his face. Turning his head, he reached for his phone.

She was headed to the bathroom when her phone dinged with a text message.

Mac: Need you to get this done today. Things are starting to close in at CZR.

She deleted his message right away, dreading her next mission.

Chapter Twenty-Three

RAQUELLE'S SURRENDER had given him freedom and one of his best night's rest in recent memory. Misha couldn't wait to get her fully bound in his ropes. Knotted patterns formed in his mind, distracting him, but after last night's conversation, he had come to a decision that wouldn't make his father happy.

"Audrey, can you come in here please? I have something I need you to put together."

Audrey entered with her iPad in hand. Her fingers flew across the screen. "Yes, what can I do for you?"

"I need you to send out invitations to all the gallery owners in the city to come and see our collection. I also want Raquelle's family there as well. It needs to be short notice so make it for this Friday night."

Audrey looked at him like he had three heads. "I'm sorry. What? You can't show that collection. Everyone will know—."

"I'd like to shock some people. It's about time we share it with the world. I have always disagreed on this point with my two colleagues and it's long overdue. Oh, and make sure

Akari Aurtoro gets a personal invitation. I want her here to see Raquelle's work."

Her eyes peered over the iPad. "I'm on it. Are you sure about this?"

He folded his hands in his lap. "Are you questioning my decision?"

"Won't there be repercussions?" Audrey questioned.

"Someone would have to prove ownership, which is very difficult to do since so much time as past. We'll see what comes of it all," he said confidently.

Raquelle came in the door with her signature Louboutins; nude was the day's color.

Audrey nodded to Raquelle and turned on her heels, closing the door behind her.

"What was the Mexican stand-off about?" Raquelle asked.

"Nothing. Can you be done with my portrait by Friday?"

"I can try but it'll be nonstop work. Why? And by the way, good morning to you too." She dropped Titus's leash and gave Misha a stern look.

"I'm sorry." His heart raced at the thought of defying his father, consequences be damned. "I'm inviting some people to come and view your piece." He left out the details about her art hanging among the greats of the art world and the fact that the owner of Aurtoro Gallery would be in attendance.

He came out from around the desk and reached out to her. He held her hands in his as his forehead touched hers. "You're still in your shoes."

"I like the air up here. Why do I get the feeling I'm not getting the full story?" She kissed his lips the way he wanted her to do every morning.

He smiled. "I can't give all my secrets away." Something passed in her eyes and faded just as fast.

He cupped the back of her head and held her in his kiss. When he released her, she panted. "I need to get to work. Your kisses are powerful, but if I don't stay focused your portrait is never going to get done." Her cheeks flushed pink.

"Let me know if you need a break. I have a couple of things in mind."

She turned away from him and he smacked her ass. The Louboutins came flying in his direction as he ducked, leaving them both laughing.

He couldn't stay and play with her. His weekly meeting was about to start in the conference room and he had been warned that his presence was required. Something was about to go down.

The floor was unusually quiet as he walked down to the conference room. When he opened the door, he expected to see a room full of directors from each department. Instead, only Zane and Andre were present as they stood at the window waiting for him.

"Misha," Zane Cavit said with cold eyes.

"Zane, Andre, please have a seat," Misha said trying to take control.

Zane pushed a button on the wall to black out the glass making it opaque.

"We need to talk privately without eyes or ears." Andre spoke in Russian.

The tone of his voice made Misha nervous. Years of experience had taught him not to show what went on beneath the surface. The three of them had been brought up in the United States but with strong ties to their Russian roots. Zane and Andre's mothers were American but Misha's mother was Russian. She worked hard to rid herself of her Russian accent, which was almost undetectable. His friends never questioned her heritage, assuming she was American. They were told specifically not to flaunt their Russian sides, but they'd been brought up bilingual. When things got intense they fell back into their Russian.

"What's going on?" he replied.

Andre looked at Zane and then back to Misha. "I have it on good authority that the FTC and FBI are closing in on us. We will probably get shut down."

"What? Why?" This new information puzzled him. They always traded above board and were transparent with everyone from the government to clients.

"The trigger was Brock taking off with Russian money. I don't know all the details of that client list but there were some questionable clients." Andre's lips tightened.

Zane held his hand up. "Wait for it. It gets worse. None of our fathers can be reached."

Realization hit him that he hadn't heard from his father in two days. His father never missed an opportunity to tell him how to run the business.

He sat back in his seat. Heaviness hung in the air.

Andre leaned on his hands. "Our only way out may be to leave for Russia."

"What the hell is going on? You would leave all these people to take the fall for something they didn't do? I understand Brock made off with millions, but we've covered that and complied with the FTC. There's something going on we know nothing about."

Zane spoke up. "Do you find it interesting that our fathers suddenly can't be reached, leaving *us* to hold the bag? I will save my own ass and go to Russia and when I find him my old man will have some explaining to do." They all carried dual passports.

"I'm staying. My allegiance is to this company and the people who work here. We'll get through this. Keep me in the loop on when you think the agencies are getting closer. I'm having a private gallery showing this Friday and I'd like you to be there."

"Are you crazy? Don't you think that's like waving a red flag? Word will get out." Andre scowled.

"It may show confidence that we have nothing to hide. I'm tired of hiding who we are and what we have. Let's get out it out in the open. It can't hurt at this point." He was determined.

The meeting adjourned without any real resolution. Each of them had been groomed for these jobs and could keep the company afloat without their fathers. He was confident the three of them could and would handle anything.

Misha had had enough of his father's meddling. He would be making the decisions from here on out. His head spun, trying to anticipate the possible fallout from the government agencies coming in and turning the firm upside down. What bothered him was what he didn't know and what his father might really be up to with the firm.

He entered Audrey's office. "I need some time alone. I don't want any interruptions."

He stepped inside his office. Raquelle stood at her easel with her earbuds in as her whole body swayed to the music in time with the strokes of her brush, oblivious to the world around her.

He dropped his jacket on the couch and loosened his tie. His fingers itched for the black silk ropes hidden in the top drawer of the bookcase. He decided on the thinner rope.

He came up behind her, covering her hand with his, following her strokes. She pulled out her earbuds and started to turn toward him.

"Don't turn around," he said close to her ear.

She nodded, sensing what he needed without words. He

knew she was on a deadline but he needed what she had to offer, calmness.

Pulling her hands behind her, he tied her forearms together in an intricate weave of knots, avoiding her injured wrist.

"You won't be able to get out of this one. Are you okay with that?" He needed her confirmation and held her arms firmly.

"Yes," she said confidently.

He turned her to face the windows. The sun peeked through the clouds in the late afternoon. He unbuttoned her shirt and pulled it down off her shoulders, hanging over her bound arms. His fingers skated across the skin on her belly and he felt her tremble. He cupped her breasts and then freed them from their lace confines. Sucking on her neck, he tugged at her nipples, making her arch her back as her ass hit his hard cock.

"Someone is ready for action," she moaned.

"Shh, *malen'kiy*. I need you to be quiet," he whispered. "I just need you to focus on what I give you."

He wanted to feel her in the moment without the distraction of words. He led her to his desk, never letting her go, and turned to see her flushed face open to him.

"I think someone craves my rope. And to think, we're just getting started." He pulled down her pants and helped her step out of them. She stood before him naked, with her chest pushed out and arms bound by his rope. There was no fear in her face. She seemed to sense that he needed this.

"On your knees." He waited for her smart response. Instead, she delivered a devilish smile.

Her eyes bored into him as she knelt onto the carpet, licking her lips as he unzipped his pants and pulled his cock out, stroking it up and down. The trust she placed in him was evident in her vulnerable position. Her surrender loosened something in him.

He slid inside her warm, wet mouth and she sucked generously. Her hair was like silk in his fist, forcing her to take all of him, which was no easy feat, as her lips hit his zipper. She gagged once and opened her throat. Her experience showed as she adjusted her mouth and moved with him. As her eyes locked with his, they spoke of surrender and understanding. She trusted him and accepted his dominance of her. This was what he needed from her. He also needed to be inside her.

"Get up, little one." He slid his hands under her arms and lifted her.

He started at her neck and made his way to her lips, pushing his tongue into her mouth, invading her. He unbuckled his belt as her breathing increased and his pants fell to the floor. He stepped out of them and carried her to the chair behind his desk.

He sat down. "Ride me." He sounded harsh in his own ears but she complied anyway.

"Condom?" she asked.

"I'm clean. Are you on birth control?"

She stared at him for a moment. Her head bobbed up and down. "I've never been with anyone without a condom," she whispered.

"Good. I'll be your first and last." His dominant tone left no room for an argument.

She gasped as he pulled her to him. "Are you okay with that?" he asked.

She smirked. "I thought you said no words."

Angling her hips, she slid down, surrounding him in her tight, wet pussy. He grabbed her legs, putting them over the arms of the chair. He raised the chair so she could lean on his desk with her hands from behind.

"My God, you feel incredible." She threw her head back, exposing her neck.

His hands grabbed her hips as he thrust into her, unrelenting. At this angle he could hit her sweet spot. He pushed her off him and she cried out in protest.

He took two fingers and pushed them up inside her, coating his fingers, and started to rim her backdoor. Her eyes flew open.

"I see we have a virgin. I have so much to explore with you."

He watched as she accepted a little more of the invasion. If he kept this up, he would come without being inside her. He pulled away his finger.

"Wow. That was different." Her eyes glazed over.

He positioned himself at her pussy and glided in with ease. The pace he set was controlled, his rhythm torturous, aiming for a slow undoing. He watched in awe, peeling away one layer at a time until she revealed her true self. No woman had ever sacrificed her defenses for him, giving herself so completely. The sense of power he possessed over this woman pushed him to the edge of euphoria. Her pussy clenched down on him and he came with her. They panted in unison, touching foreheads.

Sweat covered her and hair clung to her forehead. He made short work of getting her untied. He laid her on the couch and rubbed her shoulders all the way down to her wrists.

"Thank you," he said.

"You're thanking me? I should be thanking you. That was incredible. I've never accepted offers on my ass." She laughed.

"Your surrender was amazing. It's been a rough day and I needed you." He brushed his thumb across her lips. A bond was beginning to form, a bond he shouldn't pursue. Given the new information about the company, he didn't want to take her down with him.

"I could tell something was wrong. My intuition always works overtime." She played with his tie.

"I have a surprise for you tomorrow." He wanted to give her something in return.

"I need Jonas to very carefully take my painting back to my studio in my special carrier. Some of the paint has dried but other parts are wet. I'll be working through the night. I'll call you tomorrow."

He was torn between wanting her forever and protecting her from his undetermined future.

Chapter Twenty-Four

SEX WAS the fire that lit Raquelle's wick, keeping her energy up to work on her art through the night. She exiled herself to her studio, grounding herself after flying so high. Misha had strummed her body to perfection. She had never submitted to anyone until he came along. He was a double-faced portrait, caring on one side and dominant on the other. She was committed to the idea that he wasn't dirty in this spy game with the Russians and she failed to see his connection to her father. There was a chance that someone was working behind the scenes or even within the company. Resolution and closure were what they all sought and there was only one way to get there, through Misha.

Following the rendezvous in his office, spying on her lover felt more like a betrayal than ever before. Her feelings for Misha were confusing at best. She needed to take a step back and take a hard look at those feelings, because she was starting to soften when it came to him. On the other hand, the angst worked in her favor. His portrait put her other portraits to shame. But she wanted to get rid of the monkey on her back: her secret spying.

Her finger stalled over the button on her cell phone. She had completed her mission earlier in the day by downloading the information off his computer onto the zip drive. Maybe she should get rid of the drive and be done with it all, but without it, she would never know for sure if what was going behind the scenes at CZR was related to her papa's death.

Mac answered after the first ring. "I got what you asked for. You can come by and get it. I'm here all night," she said.

"Thank you. I'll be by later." Mac clicked off.

Sadness spiraled around her as she thought about her beginnings and soon-to-be ending with Misha. She didn't know what he would do when he found out about her lie. Would he accept her rationale on why she had to spy on him? If he didn't, she would be a wreck.

Turning on her Sonos, music filled the room. Every mood was wrapped up in her playlist. Sarah McLaughlin's song *Angel* reached deep down inside her, pulling something from within. Her small brush made long strokes when she was sad, caressing the sides of his face. She saw many things there: hope, strength, determination, caring, and loneliness, but never deceit. And of all the emotions to recognize, deceit was the one most familiar to her.

The knock at the door signaled Mac's arrival. She threw on her oversize paint shirt and opened the door.

"Hey. You okay?" He wasn't a top spy for nothing. Being able to read people could be a matter of life and death.

She turned to get the zip drive, then curled it in her fist. "First off, this was the most nerve-racking experience of my life. I don't know how you and Dean do it. I was sweating bullets."

He smiled. "Aye, it's not for everyone. I have to be honest. It's a little bit of an adrenaline rush." He put his hand out for the drive.

"Oh, I'm not done." His smile faded. "Second, I am done, out, over, *fatto, su, al di sopra di.*" She gave him the words in Italian. "I don't care what you say, he's not your guy. I don't know what's going on at CZR but he's not involved."

"You've fallen for him, haven't you?" Mac asked with a knowing look in his eye.

She stalled. "You're not the only one with a sixth sense. Maybe I have. But I can handle him."

"He may look like the good guy but you and I both know looks are deceiving. We didn't even know he was Russian until you told us. We still don't know the connection. He was born in the U.S. without his father's name on the birth certificate. Maybe he's a puppet for someone else. We won't know until we look at that drive." His jaw tightened as the muscles twitched. "There have been some new developments. I'm not going to tell you what they are because I don't want to compromise you. The less you know the better at this point."

He opened his hand as she slapped the drive in it, leaving her hand over his. "Be careful," she said. "Don't bury an innocent man. There's a trail of dead people. We don't need to add to the list."

"You need to be careful too. Create some space until we get this figured out." His eyes surveyed her from head to toe. "Are you wearing anything under that shirt?"

"I paint in the nude. What do you think?" She smirked.

"TMI, I got to go. Mara's still not feeling well." He sighed. "Hang in there."

As he left, the phone rang with Rhianna's song *S&M,* which meant Brie was calling.

"Hey."

"Wow. Ball of fire, eh?" Brie knew her like her sisters did, maybe even better.

"I'm in the deep end here." She explained everything that had been happening between her and Misha.

"You got it bad. He sounds like an incredible guy. So what's stopping you, all your wonderful one-night stands? Last time I checked, they weren't so wonderful." She had left out the part where she had not only been spying on him but hacked his computers. There had been a small relief in telling Mac she was done. Unloading completely might do her some good. On the other hand, she needed to protect Briella.

"We're still trying to get information on my father's death and Brock's role in all of it. That's all I can say." She left it there. Brie didn't need all the gory details and could read between the lines.

"No wonder you're conflicted. You've got a lot on your mind. Lucky for you, I have a distraction to all of this. Let's go out tonight and drink the night away."

"Shouldn't you be slowing it down a bit now that you have a boyfriend?" she asked.

Brie sighed. "It's kind of hard when your boyfriend's in a rock band and on the road a lot."

"I'll take a rain check. I'm emotionally spent and Misha wants his portrait done soon for a private showing. I've got to pull an all-nighter."

"Hi, it's Briella. Could you put Raquelle on the phone? I think we got disconnected."

"Ha, Ha. You're very funny."

"I've never known you to turn down a night out. Things are changing, my friend. Just don't change too much. I want to be able to recognize you."

"Oh, you mean like the way you're a rock star's girlfriend?" Raquelle laughed.

"Don't go there, *chica*. Remember I love you. You might

209

need to slow this down. I don't want to see you get hurt. I'll talk to you tomorrow."

"Duly noted and thank you. You're the best."

She couldn't remember the last time she had turned down a night out. What she really wanted was to show up at his place and snuggle up next to him. God, she was so in over her head.

The night progressed with each stroke, her vision coming to life on canvas. Titus snored softly in the corner, used to her all-nighters. Sleep came around three o'clock in the morning. She had burnt herself out but his portrait was almost done.

Her phone rang with the song *Stupid Girl* by Saving Abel. *Misha*. She had needed a reminder not to be the stupid girl when it came to him but things had taken a different turn.

"Hello, handsome," she said with a groggy voice.

"It's eleven in the morning. Are you just waking up?" Misha sounded alarmed.

She loved the sound of his voice. "Yes. I worked on your portrait until the wee hours of the morning."

"Can you be ready in an hour? I have a surprise waiting for you and I'd like to take you to lunch."

"Sure. What should I wear?" she said coyly.

"Casual is fine, but not naked. Others might take offense. If I had it my way, you would be naked all the time." He laughed.

"Naked and bound." She laughed too. "I'll see you soon. I can't wait for your surprise."

"*Ciao, malen'kiy.*"

At least he said goodbye.

She got dressed in jeans, a sweater, a red cape, and, of course, Louboutin over-the-knee boots. The urge to cut and run away from him had vanished. There wasn't anything she didn't like about him. He was strong enough to show her his weaknesses and fears. She wanted to see what else lay beneath his alpha exterior.

Downstairs, Jonas opened the car door for her. She slid in and feasted her eyes on Misha dressed in his signature dark suit, white dress shirt, and a tie with a hand-painted elephant design.

She moved closer and stroked his tie. "I like it."

"I like your collection of everything Louboutin. I think I'd like to see you in nothing but those boots." He cradled the back of her neck and pulled her to him, kissing her mouth as if he owned it.

She returned the kiss with passion. "I can make that happen." When she sat back from him his eyes were turbulent and dark. "Where are we off to today?"

"You'll see. I don't want to give it away. But I think you'll like it."

He put his arm around her and pulled her close as she laid her head on his shoulder. Words weren't needed. The traffic up the FDR was light. Their fingers found each other with small gestures of rubs and squeezes. His focus was out the window but he didn't seem to be seeing anything. His body felt tense.

"What's going on? You don't seem like you're really here with me."

He turned to look at her as if he doubted whether he should share what was going on. He ran his finger down her cheek.

"I got some bad news at work." He paused, looking for an answer in her eyes. "There are two government agencies that will be coming to the firm looking for God knows what." He sighed. "I have no idea what they're looking for and I don't have any answers but it doesn't look good for us."

Her heart ached, hoping she hadn't contributed to his new circumstances. "I'm sorry."

She turned her head to look out the window avoiding any more discussion and noticed they were going through the entrance to the Bronx Zoo.

"Oh no. I don't like zoos. I hate to disappoint you. Animals need to be free and not caged in."

"Spoken like a true animal lover. I agree whole-heartedly. However, I support the zoo as a way to help educate people on animals and the study of endangered species. This one happens to be a conservation. Many animals in our world are in crisis. This is one way we can give them a fighting chance."

"Okay, you win this round. Are we seeing anything in particular?"

He tapped her nose with his finger. "So many questions. You'll have to wait."

Jonas opened the door for them. Misha grabbed her hand, lacing his fingers with hers, and slung his camera around his neck.

They entered at the back of the zoo through the employees' entrance.

Trumpeting could be heard loud and clear. "Is that an elephant I hear? They must be celebrating something."

"They are. The zoo has been gifted with the birth of a baby elephant and we get a chance to see him."

She stopped with her hand still attached to his. "Are you kidding me right now? Because it's not funny. Do not play with me. I've always wanted to see a baby elephant but thought I had to go to the orphanage in Africa."

He turned to her and curled his finger for her to follow. He led her through a door to the back of an enclosure. Fresh straw covered the floor as they tiptoed in.

The sight took her breath away.

Misha said in a hushed tone, "His name is Romeo because he likes to roam away from his mother. You can go in but he can't be separated from his mother for very long. She's in the next stall. She'll charge the fence to get to him."

Without taking her eyes off the baby elephant, she bent down to unzip her boots and handed them to Misha. She opened the small door and walked in, barefoot. Romeo came right up to her out of curiosity. Her hand caressed his soft head. This was the most incredible gift anyone had ever given her. She was in awe of the little gray bundle with big ears who would grow up to weigh tons and have family ties not unlike her own.

Romeo's trunk played with her, exploring her legs and hair. She giggled as her hand stroked down his body, feeling the tender skin of the newborn.

"He's incredible." She looked at Misha for the first time being in the enclosure. His whole face lit up watching her as he continued to take photos of her with Romeo. "How did you know I wanted this?"

"I guessed that you hadn't been to Africa or India. It brings me great joy to see you so happy." He stood leaning on the fence, holding her boots.

In that moment, it all boiled to the surface. Her lies, spying, deception, and the fact she was possibly falling in love with a man who might have ties to the people who killed her papa. Mac's words rang in her ears: *new developments*. She didn't want any new developments. She wanted to capture this moment and stay here forever, but that wasn't an option. Tears began to form in her eyes. She wouldn't let them fall.

A loud trumpet from Romeo's mother snapped her out of

her head talk. One of the zookeepers came over. "It's time to go. Mama is getting restless."

She headed for the gate and grabbed her boots from Misha.

"What's wrong?" he asked with concern on his face.

"Nothing. This was an incredible experience. Thank you. I'm just overwhelmed." She leaned down, focused on her boots.

He wasn't going to let up. "Something happened in there. Now, what is it?" he demanded.

"I have a lot on my plate right now. Can you just take me back to my studio?" She turned away from him.

Disappointment flashed across his face and he nodded. "Are you going to run now? Are you getting too close? Or have I done something to offend you?"

"It's not about you," she said without looking at him.

The car ride back to her studio was shrouded in tension. She could feel his eyes on her but she stayed staring out the window, willing her tears not to fall. As the car came to a stop, she turned to him.

"I need to finish your portrait. I'll see you in a couple of days." Her heart dropped to her stomach.

He grabbed her hand and pulled her close. "I want to tie you up and make you tell me what's going on in that head of yours. But I won't. That's not what it's about." He glared at her.

"I have a feeling you'll find out soon enough." She tugged her hand away.

He jerked back at her words. A frown appeared between his brows. "What the hell is that supposed to mean?"

She attempted to smile and rushed to get out of the car, making her way to her studio. The next couple of days would be agonizing in so many ways. She wasn't sure she could live with the guilt. Confessing to him might be the only way to clean her marred soul. When Misha found out what she had done, he might want to tie her up and burn his portrait before her eyes, making her watch everything she had worked for go up in smoke.

Chapter Twenty-Five

THE SOONER RAQUELLE finished his portrait, the better. Things between them were falling apart. He would show it to his friends, family, and colleagues and then she would have to be done with him. Her heart flip-flopped between the need to have him in her life and not wanting to face his wrath when he found out what she had really been up to in his office. Determination and anxiety were at war.

Based on the information Misha had shared with her, she knew she had a phone call to make.

"Hey, I have something to pass along to you and the rest of the gang in *The Spy Who Loved Me*," she said without regret or apology.

Mac cleared his throat. "Look, I know this has been hard for you, but try to understand. We're working as hard and as fast as we can to get this resolved so you will be out of it. What's going on?"

"First off, you need to know he took me to see a baby elephant. That's a huge deal. How bad could he be if he even thinks of doing that for me?" she said in anger.

A deep sigh came through the phone.

"Just sayin'." Her petulant child came through. She proceeded to share Misha's news about the federal agencies that were bearing down on CZR.

Mac cut in, "Did he say how he knows? That's top-level information."

"If it's so top secret, how do you know about it?" she bit back.

"I have friends in high places," he said coolly.

"He didn't say how he knew. What's going to happen, Mac?" Her voice broke.

"You need to stay clear of him for now. I don't know when this is going down but it'll probably be sooner rather than later."

She gulped down her tears. "He's showing his portrait in a couple of days. I hope it doesn't happen before then."

Mac's voice softened. "I got people I have to get in touch with. I'll talk to you later. Be safe, Raquelle, and stay clear of him."

"Yeah, you too."

She hung up not feeling any more optimistic about the future as she stared at the portrait of Misha. He stared back at her with soft hazel eyes and a hint of a smile. Behind the smile stood a man with determination, passion, and kindness. This was how she wanted to remember him. But what she also saw she couldn't deny: loneliness. When painting a portrait, loneliness always sat at the brow in a person's face. A slight downward curve in his brow was his tell. She understood his need for the ropes, his need to tighten things up in a world out of his control. Most people were takers, not givers. Givers fought to survive in a taking world. He had given her so much and taken so little. With a few small brush strokes, she could change what she saw in his brow. But a painter worth their salt always portrayed what was there and not what they wanted to be there.

She worked on his portrait through most of the night and into the next day. Her brushes caressed his cheeks, nose, and lips. Overwhelmed at times, she would take a break to let her feelings come through from rage to tears of sadness. He was the one who had broken through her toughness and had seen her for who she really was, as loneliness called to both of them.

The hours sped by so quickly, she had lost track of the day. Misha texted her a few times but she ignored them or sent him her automated "I'm working" reply. She was putting the finishing touches on her work when a buzz came from security.

"Who is it?" Her voice was muffled because she had a brush in her mouth.

"Delivery from Neiman Marcus."

The brush fell and hit the floor. "Send them up." Intrigue had gotten the better of her.

She opened the door to receive a huge gold box.

Her hands shook as she opened it, knowing exactly who it was from. She gasped. Inside, wrapped in tissue, was a Carolina Herrera strapless red gown. The embroidered white and pink flowers spread around the front and back, accented by gold and green leaves reminiscent of a Japanese garden. A red train flared out from the waist down to the floor. She knew every detail because she had spent time drooling over it in the window on Fifth Avenue. Included in the box was a pair of Badgley Mischka black satin pumps. She opened the card.

Malen'kiy,

I want you to wear this classic gown to your presentation

of my portrait. You will be nothing less than a queen in it and carry it beautifully.

Please have faith in us. Don't run away from me. I feel connected to you in so many ways. We can weather any storm. I promise. I'll see you soon.

Yours,

Misha

XXX

She didn't think they could weather the storm she had brewed up. The showing was tonight and her family would be there. He had insisted they be invited to share her triumph. She was unaware of anyone else on the guest list but the dress would be making a statement.

Jonas contacted her to tell her a van would be by to transport the portrait in its special carrier to the location. He would be by later to pick her up. She still had no idea where this was all taking place.

The thought of the night ahead had her nerves on edge. She had decided on a chignon for her hair and a touch of makeup. Jewelry wasn't required. The dress spoke for itself.

"Hi, Jonas. Where are we going?"

He looked at her in the rearview mirror and smiled. "The firm. You have no idea what's going on, do you?"

"No. Would you like to clue me in, handsome?" She tried to charm him.

"Nope. Sit back and enjoy the ride. I think you're going to be surprised." He smiled.

"We'll see." Her polished nude colored nails shone in the flecks of light in the car. She was either going to her coronation or the guillotine. A drop of sweat ran down her back in an effort to escape her nervous energy.

The car pulled up to the building and Jonas jumped out to open the door. Memories flooded her mind of the first time she had come to CZR and met Misha. He had glanced her way as she stumbled into the lobby. She didn't miss his eyes and sharp suit. This time she hoped something even greater waited for her.

Misha exited the front lobby and walked toward her with his hand stretched out.

"My God, you look incredible." He held her hands as his eyes took her in from head to toe.

"Thank you for the dress. I don't know how you knew but I've been eyeing this dress for a while. I didn't get it because of the price tag. You have excellent taste." She tilted her chin up.

"A classic for a classic. Nothing is ever too much for you." He held out his bent arm. "Come with me, beautiful, I have a surprise for you."

"So I heard. You'll be happy to hear Jonas didn't give you up."

"Loyalty is hard to find." He smiled.

She almost stumbled at his words. The ride on the elevator was quiet between them as she used her breathing technique to keep her calm. Her nerves were already running fast. She didn't need to add to it.

"I hope you'll be happy with what I've done." Worry crossed his face.

"I'm sure it'll be fine." The night would be full of surprises.

They entered the gallery to a crowd of people milling around, looking at the artwork on the wall. In the center, under proper lighting, stood his portrait.

She stopped and tried to catch her breath. Not only was he publicly showing the firm's private collection to the world, but also he had spotlighted her work among the masters. Soft classical music played in the background as the waitstaff served drinks and appetizers to guests who marveled at the sights before them.

He leaned down, "What do you think?"

"My God, what were you thinking? Your father is going to have an aneurysm. Everyone who's anyone is here," she said in a hushed tone.

He grinned. "Isn't that the point? I believe your words were, *do something bold*. Is this bold enough for everyone?" He held her by the elbow as they toured the paintings. There were other works she hadn't seen before.

"Aren't you afraid of the repercussions?" She smiled at people who nodded in her direction.

"Which ones, from my father or the world?" He nodded at someone who waved from across the gallery.

"How about both? The world will not be happy that you've hidden these or that you own them. You could lose some of them if anyone claims ownership."

"Let the chips fall. I've wanted to share these with the world for years. My father is not an honorable man." His face grew dark.

Before she had a chance to ask him to elaborate on his comment, Akita Aurtoro interrupted them.

"Misha, thank you for the invitation to this exceptional collection. You'll be the talk of the art community." She turned to Raquelle.

"You must be Raquelle Luccenzo. Your father used to gush over your talent. I'm Akita. It's nice to meet you. Your portrait of Misha is not like anything I've ever seen in contemporary art. I've known Misha for many years and you have captured all his facets. Congratulations. You've surpassed your father's talent. I wanted to say how sorry I was to hear about his untimely death." She turned toward the portrait. "I see you have many admirers. We'll be talking later."

Akita's comment cut both ways. On the one hand, she had acknowledged Raquelle's work and dropped the comment about her father's compliment. But then she'd compared her to her father's talent. Raquelle wanted to stand on her own. Maybe she should consider changing her last name.

"See, I recognized your talent from the moment I saw your portfolio. I'm glad I talked to Akita. This could turn into something big." He was so proud, she didn't have the heart to burst his bubble with a cutting comment.

"Thank you," she said through tight lips.

More gallery owners as well as agents came by to greet her and congratulate her on the portrait. Many left with an underlying comment about her father, either offering condolences or about how his talent had somehow rubbed off on her.

After an hour, she had had her fill. Her gut churned with regret for doing the portrait and she was tired of hearing about her father. His ghost never gave up.

As she was about to leave, Akita stopped her. "I wanted to talk to you about showing you in my gallery."

Raquelle was taken aback. "I submitted my portfolio. Did you have a chance to look at it?"

She let out a short laugh. "Oh no. We don't look at anyone without an agent. I'm here because of Misha's invitation. He's been involved with my gallery for a while and sits on the board. He has an eye for new talent. I had to check you out for myself. I expected to see a copy of your father's work but what I see is very original. I'm impressed. Here's my card. Please give me a call so we can set something up." She handed Raquelle her card and turned to leave.

Fury built and her eyes were like heat-seeking missiles looking for their target. Misha was across the gallery, laughing, with a glass of champagne in his hand.

She turned on the charm before she let loose. "Can I have a word with you, privately?"

He took a sip of his champagne then placed it on the table behind him.

She hiked up her train so she could move faster to his office.

"Why do I get the feeling you're about to unload on my ass?" He stood with hands in his pockets.

"Unload would be about right.".

"Have at it." She could see him smile out of her peripheral vision.

She walked into the space where they had argued, bantered, painted, had a therapy session, and made love. Made love? She spun around on her heels only to have him push her against the door and kiss her as his tongue took over her mouth.

He pinned her hands above her head, restraining her. His mouth moved down her neck and across her chest, dipping his tongue between her breasts.

"I've missed you. I want to peel you out of this dress and worship your body, tie you up in my most beautiful rope creation, and take your photo. You stir something in me I can't ignore and neither can you, as hard as you try."

She pulled her hands free and shoved him off of her. He took a step back and slid his hands into his pockets.

She panted, letting his words settle in where they didn't belong. He was right. There was something between them that couldn't be ignored. But right now, she was pissed as hell. Passion was the instigator.

Standing up straight, she crossed her arms over her chest.

"Akita approached me and offered to show my work. Know anything about that?"

"I know she has excellent taste."

"But I wouldn't have been on her radar had you not talked to her. I wanted to do this on my own."

"Everyone needs a little help sometimes. Your work speaks for itself." He didn't back down.

"I have lived in my father's shadow and with the Luccenzo name my whole life. I'm sick of it. Everyone sings his praises. I want people to see my work for what *I've* done." She took a step toward him. "I didn't ask for your help. Akita told me you sit on the board for Aurtoro Gallery. Funny how you left out that little fact. And in addition to all this, I come to find out my father was also less than honorable. He may have been involved in some shady shit."

"Reality's a chilly bitch. I'm not apologizing for giving you an opportunity to get your foot in the door of the Aurtoro Gallery. You belong there despite your father. Maybe he was good for something after all."

She held back her tears. "You know what? You don't get it. You've had everything handed to you. I've had to fight to get recognized."

He stepped closer, towering over her. "Don't talk to me about having anything handed to me. It came at a price you know nothing about. My life is not my own. Show a little gratitude for the fact I could give you this opportunity," he said through gritted teeth.

Rage rushed through her veins where she couldn't see straight. "I don't want you to *give* me anything. I didn't ask for you to give me anything. I'll take my life over being imprisoned up here in your cage."

She turned and yanked the door open, jogging for the gallery even in the high heels, tears of anger crested in her eyes. When she got there, she found her sisters standing with Mac and Dean.

Mara saw her first. "What happened?"

"All men are assholes, that's what happened." Mac and Dean stepped away.

"This was all a hoax. I'm going home. I'll talk to you later." She left before she heard anyone's reply.

Chapter Twenty-Six

OF COURSE MISHA had had to open his mouth instead of letting her vent. He pulled his hands through his hair. "Shit."

He poured vodka on the rocks from his private stash and made his way back to the gallery.

"Hey, buddy where've you been? I've been looking for you. Showing the collection made quite the statement. Someone's going to have a meltdown," Lucas said from behind him.

"Yeah," he said without processing a word.

"You're drinking the hard stuff. That's never a good sign. Let me guess. The little dynamo finally went off."

"Something like that," Misha said into his tumbler.

Lucas put a hand on his shoulder. "I know what you need. Let's go after the show. My car's waiting downstairs."

Misha was a balloon on the end of Lucas's string. He followed without question. They ended up exactly where he needed to be, Club 24K. One of his regulars would be available to be tied up. He needed to feel the silk in his hands. Things with Raquelle weren't going where he had wanted them to go. She had cut and run, spitting mad.

226

They headed upstairs to the elite-members-only, platinum lounge and sat at the bar. The chairs and couches were made of Italian leather and suede accented by brushed silver. The liquor was top shelf and kept in private stashes for its members. His Stolichnaya Elit vodka would be waiting for him, but Misha opted for water. Given what he wanted to do with the rest of his night safety came first.

"So talk to me. For someone who has it so together all the time, you look like you're about to come undone." Lucas stuck to his bourbon.

"Well, it goes something like this. Man meets woman who gives as good as she gets but is a tad on the skittish side. There are ghosts in her closet but nothing I can't handle. The worst part is, I can't stop thinking about her and I definitely want to get her in my ropes, permanently. She's made for them and she's made for me." He looked at Lucas, knowing what the next words would mean. "We have that chemistry, the person you find where you begin and end."

"Okay. So you got it bad. It doesn't look like things went well tonight, though." Sorrow touched Lucas's eyes, for himself or Misha, he wasn't sure.

"That's an understatement. I may have fucked things up royally and I don't know if I can fix it. I invited Akita to see her work. Raquelle saw it as me handing her the key to the Aurtoro Gallery." He swirled the ice in his glass.

"She'll come around. I'd say you need a distraction. Oh, and look, here it comes." Lucas chuckled.

Misha looked over his shoulder to see Victoria sauntering toward him.

Her face lit up. "Hi, Misha."

"Hello, Victoria." His words were icy. This wasn't a distraction. This was sabotage.

"How are you?" Her words were tentative.

He didn't want to engage her any more than possible. "Fine."

She stepped closer, her breast brushing against his arm. "Do you want to play?"

"I think you already know the answer. It was good seeing you." He watched her reflection in the mirror behind the bar.

Disappointment covered her face. "It's always good to see you, Misha." She walked away.

"That was a little harsh, don't you think?" Lucas stared at him.

"It seems to be my night for harsh. But what you don't know is that Victoria has been hounding me even after I told we were over. I need to create distance and she's not getting the message." He downed the rest of his water and turned to look for one of his regulars.

Across the lounge sat Zanna in a short gold lamé dress. She was tall with blonde curly hair and big brown eyes. She knew the drill and was very clear on boundaries. He caught her eye and she smiled, making her way to him.

"Hi, you look like you're in need of something I might be able to give you." She kept her hands at her sides.

"Yeah, it's been a shit night. What do you say I show you off? You look great. Keeping in shape, I see." His eyes lingered down her arms.

"Sounds like a plan." She waited for his lead.

His blood pressure went down as she followed behind him. He took her to one of the rooms that had a viewing window. Lucas would lead a small group down there to see the performance.

Zanna was perfect for him in every way except the one that mattered. He didn't have any deep feelings for her or that connection he craved. He had found that connection in Raquelle and he knew that once he had her in his ropes, they would reach a whole other level. But he needed to center himself before he tackled trying to mend things with her.

He loosened his tie and discarded it on the floor with his jacket. The shirt and pants would stay on as always.

"Can you strip for me, Zanna?" He wanted it all tonight.

She smiled as she took her clothes off piece by piece, putting on a show for anyone who was watching.

He grabbed a black silk rope and wove it between his fingers, gathering its power. The rope always grounded him and gave him pleasure.

"Lie on your stomach," he said softly.

She complied and he stroked her skin with his fingertips from head to toe, making sure she was relaxed. Purrs came from her as she closed her eyes and surrendered to his touch.

He started with her arms and bound them using a loop and knot design. His fingers knew the configuration, like playing a piano. He wrapped the rope around her breasts, lifting them, and then down the front to her legs. With each knot, his fingers snaked between her skin and the rope, checking for tension. All he could picture was Raquelle's olive skin under the rope.

He finished his design, adding a couple of rings for suspension. He hooked Zanna to the rope that hung from the ceiling and used the pulley to lift her. The lights dimmed as the spotlight shone on her. The eyes behind the one-way mirror were watching his every move but there was something more, almost as if he could feel *her.* He stood back and admired his artwork but his intuition wasn't letting up. Was it possible to feel Raquelle without seeing her? Was she here?

"Misha?" Zanna caught his attention. "I want all of you tonight."

He knew what she wanted and what she was asking for.

As badly as things had gone with Raquelle, he couldn't push himself to be with anyone else. He could feel the heat of Raquelle's stare but it wasn't anger, it was something else.

"You've been absolutely magnificent but not tonight. My head and heart aren't in it." *Heart?*

He pulled over a soft mat and eased her down. Grabbing the knife he always carried, he cut the ropes free, massaging her muscles from head to toe. She stood up with a glazed look in her eye and he helped with her clothes. He finished by kissing her on both cheeks.

"Thank you. You were just what I needed," he said.

"Thank you. I always feel better after one of our sessions." She smiled.

He put his jacket on, stuffing his tie into his pocket, then opened the door to a hallway full of people. They nodded and smiled his way as words floated by him like *beautiful, lovely, and exquisite.* He was looking for only one person and as the onlookers left, he saw her turn toward him.

RAQUELLE MOVED as if being pulled by an invisible thread. His performance and expertise with the rope was moving but lacked sexual energy.

He waved his hand toward the viewing room and closed the door.

"Enjoy the show?" he said smugly with his hands stuffed in his pockets.

"Yes. More than I should have. You have talented hands and she seemed to enjoy it as well."

"She always does." His jaw twitched.

Her body retracted. As pissed off as she was at him, she didn't want him to be with anyone else. The thought entered her mind and feelings followed before she could process it. She always took the spotlight during her one-night stands and shouldn't care if he did so with someone else. But she *did* care, and that fueled her fire.

She hadn't noticed he had stepped toward her.

"Tell me, what did you like about it?" His stare was so intense it made her squirm. His finger skimmed under the bracelet he made for her.

She hadn't planned on revealing much but then the words came of their own volition. "She looked so peaceful and trusted you so completely."

She looked into an empty room through the window, remembering how she had pictured herself in the scene, tied up and available to him.

"Interesting choice of words, don't you think?" His mouth turned up at one corner.

If he wanted this discussion, she would bring it. "I don't think you understand what it feels like to live in the shadow of your father. He was internationally famous and I admired him as an artist most of my life until recently. The Luccenzo name has not benefited me in getting people to recognize my work. I wanted to get discovered for who I am as an artist. Not because I have his genes."

His hands balled in his pockets. "I know excellent artwork and talent when I see it. You needed to trust that I could put you in a position where your work could get exposure. That's all I was going for. Besides, you don't need to be a world-famous artist to see how wonderful you are as a person. As for fathers . . ." He sighed deeply.

"Misha?"

"I'm so tired of taking orders from my father. He acts as if I'm useless. Daily, he tells me how to run the business while my mother tells me how to run my life. Showing the collection with you in the spotlight was my way of taking something back, making it solely my decision. My father is not who he pretends to be, a man who won't even let me see my half sister. Yes, my father had a child out of wedlock. My mother knows nothing of it. Our father weaved in and out of our lives growing up. My brothers and I want to know her and who she is. She must be special to him. He calls her his Little Angel." His eyes were glassy.

Her mouth went dry. "He calls her what?" She wasn't sure she had heard him correctly.

"Little Angel. Why?" His brows furrowed.

"Just interesting, that's all." She laced her fingers together listening to the blood rush in her ears.

He took a hand from his pocket and held her cheek. "Are you okay? You just went pale. Do you need to sit down?"

Her eyes were locked with his as the puzzle pieces flew together.

His phone rang from his pocket. "I'm sorry. I have to take this. It's my emergency ring. We'll talk more later."

He opened the door and left.

She had to gather the troops. This information was about to rock everyone's world.

Chapter Twenty-Seven

RAQUELLE SEARCHED the club for Brie but couldn't find her. Brie and Logan were probably getting their freak on in a private room. She shot her a text and made a beeline for the exit.

She requested an Uber and dialed Mara.

Mara answered the phone, groggy. "Raq, why are you calling me at this hour?"

"You better get your boyfriend out of bed and call Leigha and Dean. I found out something tonight that can't wait." She was in a rush to get this out. "I'll be there in fifteen minutes." She hung up.

Her phone dinged with a text.

You're getting as bad as the boys with no goodbye. Followed by an emoji sticking its tongue out.

She laid her head back on the car seat. How was she going to tell them what she suspected? This answered a lot of questions and raised hackles in other ways, but this might finally bring some of this mystery to an end.

Leigha and Dean arrived the same time she did and rode up with her in the elevator. Her mind was so focused on the new information, she forgot to do her deep breathing exercises.

Dean's hair stuck out every which way. "This better be damn good. You're interrupting my beauty sleep with my queen."

"Oh, trust me. This is more than anyone banked on, including me." She looked over at Leigha, who was half asleep but gave her a curious glance.

The rest of the ride was quiet. They stepped off the elevator and headed for Mara's apartment. The door was unlocked so they let themselves in and sat in the living room.

Mara and Mac stumbled in with Mac wearing Mara's pink fuzzy robe that didn't fit him.

"Nice robe," Raquelle remarked.

"It was this or naked. My gorgeous physique is only for my Leannan." Mac smirked.

Mara blushed and smiled.

Mac continued, "What is so earth-shattering that we're gathered at this ungodly hour?"

Nerves knotted in her stomach as she tried to figure out how to phrase her newfound information. "Well, I know who Misha's father is." She paused.

"Don't keep us in suspense," Dean said with a yawn.

"Alek Romanowski. Ring any bells?" She played with her fingers and peeked up to see Leigha's reaction.

"What?" Everyone said in unison.

"Of course. How could we not see it?" Mac threw his hands in the air.

"But why is Misha's last name Raines and not Romanowski?" Dean asked.

"My guess is he set his son up from the beginning. He made sure he was born here and changed his name on the birth certificate. The question is why." Mac surmised.

"Sons." Raquelle reported. All eyes turned to Leigha.

"I have half brothers?" Leigha's eyes were unfocused and hazy.

Raquelle waited for more to come as her fingers twisted painfully in her lap.

"Oh God! Are you sleeping with Misha?" Leigha said, alarmed.

"Kind of," Raquelle responded, curling her body inward.

"You don't kinda sleep with men, Raq. The good news is, you're not related to him in any way. The bad news is I *am* related to him and he might be as bad as his father." Leigha's face fell.

Dean put his arm around her and pulled her to him, kissing the top of her head.

"As much as it pains me to say this, Raquelle's instincts may have been correct. The information we got from Misha's computer indicates that there's a whole other operating system behind the company's operating system that contains the information about whose money was stolen. I can't get into all the details but let's just say the mob is involved in a big way. It's pretty sophisticated technology." He steepled his hands in front of his mouth. "Remember how you wanted out of the spy game?"

"Yeah," Raquelle said warily.

"Well, you're back in it. We need you to turn Misha against his father and get Alek to come back to the US." Mac's voice broke through her bubble.

"Oh, hell no. He and I are barely on speaking terms. As much as Misha is not in a good place with his father, I doubt he will turn against him. He's very loyal."

"There's more." Mac looked at Dean. "We think the only person close enough to your father to poison him was Bernardo." Mac stared at her.

That caught her attention. A small gasp came from both her sisters. She would love nothing more than to catch her father's killer and make Bernardo pay for all his evil doings over the years. She nodded at Mac.

Mac continued, "We're in the process of bringing him in and questioning him. You in?"

She waited a beat. "Yeah, I'm in. I just don't know how it will go with Misha."

"I'll help you through it and we'll come up with a plan." Relief came over Mac's face.

Exhaustion and sadness hit her like a ton of bricks. "I need to go home and go to bed." She hugged both of her sisters, especially Leigha who had a lot to sort through and had gotten very quiet.

She leaned back from Leigha. "He really is a special man. You should get to know him."

"And you shouldn't give up on you and him." Leigha put on a weak smile.

Raquelle was too tired to think straight. "I'll talk to all of you later."

She let herself out and waited curbside to catch her ride. A city filled with millions of people and yet her life came down fate and DNA. Six degrees of separation was narrowed down to two degrees in a heartbeat.

When she got home, she left a trail of clothes leading to her bed. Titus was already on the bed, sprawled out on his back. Sleep wouldn't come for either of them until she had thoroughly kissed his face and tucked him in, under the covers. At this point she was convinced he would be the one and only male in her life. Her record spoke for itself. She had breached the trust of the one man she wanted to be with for a long time. Deep sleep took over without a prelude or dreams.

In the early morning, Titus lifted his head to a heavy

knock at the door. The knocking didn't let up. Titus jumped off the bed and barked at the front door, wagging his tail. She dragged herself out of bed, put on one of her silk robes, and looked out the peephole. She wasn't particularly friendly with her neighbors. The person that stood in the hallway surprised her as Titus started whining for her to open the door.

The fact that Misha wore the same clothes as the night before was not a good sign. She opened the door slowly. Titus squeezed himself out the door to greet his friend. Misha bent down to get kisses from him, a far cry from where he'd been a couple of weeks ago.

He stood up, gone were the tie and jacket. His hair was a mess. He smiled without it reaching his eyes. "May I come in?"

"Sure." She moved out of the way for him and Titus.

The air thickened and anger flashed in his eyes.

He knew.

His finger and thumb stroked his chin. "So, I had an interesting rest of the evening. Tell me, how was yours?" His hands rested on his hips while his fingers curled into his hipbones.

She had fought for everything in her life and was never afraid to speak up until this moment. Turbulent waters of emotion and betrayal surrounded her. She pulled her robe tighter. "Fine."

"Funny. You don't look like you got a lot of sleep. Where'd you go after the club?" He moved toward her.

She took a step back. "I came home and went to sleep."

He chuckled. "You can't even tell the truth about where you've been."

A lump formed in her throat.

He took another step forward. She moved back until she had nowhere to go. Her back hit the wall.

He bent over her. "Look at me," he yelled. "I want to make sure you hear every word."

She looked up at him. "Here's what I know. Marco called while we were at the club. After the last security breach, he decided to set up cameras in my office because he suspected you weren't on the up-and-up."

Hot tears burned in her eyes.

"You know what he saw? He saw you putting a drive in my computer. Did you get everything you needed between hacking the company Wi-Fi and my computer? How stupid I must look to you. Was it a setup from the beginning? Is that the only way the FTC and FBI could get what they need? Yes, I know you've been watching us since Brock fucked up and now you're coming after me but you won't find anything," he said through gritted teeth.

Tears streamed down her face, burning their path. This wasn't how she'd wanted this to go.

He leaned back and breathed out, nostrils flared like a bull pierced by a sword.

"Here's what else you got. My heart, my loyalty, my belief in you, and my love. That's right, Raquelle. I've fallen in love with you. Bravo, you're quite the little actress." His sarcasm was thick.

She shook her head. "No," she whispered.

"Tell me, was it all worth it?" His breaths became rapid.

"Tell me!" He yelled and smacked the wall behind her head.

She jumped. Titus growled and got up from where he was laying on the floor. He wedged himself between them and gave him a warning bark. Misha backed away and Titus stood in front of her for protection.

"Betrayal's a real bitch, isn't it?" His face flushed and he headed for the door.

Her voice was barely above a whisper. "You don't know the half of it."

"I think I've had my fair share. Stay away from me and keep my portrait. I don't need any reminders of you." He slammed the door as he left.

She stumbled to the couch and Titus laid his head in her lap, nudging her hand to pet him. He wanted to make her feel better, but nothing could at this point.

Her bed called to her. Hiding under her comforter for the rest of the day sounded like a good plan. As she drifted in and out of sleep, the phone dinged as people left texts and voice mails.

She didn't have the next move.

The clock kept moving forward but she stayed still. A knock came at the door she refused to answer. She could hear the key turn in the lock. It could only be one of two people.

Chapter Twenty-Eight

MISHA'S DAY had started off with devastation and only got worse. When Marco informed him about Raquelle he'd been gutted, his feet kicked out from under him. He had never known that kind of pain. Betrayal ripped him from the inside out. The woman he had found a connection with was also one who played him. So much for his instincts. She was good, maybe too good at her job as a spy. He should have paid closer attention and seen the signs especially given his father's warnings. His focus had been on her achievements as an artist instead of on the firm. This would only give his father more ammunition.

He sat back and watched the video several times. A couple of things struck him. She was tentative and fumbled with the drive before she found where to put it. Her eyes constantly scanned the office and door to see if anyone was coming. She talked to the computer telling it to hurry up and fanned herself with her hand. These weren't the actions of someone who had the confidence of doing this kind of thing many times. He remembered the day it happened. He'd been in a conference with Zane and Andre.

Then there was Marco's report. He had carefully chosen his words, telling Misha what he wanted him to hear, putting the entire security breach on Raquelle's shoulders. When he'd pressed Marco about what she would find on the drive, he evaded answering the question.

"Audrey, can you come in here, please?" He released the intercom button.

He walked over to the window, enjoying the last few moments of his empire in the sky before it fell. The troops were already formed and poised for action. The door opened and he turned around.

Audrey came in wide-eyed. "What's going on out there?" She pointed to the flurry of activity out on the floor. He couldn't tell her they were getting rid of sensitive information.

"Nothing. It's just a busy day on the market." He remained calm amidst the storm.

For once Audrey looked nervous. She wasn't one to crack under pressure but this was bigger than both of them.

"I need you to follow my next set of directions explicitly." He wanted to make sure she understood the gravity of what was happening. He handed her an envelope. "I need you to follow through with the set of directions in this envelope."

Her hands shook as she opened the flap. There was a handwritten note from him.

There are eyes and ears on us. You'll pretend that everything is operating normally in the office. Federal agencies are coming soon and CZR will no longer exist. I need you to spend the day dismantling the art collection. You'll work with Akita and Enrique. They know what to do.

Her eyes glassed over as she looked up at him. He walked toward her. "Please read all of it."

This is very important. I need you to go home and pack a

bag. You're going to be gone for a little awhile. Jonas is going to take you to the airport. Follow his directions. I've taken care of everything. I don't want you caught up in any of this. My office is probably bugged as we stand here.

Her arms flew around his neck. "Are you going to be okay?" she whispered in his ear.

"I don't know. But you've been loyal to me for many years and I need to make sure you're out of harm's way."

"Be careful." She nodded, wiped her tears, and left without another word.

He took out his cell phone and dialed his next order of business. "Marco, I need you in my office now."

Mister Nice Guy had left the building. Misha couldn't get rid of the loud gong in his head that told him something was very wrong with everything in his life. Things weren't adding up. He had to stand strong before his collapse.

Marco knocked and entered his office in his usual state, his face in his tablet.

"What aren't you telling me?" Misha demanded.

Marco's head snapped up. "Excuse me, sir?"

At least he had the decency to call him *sir*. "You heard me. I didn't stutter."

"In terms of what? I told you everything you needed to know." He'd become defensive.

"And there it is. Everything *you* wanted me to know. I want to know more about Raquelle, security, and anything else going on. I watched the video and she didn't look like a professional who knew what she was doing. In fact, quite the opposite. So what's the real story?" He clenched his jaw so hard it hurt.

"Are you going to let your dick dictate over logic and proof?" Marco's eyes darkened. His response was out of

242

character for him, causing Misha to pause and take stock of the situation.

Misha raised his voice. "You're out of line. I know what I saw on the video. She's not a trained agent. Are you going to tell me she works for the FBI? What are we talking about?"

"I'm not sure. But I do know the FTC and FBI are bearing down on you." Marco's lips drew a tight line.

He was hiding something. "Where are you getting your information from?"

"I have my sources and that's all you need to know." He stared at Misha, daring him to ask more questions. "If that's all, I have things I need to get done." Marco turned to walk out the door.

"One more thing. If Ms. Luccenzo shows up make sure she doesn't make it in here. You can go now." He'd be calling all the shots from here on out. *Keep your friends close, keep your enemies closer*. Marco was definitely hiding something.

Marco pulled the door shut with a bang.

Misha's adrenaline spiked. He was lost in a fog that blinded him to what might be right in front of him. As he contemplated his next move, his mother came barging through the door, minus shopping bags.

"Misha, what's going on?" Her perfect hair was in place.

"It's nothing. Can I get you a drink?" Misha started to pour two drinks without hearing her answer.

"It isn't even noon yet. Is everything okay?" She reached for the tumbler he offered her.

He laughed. "That's a loaded question at this point. I'm surrounded by betrayal and it feels fantastic."

She looked into her glass. "Who has betrayed you?"

"The woman I've fallen in love with, Marco, and maybe even this firm. To top it all off, Father is nowhere to be found.

It's as if he's disappeared off the face of the earth. I guess after all these years; I finally get to make decisions for the firm as it's in the greatest jeopardy. I'll go down with the ship, I suppose."

Her face paled. "What do you mean?"

"The federal government is coming to get everything in this firm and close us down. I never really cared for the world of finance so it won't be a total loss for me." He threw back the rest of his drink as it scorched down his throat.

"But I thought you excelled at it." She frowned.

"You can be good at something and not love doing it. My passion is fine arts and art history. That's where my heart lives. Father is the one who pushed me into finance, as you recall."

Quiet shrouded them.

"I didn't know. Your father was always convinced this was your calling." She placed her full glass on his desk and gave him a sad look.

"Father was convinced it was my calling because it was convenient for him. Interesting how it's convenient for him to go missing now," he said bitterly.

She gave him a weak smile and hugged him tightly for longer than usual. "Oh, *malen'kiy krolik*, I'm so sorry." Her hand stroked his cheek.

"Sorry for what?" He held her hand to his face.

"Everything. I wanted a better life for you and your brothers." She put on a sad smile.

Her words hit him as the hairs stood up on the back of his neck. She left before he could ask her what she meant.

Chapter Twenty-Nine

MARA PEEKED her head around the corner. "Raquelle?"

Leigha turned the lamp on by her bed.

The covers were up to her chin. Titus had kept her company all day but now stepped over her to get to Mara, whining for attention. Mara grabbed the top of the covers and tugged them back. Titus jumped to Leigha to be taken out for a break.

Her eyes stung. There were no tears left. Her heart was empty. In her head she'd known this would end badly but her heart wasn't prepared for the obliteration.

"Oh, honey. Come here." Mara pulled Raquelle in for a hug, but drained of strength, Raquelle fell limp and sagged into her sister's arms.

Betrayal was the poison stringing the three of them together. They had each tasted the poison by the hand of a toxic man: a husband, father, or lover. Each bitter experience came at a higher price.

The front door closed as Leigha and Titus returned and sat next to Mara. "What happened?"

"He came by this morning. He knows everything but he

thinks I work for the FTC or FBI." She let out a snort. "I didn't correct him. What difference does it make who I betrayed him for?" She lay back on the pillows.

As she said the words, the one tear left in her heart leaked out. "He said he'd fallen in love with me. What are the chances that he saw me with all my smeared colors and accepted and loved me anyway?"

She wiped away the tear with the back of her hand. "I don't know how to fix this. I don't think I can." Worry covered her sisters' faces.

"I hate to be the bearer of bad news but things are moving at a rapid rate." Leigha looked at Mara. "How about you get a shower and we'll make you dinner and talk."

"I don't wanna. I want to sit here in bed for the rest of my life and rot away." Raquelle sniffled.

"That's not an option. Mac and Dean have to talk you through what needs to happen tomorrow. You can throw a pity party for yourself later. As they say, it's not over till it's over. Come on, get up." Leigha took charge of Raquelle while Mara made her way to the kitchen to make dinner.

Raquelle let the water run over her body. She had become two-faced, smiling at a man who adored her and took care of her but at the same time trying to find dirt on him to find her father's killer. In the end, it had been a necessary evil. No apologies would be coming from her. She wanted to bring closure to the nightmare her family had endured, but she had miscalculated the hellish fallout.

Her sole focus had been her artwork. She'd never anticipated falling in love with her sister's half brother. The absurdity was almost comical. Her groan echoed off the tile walls. This could only happen to her. She'd spent her life avoiding any love connections. Most men were users, but this one had had all her best interests at heart. In return she would be his downfall. Betrayal was a bitch she was too familiar with and she needed to kill her.

She managed to pull on a pair of sweats and an oversize shirt. Her body felt drained and weary as she made her way to the kitchen, and plopped herself into a chair.

"The boys are coming over to talk about your next move," Mara said while stirring the sauce.

"Oh, yeah. To tell you the truth, I really don't give a shit at this point," Raquelle replied.

When Mara served her the pasta, Raquelle pushed her food around on her plate and made a few attempts to eat without success.

"You know there'll be someone else, right? Misha may not be your forever." Mara tried being positive.

"There won't be anyone else. He's got me hook, line, and sinker and I'm done," she said without looking up. "My mojo has left the building."

The doorman called up to announce Mac and Dean had arrived. "Oh, good. My evening just got better. Two of my favorites."

"Don't blame them. They're just trying to do their job." Leigha would defend her man to the end. "Besides, they want this over as much as you do."

They convened in the living room. Titus lay on her feet. Mac sat across from her and spoke first. "I heard you had a visitor today. I'm sorry things didn't go well." He gripped his hands together, leaning on his knees.

Dean picked up the conversation. "We have some good news. Bernardo was brought in for questioning. The police have evidence that suggests he's the one who poisoned your father. He gave us some information before he asked for a lawyer. He isn't confessing. Our guess is Alek offered him a lot of money to do the job. Apparently, your father was packing money, gold, and artwork inside his installations for Alek and moving them around the world. What we don't know is why."

"I know why." Mama stood in the doorway. She had used her key to get in.

Raquelle waved her over to come and sit with her on the couch. She hugged her.

"Your papa was a good man. He wasn't perfect but he tried to protect all of you." She sighed and put her arms around Raquelle and Leigha. Mara sat on the other side of Raquelle.

"I finally found the courage to read the letter you gave me from your papa. After Leigha was born, they made a deal, of sorts. Alek agreed not to be a part of Leigha's life if your papa agreed to do things for him. Your Papa kept Alek and his men as far away from you girls as he could. It's why he hired security for us. I had always had my suspicions about what happened between them. I didn't know it went this deep." She stroked Leigha's face. "He loved you all very much, despite what you think. I know he was distant. He had to be in order to protect you."

Their sniffles punctured the still air.

Mac interjected, "Bernardo said Antonio knew too much about the Russian mob. Your father would have had the upper hand and that wasn't going to sit well with Alek. When your father retired, he had an expiration date."

"Excuse me." Mara left the room with Mac in tow.

Dean filled Raquelle in on the plan for Misha. "Tomorrow the FBI is coming in to shut down CZR and collect evidence. There was enough on the drive to put them out of business for good. What we don't have is Alek. You need to get to Misha and convince him to give up his father."

Raquelle dug her heels in. "No, I don't. We know

Bernardo murdered Papa. Case closed. And what about Misha? Is there evidence against him?"

Dean looked at Leigha. "It's going to take some time to connect all the dots. The case is open until we get Alek. By getting Bernardo, we only know one-tenth of what Alek was doing behind the scenes. He used CZR as a front to move all his money and investments." He paused. "It gets worse. From what we can tell, Misha was born, I mean literally born, to run the company as a front for all of the Russian mob's illegal activity along with the sons of the two other families. I'm not sure Misha is involved or knows about any of it."

"He won't see me. I've betrayed and hurt him badly." Tears welled up. "While he did everything for me, I was plotting behind his back. To top it all off, he's the best sex I've ever had, even though he's a little kinky. I've never felt that deeply for anyone. We have that connection that makes you feel like you've known that person forever. He opened me up and stepped into my soul."

Leigha spoke up, "Having feelings like that will take sex to a whole other level." She looked over at Dean.

Dean stood. "Okay, TMI ladies. I don't need to hear about your sex life with your mother sitting here."

Guilianna said, "What's the matter with you Dean? Everybody has sex. It's especially good when you're in love." Her voice faded.

He held his head in his hands and muttered, "Someone help me."

Mac walked in the room. "Did you fill her in on what needs to happen tomorrow?"

"Sure, after we talk about everyone's sex life. Would you like to join in and tell us about you and Mara?"

Mac looked at each of them, shrugged and said, "They're hot Italian women, what can I say? You gotta roll with it.

Now, back to business." He turned to Raquelle. "We need you to get to Misha somehow, pull out all the stops, and convince him to get his father to come back to the US, if it's not too late."

"What do you mean, *not too late*?" Raquelle asked.

Mac's faced hardened. "We have intel in Russia. The mob and the government may be turning on him, realizing things here aren't going well. He won't live to tell about it if he stays in Russia. Coming to the States maybe a better option for him. It may not be a hard sell for Misha, who's still loyal to his father."

Raquelle rubbed her temples. "I'll see what I can do. It won't be easy though." She looked at Mac. "What's going on with Mara?"

"She's going to see the doctor tomorrow." Mac's face showed concern.

Mama smiled.

"Mama, why are you smiling?" Raquelle thought it was an odd reaction. The family didn't need one more piece of bad news.

"Everything will work out." She patted her hand and got up. "I have to go. I've got things to do. *Mia bellas*, I'll see you soon." She kissed everyone on the cheek and left.

"I need everyone to get out. My head is ready to explode. I'll figure something out tomorrow." Raquelle was exhausted. Her emotions were on overload and psychologically she didn't know which end was up.

She closed the door to a quiet apartment, alone again with her thoughts and pain. There was only one way to get Misha to see her again and she had to play that card.

Her phone rang from her handbag. The number was unfamiliar.

"Hello?"

"Raquelle, this is Akita Aurtoro. How are you?"

"I've been better. I'm sure you are calling to tell me Misha has withdrawn his recommendation of my work being shown in your gallery." Raquelle held her head in her hand.

"Misha never recommended your work be shown in the gallery. But after seeing it, I want in on what you have to offer. I showed it to the board of directors and they are very excited to see the rest of your collection. We're looking to put your pieces in a show with some high-end buyers who are already very interested. So what do you say?" Akita sounded excited.

"Wait. Misha never made a recommendation?"

Akita paused. "Oh, no. He invited me to the show to see everything in his collection as well as your piece, which was remarkable. We need to get you to the buyers. I'd like to set up an appointment in a couple of days to see your portfolio. Please call my office at your earliest convenience. You also need to get yourself an agent. I have some excellent ones I can recommend."

Raquelle couldn't believe what she was hearing. Misha had put her work in the collection to be seen, but hadn't done anything else on her behalf. Which meant that she'd gotten into the gallery on her own. She should be ecstatic but this was just another tear in her bond with Misha. When she thought back to their conversation, she realized he had never said he had recommended her work.

"Thank you. I'll give your office a call. I'm looking forward to partnering with you."

She hung up and hoped her plan for tomorrow would work. There was no other way to get him here than to tell him the one secret he wanted to know.

Chapter Thirty

WHEN RAQUELLE HAD MADE her way to CZR Investments for her interview, she had no idea what to expect. This time she was pretty sure she knew the outcome. None of the scenarios went in her favor.

Clouds hung in the sky, vacillating between dark and light gray as if they weren't sure if they should be angry. No rain meant she wouldn't be dripping wet like last time. She put herself together for the confrontation, wearing a black skirt with a high slit, her favorite Louboutin shoes, and a red cowl-neck blouse. He needed a good look at what he was throwing away.

Tears pricked her eyes. She squeezed her hands together until they were white, stopping them from falling. The cab lurched forward and came to a stop, snapping her out of her thoughts. She stepped out onto the street and was surrounded by the lunch crowd. In some ways it was a relief. Getting lost in throngs of people would give her some cover going into the building.

She moved with the crowd to the elevator but stepped back as men in dark blue coats rolled out boxes of files.

Something wasn't right. The elevator ascended at a snail's pace, stopping at almost every floor. Her anxiety flared up but she was too exhausted to go through the paces of her breathing exercises. She shook out her hands and mumbled, "Come on."

When the doors opened, a scene of chaos confronted her. People moved like speed walkers, scurrying around, while others were shouting orders.

The front desk stood vacant, several phones ringing at once. She turned down the hallway to Misha's office and made it halfway there before she encountered Marco.

"Oh, look who it is, the *Spy Who Loved Misha*. Look around you. Do you like what you see? It's because of you," he sneered.

He took out his cell phone. "I need security."

She prevented herself from lunging at him and grabbing his throat. "I'm here to see Misha. Where is he?"

"He doesn't want to see you." He turned away from her but not out of earshot. "Yes, could you send someone up right away? We have a situation."

"I have to speak to him. It's urgent," she pleaded.

Marco motioned over her shoulder. She whipped around in time to see two security guards heading her way. Her only hope was to make a run for it. As she jolted forward, two arms caught her in midair. She wrestled with them, jamming her heel into one guard's foot. He cursed and gripped her arm harder. "Misha!" she yelled.

Misha came out of his office. "What the hell is going on out here?"

He started to move toward her as Marco grabbed his arm.

"Don't. Just let her go. She's not worth it." Marco held him there. "Take her out of here," he ordered the guards.

"You don't get to tell me what to do." Misha barked at

Marco, yanking his arm away. "Get your fucking hands off her." His face reddened.

The guards looked back and forth between Marco and Misha and turned her around as she yelled over her shoulder, "I know who your sister is."

Misha moved toward her. "Stop. Let her go. Now!" He turned to Marco. "And by the way, she *is* worth it."

She pulled herself together and walked toward him. The air was charged with trust, mistrust, lust, lies, and loyalty all tied together by a red bow of anger.

"Let's go to my office." He waved in the direction of the double doors.

She came to a stop in front of Audrey's abandoned desk. "Is she gone?"

He motioned to his office door. "Go."

He closed the door behind them.

"What's going on out there?" she said.

"As if you don't know," he sneered. "Haven't you done enough damage?"

She waited. "I'm trying to make things right."

He stared at her for a minute. "Damn it. We can't talk here. I have a lot of questions for you."

He pulled her forward by the back of her neck and leaned toward her ear. "Do you really know who my sister is or are you just playing me again?"

His hot breath brushed her ear. Her heart fluttered in her chest. "Yes, I know her very well. And no, I'm not playing you."

He pulled back and frowned. "Really?"

She nodded. "Is it possible for you to come to my place later?" She slid her hands around his waist and slipped something into his pocket. "Please."

He swallowed and nodded. "I'll be there. But this better

be good and you better have the answers I want," he whispered harshly.

She gave him a hug and whispered in his ear, "Please listen to your heart. You can trust me. Things are not what they seem," and she kissed him, wanting him to feel her honesty, love, and devotion.

He grabbed her shoulders and pushed her away. "Don't."

She felt defeated but left without another word. FBI agents rushed by her in the direction of Misha's office. Pain tore at her. She wished she could have done things differently for him.

Marco—and Bernardo—came into view across a row of cubicles. What the fuck? Every memory of every evil thing he had done to her flooded back. In the past she would have been intimidated by him but not anymore, now that she knew he'd killed her father.

She walked toward him with fists at her sides. His look of surprise at seeing her there didn't stop her.

"What are you doing here?" he said.

"I think the better question is, why aren't you behind bars for killing my father?" she said in midstride.

He smirked as she sucker punched him square in the jaw. His look of shock was priceless so she hit him again in the eye. When he put his hands up in defense, she nailed him in the balls with her knee. He doubled over, breathless.

She spoke to him in Italian. "The first one is for my sisters, the second for my mama, and the last one is for me. I suggest you look over your shoulder from now on because you will never be free."

MISHA CAME out of his office in time to see Raquelle beating the crap out of some guy and he wasn't about to stop her. She looked over her shoulder at him and strode to the elevator. He walked over to where the man lay on the floor.

"What happened?" he asked.

"That crazy bitch beat up Bernardo," Marco spit.

Misha moved fast and cornered him. He kept his hands at his sides to avoid grabbing him by the throat. "First off, don't ever talk about Raquelle like that. Second, you're fired. Third, why the fuck is Bernardo here? You better get him out of here before I kill him." He pointed to Bernardo, who was still doubled over on the floor. Marco paled and moved past Misha, ramming his shoulder into him, but Misha didn't budge. What the hell was going on? His world made less and less sense by the minute.

Before Misha left the office, he looked over the company he had helped build, knowing it would be the last time he would be coming here. Depending on the outcome of the investigation, he was either going to jail or taking his mother and leaving the country forever.

He went back to his office to have one last look around the place where passion met heartbreak. The crumpled piece of paper Raquelle had slipped to him itched in his hand. On it was an Upper West Side address not familiar to him. He wanted to trust her and, based on her reaction to the chaos in the office, his instinct was correct. She wasn't FBI or any other agency. What was her story and how did she tie into all of this?

The evening was just getting started with no end in sight. Before he went to see Raquelle, he needed to call his mother. He told her about the raid by the FBI and the closing of CZR Investments. She seemed sad but not surprised.

Misha wanted answers. "Is there something you're not

256

telling me? I get the feeling you know more about all of this than you're letting on."

"I see the way you look at her. It was how your father looked at me in the beginning. We were young and not in a good place in so many ways. You need to know that I had to do what was best for my children. You and your brothers are all that matter to me." Her voice was distant, speaking to him from somewhere in the past.

"What do you mean?"

"Your father and I had to make some choices in order to protect you. That's why we came to the US." Her voice sounded sad.

He waited, contemplating his next comment. "Do you know about our half sister?"

"Of course I know. Did your father really think he could keep a child hidden from me? Go to Raquelle. She has the answers you're looking for." Without another word, she hung up, leaving him with more questions than answers.

His life was a photo montage with missing faces. A piece of him didn't want to go and see Raquelle. He wanted to pack a bag and take a long vacation where no one could find him. His entire life had been mapped out for him, yet in a matter of a few hours, that life was gone and he had no idea who he was or how he had gotten there. He was falling apart on the inside like pieces of shattered glass.

After the FBI was done for the day, he left to see the one person who might have the answers he needed to put this all to rest. He showed up at the specified address and, according to the directions, he came alone and checked to make sure he wasn't followed.

His nerves were raw and muscles tight, cocked like a loaded gun. The doorman announced him and he made his way up. After one knock, the door opened and Raquelle let him in with a worried expression on her face.

"I have to ask if you were followed." She gave him an apologetic look.

"No, I made sure of it. Where are we?" He stuffed his hands into his pockets to keep from holding her face and kissing her. His heart didn't know the difference and wanted her, craved her, despite the betrayal.

"This is my sister Mara's apartment. We needed an unknown location." She let out a nervous laugh.

"This is funny?" he said sharply.

"This is what my life has become. I never would have guessed. Please have a seat." She motioned to the living room couch.

She sat down opposite him in a high-back chair. "I don't even know where to begin. This is all such a mess. But there are some things I need to say first." Her fingers twisted in her lap and then she gripped onto the arms of the chair as if it would hold her in place.

"I took the commission with you, not to spy on you but because I wanted to do your portrait. I am not a portrait artist-slash-spy. I was asked to look into things after you hired me."

"By who?" He wanted to know the Great and Mighty Oz.

"Mac. He has been investigating my father's murder and is ex-MI6. His bosses at MBK allowed him to continue to pursue the case."

"Interesting."

She paused as if she wasn't sure where she wanted to take the next turn. Her head snapped up and she said, "First, tell me about your father."

He sighed. "I don't know what good that's going to do but I'll tell you again. Like I said before, my father is Alek Raines. He's Russian and deals in imports and exports." He picked a piece of lint off his pant leg. "He also calls a lot of the shots at CZR Investments, or at least he used to."

"Why?"

"Why what?"

"Why did he call the shots at an investment firm? What does he know about investments?" Raquelle held his gaze.

He thought about it for a minute. The question hung between them. "I guess I never thought about it. The import-export business deals a lot with money. He's always been involved in investing money and has some good advice."

Her eyes dropped away from his and he got the feeling a bomb was about to drop.

"Do you know who your half sister's mother is?" Pain clouded her eyes.

"No. But I'm guessing I'm about to find out."

She sat back in the chair. "Your half sister is *my* half sister. She and I share a mother. You and she share a father."

He didn't know how to respond to this information. His mind tried to follow the family flow chart. He had slept with his half sister's half sister. What the hell?

A ghost of a smile graced her lips. "No, we're not related. But you and Leigha share a common passion."

"The photographer?"

Raquelle nodded. "She recently found out that her biological father is Alek and he called her his Little Angel. That's how I made the connection." She rubbed her hands on her legs. "This next part is really hard for me to tell you."

God, how could it get any worse? The gut feeling that things were not as they seemed hadn't left him in days. One clue built on top of another like some crazy game of Jenga.

"Your father is actually Alek Romanowski, the head of one of the most powerful Russian mob families." She held her breath.

Nervous laughter bubbled to the surface. "You have to be joking. This is absurd. My father, head of the Russian mob? Come on. Besides, my father's name is Raines not Romanowski."

Her face remained unmoved, no smile, no wink. The knife began to twist.

"After Leigha was born our fathers made an agreement. My papa would move money, gold, and art around the world if your father stayed away from our family. Alek paid Bernardo a large sum of money to have my papa killed so he wouldn't talk. Papa knew too much about the workings of the Russian mob and your father was afraid my papa would have leverage on him. CZR Investments was a front for your father's money laundering, among other things."

His heart dropped to his stomach. She stopped talking long enough for him to process. He shoved his head in his hands, staring at the floor. Ever so quietly she said, "I'm so sorry."

His head shot up. "This is some sick joke. There's got to be a mistake. You have the wrong man. My father is a lot of things but criminal is not one of them."

"Have you ever looked closely at your birth certificate? Your father's name isn't on it." She pushed him further into his hell.

He stood up, ready to leave. "I think you've lost your fucking mind. I have to go. This is too much bullshit for one night. I don't know what your game is, but you're twisted and you have absolutely no proof."

He turned to head out the door and bumped into Mac and Dean. "Have a seat, mate. You need to calm down so we can talk," Mac said.

"We have your proof," Dean finished.

Mac and Dean sat on the couch across from him as

Raquelle sat next to Misha. The only thing that separated them was a table. A thick manila folder landed on the table, marked with official red stamps. Mac opened the cover to a photo of his father.

Mac said, "This is the dossier on Alek Romanowski. I want you to look through it. Take a look at his accomplishments as head of the Russian mob."

In a voice he didn't recognize as his own, he said, "He's my father." Misha waited to look through the rest of the folder. There were so many questions running through his head from his name change to years of his father being absent. He had abandoned him and his brothers as his mother suffered like a widow. His father had been overly involved in CZR. If his father *was* Alek Romanowski, head of the Russian mob, it would explain a lot.

Raquelle slipped her hand over his and squeezed it. "From the beginning, none of this has been easy. There's no joy in this but the truth may bring things to light for you, answer many questions, and set you free." She nodded to the dossier. "What's in that folder is not easy to digest but is necessary for you to know and understand."

He let go of her hand and flipped through over thirty years of information. One photo was a shot with Zane and Andre's fathers, only they too had different names, Zaretlinski and Chaplinowski. All the sons' names had been changed not to look Russian. His blood started to boil with a mix of pure rage and soul-burning hurt. He had a lot of questions for Mr. Romanowski.

He perused the rest of the information regarding years of illegal activity. Raquelle's lies were nothing compared to his father's betrayal. He had cut Misha at the deepest level, using him as a pawn. His father's knife torn at his heart as hatred bled out. He closed the folder and threw it across the room.

No one moved to clean it up. Raquelle dabbed her eyes next to him. He held his head in his hands, not wanting to see their eyes full of pity, questioning his naiveté.

"We need you to help us bring him back to the States," Mac said calmly.

Misha stood up to leave. "I have a lot to process." He needed to get out of there before he punched someone or something.

He moved toward the door and heard Mac say, "Let him go. He needs time."

Time wasn't the only thing he needed.

Chapter Thirty-One

MISHA'S PHONE registered five missed calls from Jonas. He hadn't told anyone where he was going and regretted showing up to see Raquelle. His head swam with images of the father he thought he knew. The life he had built crumbled stone by stone as he stood and watched it fall, lacking the courage to rebuild it.

He pushed open the front door of his brownstone and trudged through its dark interior. No light was needed. The light that had shone on his reality was enough for a lifetime. His home was without feeling, empty, and disconnected. As he made his way to the living room, he discarded his jacket and tie behind him and left them where they fell. He switched on the table lamp and sat back in his chair, letting the leather conform to his body. The Stolichnaya Elit vodka called to him. Drinking wasn't his favorite pastime. Being out of control always left him uneasy and now he knew why. His life had been out of his control all along.

He threw back his drink as clear liquid slid down his throat without the burn. The adrenaline coursing through his veins dulled any pain. He slammed the glass on his desk, then kicked off his shoes and peeled off his socks. His feet sank into the high plush carpet and his mind wandered to Raquelle. He couldn't blame her for wanting to discover her father's killer. Too bad it had to be *his* father at the other end.

The life his father was leading away from his family was foreign to him, out of his wheelhouse. He had always looked up to his father. He took control of everything around him, yes, but dishonest? Memories of small things leaked into his mind. He started adding them together. The missed holidays, trouble with customs, private phone conversations he'd overheard but didn't understand, all pointed to a secret life Misha didn't want to acknowledge.

Then there was the issue of his mother. What did she know about any of this? Or had his father left her in the dark too about his illegal activities? His life was a series of questions that had no immediate answers. The man *with* all the answers was MIA.

He pounded back his second drink, well on his way to oblivion. His nerves soaked in the numbness, slowing down his racing mind. This wasn't where he wanted to be. At this point in his life, he should have a solid career and family. But his best-laid plans always seem to go shit up.

The front door clicked open and shut. His body readied for the fight of an intruder until the scent of lavender wove its way into the room. Tonight would prove to be a different kind of fight.

She knocked before she entered the living room. "What do you want, Raquelle?" He pushed the glass away from him, needing to be sober for this confrontation.

"I wanted to see you and make sure you're okay even as my family advised against it." Her voice was small, her body hunched over.

"Well, I'm not okay. Now you've seen me. Get out." He

swallowed back the words he wanted to say, replacing them with venom. He wanted to tie her up, feel her surrender, and have her ask for forgiveness.

"No. I'm not leaving until you talk to me." She stood in the darkness.

He chuckled. "A typical response from a woman who never gives up." He leaned back in his chair. "What would you like me tell you?"

She moved closer to the light and lifted her head. Her eyes were red and puffy. "Anything you need to tell me. I want to be here for you. You were there for me and you can't do this alone. Been there, done that. It doesn't work."

The pit in his stomach ached. "How about, I have no idea who my father is. I thought he was running an honest business. I looked up to him. Come to find out he's a fraud, a criminal, and set me up in the process. It doesn't get worse than that."

She took off her shoes and walked around the coffee table. Her eyes focused on him as she sank to her knees.

"What are you doing?" he asked, startled.

"It feels right." Her fingers twisted in her lap.

He studied her face. Her deceit had stung. He would have had a hell of a time moving on without her. But she was here to surrender, to give herself over to him. She had put herself in a vulnerable position. For the first time in his life, someone was going to be there for him. He needed her.

"I know something about fake fathers. But sometimes there's an ulterior motive. For years, my sisters and I thought my papa loved his artwork more than he loved us. We were wrong. He stayed away to protect us from your father."

His blood boiled higher with every word she spoke. Every detail revealed another ugly side he didn't want to admit about his father. She couldn't compare their fathers. They were at opposite ends of the moral scale. Her father did things to protect his daughters. His father did things to promote his greedy agenda and manipulate the people around him.

"I can't wrap my head around the father I know and the man you revealed to me. All his motives were strictly for his benefit. It explains his need to call all the shots. I'm torn between anger in a way I've never experienced and indescribable pain in my heart." He stared at his empty glass. He didn't want to see the pity written on her face.

"Believe me. I get it. But Misha, we need you to convince him to come back to the United States. It may save his life." She went to grab his knee but let her hand fall away.

His head shot up. "What are you talking about?" He grabbed the back of her head, tilting it up.

She didn't flinch. "Your father maybe in trouble in Russia. He's involved with the Russian government and the mob. They know things are bad with the company. They may lose everything. Here, he will probably go to jail, but he'll be alive."

His eyes burned with unshed tears. "What makes you think I want him alive? He's done despicable things."

"Because at the end of the day, he's your father. He's your blood. Russians are a lot like Italians that way." She stayed perfectly still, challenging him to take over his life and make a difficult decision. He had been the pawn for too long. A new king needed to reign.

As much as he hated his father's control and his overbearing attitude, this was his father. He couldn't have his death on his conscience. He preferred him alive rather than dead. "What guarantee do I have? He could just as easily be killed here."

"Mac said they would give him top security in exchange for information about the mob and other illegal Russian activities. That's all I know. You would have to talk to Mac and Dean about the rest of it." Her eyes never left his.

He held her face in his hands like he held his father's fate. "As luck would have it, I got a text from an unknown number that said my father needed to see me and that it was urgent. I get first crack at him. Needless to say, I have a lot of questions for the fallen king."

She nodded. "Every king must give up the throne at some point." She swallowed. "I want you to know that I never doubted you for a minute. I'm convinced you'll be cleared in the end. I begged Mac to let me out of the spy game and tried to convince him he was looking into the wrong guy." Her eyes glassed over. "Please believe me. I have everything and nothing to lose."

He understood and, with her words, the canvas of illusion fell away, leaving two souls in need of repair. They needed to trust each other and take the dive. Her strength amazed him. She had left herself open to him to do with her what he wanted.

He said, "Do you trust me completely?" He would tie her from head to toe.

THIS WAS the test Raquelle had been waiting for with him. "Yes," she said with conviction.

He bent down, smashing his mouth onto hers. Scorching flames lit her need for all he had to offer. Lips bit, nipped, and sucked as she gave him everything. She knew not to touch him. He needed to be in total control of the moment.

He broke their kiss and squeezed the back of her neck. "What, no knee pads?" There was no humor in his question.

"I'm tougher than you think but not tough enough to think

I can live my life without you." No tears accompanied her statement as her hands clenched into fists.

He stood up and looked down at her. She remained on her knees and reached for his zipper. He grabbed her hands and shook his head.

"Come with me, little one." He held out his hand to her and pulled her up.

He led them upstairs in a home that had become very familiar to her. The door opened, revealing his huge California king bed.

"Take your clothes off and lie facedown on the bed." His voice changed to a deeper timbre, making her shiver.

She took off her clothes piece by piece, folding them and placing them on the chair. She lay facedown, turned her head, and closed her eyes. He knelt above her and started to massage her arms and legs.

"I need this now more than ever. You're giving me such a gift. Surrender should never be taken lightly." He stroked his fingers along her back.

"I know," was all she could say, lost in his methodical touch.

He started with her arms, tying them together behind her back. Her wrist was free of its soft cast giving him access to tie them. In this position, he would have to move her and manipulate her. The silk rope was smooth against her skin as he began to knot it down her back and wove it over her shoulders. He rolled her over onto her back, making short work of intricate knots from chest to hip.

He propped her back up on a pillow and said, "Open your eyes, *malen'kiy*. I want to see everything." His breath was even.

She opened her eyes to see him above her, eyes dilated, fingers skimming her skin under the rope.

"Tell me what you're feeling right now." His fingers didn't stop caressing her as he pulled the rope between her legs. He moved two pieces of rope so that each nipple peeked out between them.

"I'm comfortable, peaceful, and free." He stopped and looked at her. "I've never felt like this with anyone in my life. Even after everything that's happened, I give myself to you trusting you'll take care of my body, heart and mind. Does that make sense?" The friction between the rope and the softness of his caresses played havoc with her head and libido.

"It makes sense. You're a natural. I've never seen someone take to the rope the way you do. Your trust and surrender bring me peace too. Can I take your photo? No matter what happens, I want to remember this moment forever. I may have to commission another painting." He smiled.

"Yes, please." She was breathless.

He pulled his camera from his bag and began taking photos, moving her several times to different angles. His worship of her body took away all the ugly words her papa had said to her. Shame scurried away, replaced with pride, freedom, and respect.

He put his camera down as she lay on her side, her knees pulled up in a sitting position. She couldn't see him behind her but could feel his skin on hers as he tucked in behind her. He expertly worked the rope across her clit and on her nipples. Her orgasm approached at lightning speed. Being so attuned to her, he slowed down at the moment she was at the edge.

"Please," she whimpered.

He showed her the knife. "Stay very still."

Cutting the rope between her legs, he laid her on her

stomach with hips up and slid into her, pumping in and out, kissing her shoulder. "*Malen'kiy*, you are the end and the beginning for me." He slid his hand under her arms and pinched both nipples between the ropes.

She screamed his name and came harder than she had ever come before. The sensations running through her body couldn't grip onto her emotions. Her feelings were new and exciting. She wanted them to fight together for their forever. But time might end up being both friend and foe. The wild card was Alek.

Chapter Thirty-Two

MISHA LISTENED TO HER BODY, strumming it like a fine-tuned guitar, allowing her to completely let go. He followed her as they lay covered in beads of sweat. After he cut her loose from the rope and knots, he rubbed the areas that had burned, leaving red marks. She moaned quietly.

"Are you all right?" Her face was rosy and a smile spread across her lips.

"I'm more than all right. Blissful." She stroked his cheek.

He covered her in his silk sheets and walked to the bathroom to get the aloe and arnica, the two best remedies for redness and bruising. His hands rubbed into the warm areas of her skin while she purred like a kitten.

"You were magnificent." He brushed the hair from her eyes. "I have so much more to show you."

She smiled. "I take it I'm forgiven for my sins."

Her words were like spikes. "Your sins don't hold a candle to my father's lies and double life. I don't blame you for wanting to know who killed your father. You've changed my life forever, opening Pandora's box. Too bad the inside resembles a taped off crime scene. He won't ever be telling me what to do again."

Reality hit him full force, unplugging him from his father. He couldn't relate to him anymore. He needed to come to terms with the fact that the man in the dossier and his father were the same person. He continued to rub her body in silence.

She must have sensed his uneasiness. "I spoke with Akita about my work." She turned toward him. "She said you never recommended my work, just made sure she had an invitation to the show. I'm sorry."

"Your work speaks for itself. You didn't need the recommendation. Only the chance." He brushed the hair from her face. "Now, we sleep. Tomorrow is another day to tackle the big issues."

He curled up behind her as she pushed her ass against his already hardening cock. She giggled.

"What's so funny?" He began tickling her.

"I'm not tired . . . yet." She smiled.

He rolled on top of her and made slow love to her, peppering her body with kisses and soft touches. It was the two of them cocooned and safe from a brutal world.

After several rounds of lovemaking, she finally went to sleep. His woman had an appetite and he was going to need to stay in shape to keep her satisfied.

Sleep wouldn't find him easily, though. His mind went back to his conversations with Marco. He was convinced Marco had been working with his father the entire time of his employment, meaning he was the true traitor among them. Marco's give away was his association with Bernardo.

The rug had been pulled out from under him. He had nothing left to lose in this game of charades. The final mask to drop belonged to his father. His eyes closed as he tried to figure out what to do. For once, Misha held all the cards when it came to his father's fate.

The smell of eggs, bacon, and coffee permeated his senses. When he got to the kitchen, Raquelle was hustling around and had a full breakfast spread on the island.

"Good morning, sir." Her hair was tousled and cheeks were rosy.

He came around from behind and wrapped his arms around her waist. "You better be careful. I might like you calling me *sir*."

Turning her around, he took her face in his hands. His whole life had been about choices being made for him and caring for others. Looking into her eyes, he knew she was just as strong if not stronger than him. The choices were in his hands now. They could do this together. He would dig deep to finally live up to his own expectations of being a boss.

She placed her hands over his. "Have you decided to help us?" The pain in her eyes told him everything he needed to know. She knew this wasn't an easy decision.

"Yes. My father will contact me with directions. It's how he operates." He sighed. "And now I know why. I feel like such a fool in all of this."

"Don't do that to yourself. From what I can gather, he's been doing this his entire life. He's a professional at this point. I'm sorry. I know it's hard to hear." She brought his head down to hers and kissed him. "Now have a seat. You need a good breakfast after last night's workout." She rubbed her hands together.

"This is quite the spread. I didn't know you could cook." He didn't know where to begin, from the croissants to the fresh fruit and pastries.

"I don't. Half of this came from my favorite diner. I cooked the eggs and bacon with Mara over the phone."

He laughed. "Come here."

She tucked herself between his legs.

"I only need to sustain myself on what's under that silk robe." He reached under her robe and ran his thumb along her seam as she jerked.

"Don't distract me. You better eat up. I need to call the guys so we can meet with them today." The worry hadn't left her eyes.

"Don't worry about me. I have to face the inevitable with my father. When it comes to him, things are never easy." He sighed.

"We'll be there every step of the way. Besides, you're family now. I think I just grossed myself out." She made a sour face.

He slapped her ass as she walked away.

Arrangements had been made to meet at Mara's apartment again. He called Jonas to come pick them up. He needed to know where he stood with him.

He opened the front door. "I'm double-parked out here so I hope you're ready to go," Jonas said.

"Come in a minute." He closed the door behind him.

Jonas turned around with his hands gripped behind his back. "I know you need to fire me because you lost the business. I expected it. No hard feelings. I get it."

"Actually, firing you hadn't crossed my mind. You're my personal driver so I'm keeping you on. What did come to my mind is how much you knew about my father."

"Excuse me?"

"Did my father have contact with you on a regular basis to check up on me?"

Jonas looked perplexed. "I've met your father once in the ten years I've known you. He's a pretty elusive guy, if you ask me."

"So you didn't know he's a Russian mob boss?"

His eyes grew large. He shook his head. "No. What the hell? Sorry."

Misha looked at him hard. Either he was telling the truth or giving an Oscar-winning performance.

"I'm sorry. This is all new for me too. I think Marco is working for my father, giving him daily updates. I wanted to know where you were in all of this. To say I'm paranoid is an understatement."

"I never did like Marco. When did you find all this out?" Jonas's hands fell to his sides.

"Last night. It's been a whirlwind. I still haven't worked everything out. I may need you."

"I'm with you. I've always had your back, sir."

"Good to know. Thanks." He shook his hand and gave him a bro hug.

The ride to the Upper West Side was quiet. Both he and Raquelle were lost in thought but she snuggled close to him.

They arrived at the apartment as a gorgeous blonde opened the door with Titus at her feet, wagging his tail. He pushed past her jumping on Raquelle.

"Hello, brother. It's nice to meet you. I wish the circumstances were different," Leigha said.

"I had no idea you were my half sister."

She reached out her hand to him and he brought her in for a hug. "It seems we have a lot more in common than a father. I admire your photography," she said with a warm smile.

He held her back from him. "You and I both have his eyes. You have his coloring. I have my mom's but we share blood. My brothers will be excited to meet you."

Raquelle barreled in. "Could you two stop it, please? I'm not used to this yet. It's weird." She leaned down to give Titus hugs and kisses.

"Oh, grow up, sis."

Raquelle replied with something as Mac entered the room with Dean and Sean. "I see Raquelle has made an entrance," Mac said as he shook hands with Misha.

"Sean, it's good to see you outside of the club." Misha greeted his old friend.

All eyes turned toward Sean. Sean smiled and raised a brow.

"We'll be discussing that later. You can count on it," Dean said with a smirk.

"Why don't you have a seat? We have a lot to discuss." Mac waved his arm in the direction of the dining room.

The men sat around the table as the women made themselves scarce in the kitchen.

Mac started the update. "Let me bring you up to speed. Alek left a chip with highly encrypted information on the back of one of Leigha's photographs. When he needed it back, he had no choice but to reveal himself to Leigha. What he didn't know is that we changed it out for an undetectable tracking device. We'd been tracking him in Russia until we lost the signal about a week ago."

"That's about the time I stopped hearing from him, which may not seem unusual except for the fact that he contacts me every day," Misha added.

Sean spoke up, "This is difficult to tell you, but we don't know if he's still alive."

Misha sat back in his chair. "Oh, he's still alive. I got a text from an unknown number. It was from him, giving me directions, as usual."

"Well, that's good." Dean blew out a breath.

"I don't know. Is it?" Misha snapped. Everyone stopped talking, giving him a moment. "I'm sorry. This is all news to me and I'm still reeling from it. There are a lot of emotions involved when lies this big are revealed. The man in that dossier is not the man I grew up with. I suddenly don't know who he is anymore."

"Take it from someone who knows about fathers. It's a crapshoot. Mine hung me out to dry. I can't even go back to my beloved Australia. In the end, you better do what's best for you and what you can live with." Dean's eyes darkened.

"That's my plan," Misha replied.

Raquelle came in. "I made you a cappuccino, your favorite."

"Look at you being all Ms. Domesticated." Dean smiled.

"Shut it, BP." She turned around and walked out.

Mac smacked him on the shoulder as Dean laughed. "That was a good one."

Dean replied, "I thought so."

Misha gave them a hard look and had to ask. "BP?"

"Bulletproof. One of your father's goons shot me in Leigha's studio and hit my shoulder," Dean said casually.

Misha's face heated. Dean might be able to shrug it off but he had never been exposed to this side of life. And to top it off, Leigha could have been hurt had it not been for Dean. He slammed his fists on the table. "Goddamn him! What do you need me to do?"

The guys gave him a minute and then Sean took over. "We need you to bring him in. You need to get him to talk to us about what's going on and how infiltrated the Russians are in our country, including the financial arena. He'll be safe here. We'll give him top-level security. I don't know about immunity. That's for the Attorney General to figure out."

Misha nodded.

"I know this is hard to deal with and a time crunch doesn't help any. But without him, we're still left in the dark about a lot of open cases. The FBI wanted to grill you. They think you're in on it. But I talked to one of my guys on the investigation team. So far they haven't found anything linking you to what was going on at CZR. We need to do this before the agencies get involved in making arrests. Your father will be able to smell them from a mile away. Besides, I think the FBI has a mole," Sean said without missing a beat.

"His text said he's sending a car for me tomorrow morning. I'm to get in and not ask questions." Misha sealed his fate even as he clawed to get out of his newfound hell. He decided to fight for himself and what he had with Raquelle. His father could be safe but away from him. He could start again, maybe open his own gallery.

Mr. Dark and Dangerous had one last play. He would have the final word, not his father.

"So we'll tail you until we have eyes on him and then make our move," Dean said without hesitation.

"It's too easy. He knows the shit has hit the fan. But we don't have many options at this point." Mac rubbed the scar above his eye.

"We won't put you in any danger. We just need you to lead us to him." Sean rubbed his hands together. "And we need you to break up with Raquelle." His eyes swung to Mac and Dean.

Misha startled. "Why?"

"We think he knows MBK is onto him. Right now the feds don't know where he is but we have you as a link to him. He's going to want to leave the country before the feds get their evidence and find him. When we hacked into your home computer, we found the camera on your office computer was live to someone else's feed, sound included. We disabled it, making it look like a power outage. Someone has been tracking your every move from your home office. We assume it's him. We need you to go home, go to your office, and break up with her on the phone so he hears it. We'll enable the live camera again. You need to make it look like you're severing all ties, make him believe you have an allegiance to him, build his trust." Sean went into great detail about what needed to be said to her. It needed to be believable for the op to work. Raquelle had to be convinced that Misha was leaving her, giving his loyalty to his father.

By the time the meeting ended, he was emotionally spent, on a yo-yo, vacillating between truth and lies. He walked toward the front door as Raquelle approached him.

"Do you want to go back to your place?" She threw her arms around his neck.

He removed her arms. "No. I need to be by myself. I'll call you later." He looked over her shoulder at the MBK team with bitterness, turned and walked out the door.

He knew the next twenty-four hours would be the hardest of his life.

Chapter Thirty-Three

MISHA HAD FINALLY FOUND her and now he had to let her go temporarily, in order to trap one man while keeping her safe. The last thing he wanted was for his father to come after her. How sick could the world be? He would have to make it convincing, otherwise his father would be onto him. What turned his stomach more than anything else was crushing Raquelle's heart. Unknowingly, his father would have one more hand to play in this cruel twist. He was sickened by the idea that his father had felt the need to keep tabs on him twenty-four seven. He hoped his father had enjoyed the show because it would be his last. Misha would contact his mother again, demanding she tell him what she knew about his life's destiny designed by the great Alek. But he would have to wait until after he called Raquelle.

A small desk lamp illuminated his office. He pulled the chain rope to turn it off. The only light in his life was about to be snuffed out and he hated his father for it. His finger hovered over the call button on his cell phone. His father probably had that bugged as well.

"Hey, sex god." Her voice was soft and seductive. All

second thoughts were gone about what he was going to say. He had to push through the gut-wrenching conversation. The tables had turned as he became the manipulator. He realized the hell she must have lived while she betrayed him.

"Hey." Scenarios ran through his head on how they could escape together and leave everything behind. But in the end his father would find him. Besides, Raquelle could never be away from her family forever.

"You okay?"

He cleared his throat. "Yeah. I talked to the team today. I've decided I can't go through with it. I can't turn my father in. He'll run for as long as he can. I'm taking my mother and going back to Russia. It's my only play at this point. I'm afraid this is the end of the road for us. I'm sorry for everything." He waited. Silenced threaded its way through the phone.

"You can't be serious. We've just found each other. There's got to be another way. What if you go and help your mother get settled in Russia and came back? Your whole life has been about your parents. When's it going to be about you? About us? I love you. This is real for me." Desperation leaked from her voice.

He had waited for those three words from her. Looking at the camera on his computer, he tried to cover his pain. "Please don't make this harder than it already is. I need to be with my father. I can't be with you. Even if I were staying, I'd keep coming back to the fact that you betrayed me." Those were the words he didn't want to say, but it was the only way to get her to react for his audience.

The gasp was audible through the phone. "How can you say that? I explained to you exactly why I did what I did." Her voice cracked.

He cut her off. "Stop. Just stop. I can't make that feeling

go away. You cut me down to my heart with your lies and betrayal. Did you really think I could just forgive you? You can't be that naïve. And now I have to deal with my father. I've got a lot on my plate. You're not the woman I want to be with, ever."

She sniffled. "Fine. I won't fight with you. I wish I could say that I'll be here when you change your mind but I doubt it. Good luck. I'll miss you."

The line went dead and he stared at the photo of her and the baby elephant on his phone. He had used the words he knew would gut her and get the reaction he needed. He bent his head down, shielding his forehead with his hand. A tear fell onto the desk. His anger built with every one that fell, solidifying his decision to move forward. When everything was said and done, he wasn't sure she would be there but he would fight to get her back. Neither one of them was replaceable. Their bond wouldn't be broken.

He made his next phone call from the living room. "Hi, I need you to see you if it's not too late. I'll send Jonas for you," he said in a strained voice.

"Of course. Are you okay?" She had no chirp in her voice.

"I will be. I'll see you soon." He needed to regroup before he saw her.

His mother entered the coffee shop, in full makeup, dressed to the nines. "Why are we meeting here and not at your house?" Her eyes darted around.

"Please have a seat. We have a lot to talk about." Misha pulled out a chair for her. He had picked a table in a far corner.

"How much do you know about what Father does for a living?" His voice was cold.

Her eyes watered. "You know."

"Know what? Why don't you tell me?" He had never used a stern voice with her. But his tank was empty in the sympathy department when it came to his parents.

"He works for the Russian mob. That's all I know." Her face crumbled.

"Why are our last names Raines and he's Romanowski?"

Her shoulders slumped. "Before we came to the states, he got us identification with the last name Raines, dropping Romanowski. He wanted to name you Mikhail but it ended up being Michael. Misha was a coincidence. He did all of this to give us a clean start. He didn't want you or your brothers to be part of that world. But he'll explain everything when he sees you."

"You've talked to him?" He fought to remain calm.

"Yes. He said he was going to see you soon." She frowned.

He could tell by the look on her face, she didn't have the whole story. "Huh. You're right. I am seeing him tomorrow."

He pressed. "Why didn't you ever tell me and my brothers? Don't you think we had a right to know?"

Her tears flowed freely. "I . . . we wanted to protect you. The less you knew, the better."

He leaned forward into her space. "He used me as a pawn to run an illegal operation through CZR Investments. I could go to jail. How's that for protection?"

She placed her hands over his. "Please don't be too hard on him. He's doing the best he can. It's not the life he wanted. But being a low man in the mob isn't very rosy." She forced a smile.

She had no idea who her husband really was in his world. He was the king on the chessboard and he was about to get checkmated.

"Low man? Mother, he's the boss, top of the heap. He

runs the mob. He's killed many people and had people kill for him. The FBI has a file on him five inches thick. What rock have you been living under?" His father had duped everyone in his life.

Tears formed in her eyes. "You're a liar. That's not your father. He said you would do this, that you would turn on him. You've been going against his orders. I don't need to sit here and listen to this."

He needed to rescue this before it all went south. "I'm not going against him. I just want to understand. He is my father."

She gave him a weak smile, grabbed her bag, and headed for the door.

His father had fooled everyone and set him up in the process. His mother's reaction only added fuel to his need for revenge. His brothers had also been left in the dark. When he'd spoken with them earlier, they had no idea what was going on. They insisted on flying home from the West Coast to be with him until everything had been worked out. Both were well educated and had made their own marks in finances. He'd work for one of them when this blew over.

He made his way back to his empty home, undressed, and lay naked between the cold silk sheets. As exhausted as he was, sleep would not come to him. The motor in his mind went a mile a minute. He had so many questions, most of which would be answered tomorrow by a man he used to know as his father.

The sun shone through slats of the blinds, lighting part of the room. The doorbell rang three times before he could get to it. He had sent his staff home the day before and told them to take the day off. When he opened the front door, a box lay at his feet. He picked it up and opened it. There was a note and a phone.

I'll be calling you on this phone to let you know the details for our meeting. Be ready in fifteen minutes. I'll see you soon.

He dressed in his tailor-made black suit, white dress shirt, and a hand-painted tie with the American flag on it.

A man he had never seen before picked him up in a town car with the windows blacked out.

He tried to speak Russian with the driver but got no response. Oddly, he didn't feel nervous. The end was in sight and he would have the last move. There was no escape for him or his father. His need for answers outweighed everything else. Once he got what he wanted, he could be with Raquelle. The car was headed for JFK airport.

His father was a mastermind. He wouldn't make it easy, so Misha was anticipating the unexpected. As they made their approach to the terminal, a black town car turned in front of them, two more drove on each side of them, and another one was behind them, creating a caravan of town cars. Keeping his expression in check, he made eye contact with the driver in the rearview mirror. The man seemed unfazed by the fact they were surrounded. The cars rolled up in line at Arrivals and a group of men came out, headed for the cars. Each of them wore a hat, a trench coat, and carried a briefcase. Sunglasses covered their eyes and they all had blond hair. Clever move.

He laughed aloud as a man let himself into Misha's car. The driver looked at him through the rearview mirror and frowned.

"Oh, hello. And who are you?" Misha smiled at the stranger.

The man pulled a gun out of his pocket. "I'm your worst nightmare if you don't do exactly as I say," he instructed in

Russian. He looked at the driver and in a thick accent said, "Drive with the other cars. Stay with them."

"So you are the great and mighty Misha who fucked everything up." The gunman changed back to Russian and smiled with stained teeth, lighting a cigarette. "You're going to fold your seat down and crawl into the trunk and be very quiet."

Misha didn't move. "Do you work for Alek Romanowski?" he said with more confidence than he was feeling.

"Yes. But apparently you don't." The gunman motioned to him with his gun. "Get moving. We don't have time."

Misha folded down the seat and squeezed into the trunk space as the back seat slammed shut. He wasn't sure how this would all turn out. His thoughts went back to Raquelle. The last thing she would remember about him was his harsh words to her when fate had him by the balls. He'd be lucky not to kill his father when he saw him. The heat in the trunk rose and he began to sweat.

The car traveled for another couple of minutes, making many twists and turns along the way before coming to a stop. Misha's breath was shallow, his head was dizzy, and his nerves were fried but he wouldn't show fear when he was let out.

The trunk popped open and the gunman hauled him out by his arm. "You okay in there? I wouldn't want you to die on me." He laughed. If it was meant to intimidate him, it was working.

Misha stood up and noticed his father walking toward him. Behind him stood a row of goons in black suits. "Son, how are you?" He hugged him as if nothing had changed.

Misha answered him in English. "I could have done

without the gangster routine. Oh, wait. I forgot. You couldn't help yourself." He looked his father in the eye.

"Why don't you speak to me in Russian?"

Misha shoved his hands in his pockets. "Because I'm a born-and-bred American. I don't plan on speaking Russian ever again."

His father glanced at his tie. "I see you've been talking to the group at MBK. Don't believe everything you hear." His father turned away from him and spoke to the men in black suits, who were waiting for orders.

"I'm sorry. I couldn't hear you, Father," he snipped.

"I said I want them to scan you for a wire. One can never be too careful." This was a side of his father he had never seen—or maybe didn't want to see.

"Oh, please allow me." He ripped open his buttoned shirt and held it. "Remember this scar? It hurt like a son-of-a-bitch. I almost lost my life. But it's nothing compared to the lies you've spun for years at my expense."

The men in black shifted where they stood and his father grimaced. "What I did, I did for you," he said loudly. He nodded his head to one of the men standing in line.

The man carried a bulky wand and scanned him from head to toe then shook his head.

"Why don't you tell me what you did for me? Because right now, I'm jobless, without a company, and being investigated by the FBI and FTC." He kept his voice even.

His father waved his hand in the air. "They won't find anything. You are attached to nothing. I made sure of that."

"So I was the front man for your dirty operation without even knowing it, a pawn in your game. How fucking convenient for you. You're right. I have cut all my ties and am attached to nothing."

"Ah, yes. The beautiful and tenacious Raquelle. But you

never said goodbye." Alek smirked.

"And how would you know that?"

His father smiled. "I have to keep tabs on my favorite son."

"So you bugged my house. Kinda creepy if you ask me. Marco was a nice touch too. You know what really turned by stomach? The fact that you had Antonio killed. But what else should I expect from a mob boss?" He needed to stay calm. He shoved his hands into his pockets as his fingers formed fists.

Alek straightened his tie and gave orders to the suits to leave them and board the plane. "Don't talk about things you know nothing about. Antonio made a deal. He knew what he was getting into. Yes, I was born into this hell and now I might pay for it with my life. But I brought you here under a different name to give you a better life. I didn't want you and your brothers to know what Russia was capable of doing to your soul. You should be grateful." He beat his fist to his chest. "This was not my choice, it was my destiny handed down by my father."

Misha could feel his heartbeat slow down as he processed his father's words. His father would try to convince him he was the good guy. But pictures didn't lie.

As if his father could read his mind, "They showed you my dossier full of pictures. Can you believe everything you see, Misha?"

He called it *his* as if he had proudly created it. His father's life became more twisted by the minute. "You left behind a trail of bodies all over the world. I can't unsee it." He shot back. "How about you tell me the truth?"

His father shrugged. "The truth comes in many colors. Which one would you like to see today? Do you know the reasons why?"

"No. But can there really be a plausible reason?"

They were in a battle of perceptions.

His father got closer and put his hand on his shoulder. "I was forced to do a lot of things I didn't want to do, some for good, some bad. I won't apologize. I want you to leave with me. We can start fresh. I have everything we need to disappear forever. Like you said, you have no ties here anymore. The plane is waiting. You will never have to work again. Come with me and your mother."

"She's on the plane?" He tried not to register his shock.

"Of course. I wouldn't leave her behind." His father smiled slyly.

It was a low blow. Misha stared at him. "Why not? You abandoned her years ago."

Alek's face came closer. "Be careful how you judge me, son. I did what was best for everyone. Your mother knew what needed to be done."

Misha shrugged off his father's hand. As mad as he was at his mother and as desperately as he needed to break from her chains, he couldn't put her in the hands of a monster. "Actually, she had no idea. But I won't leave her behind like you did, so lead the way. You seem to be a natural at that."

Alek stared at him for a moment then led them out to the waiting top of the line luxury Learjet on the tarmac. He stepped onboard and his mother ran into his arms.

"*Malen'kiy*, there you are. What took you so long?" Worry covered his mother's face.

He hugged her tight and whispered, "Forgive me."

She released him and sat down with a stunned expression on her face. He sat beside her and rested his head in his hands.

She leaned in close. "There's nothing to forgive. I know

this is a lot to deal with but we'll be fine. Look at the beautiful plane they sent for us." She patted him on his arm.

Ignorance was bliss. She had been kept in the dark so long she couldn't even see the monster in front of her face.

The door shut, leaving him in the hornet's nest. Everyone was silent as all his father's men stared at him with questions and hatred in their eyes. Misha snapped his lap belt in place and waited for what he knew was coming.

The engines shut down.

"What's going on? We should be taking off." His father started to leave his seat just as the door opened and FBI agents stormed the plane.

"FBI. Hands where we can see them. Take a seat, pops." A burly guy with a gun entered, followed by his team.

Everyone raised their hands except Misha. He had no guilt for the first time in his life. He felt empowered, this time without the false sense of control he got from the ropes. His eyes locked onto his father's as his father stood and clapped his hands.

"Bravo, I didn't see that coming. I didn't think you had it in you. Well played. Looks like you did learn something over the years. You've just signed my death sentence and broken your mother's heart," he said in Russian.

Misha stood and buttoned his jacket. "Don't play the guilt card. It won't work. It's always all about you. You can spin it any way you want to but you hung me out to dry and used me my entire life. You showed us what you wanted us to see. But you're delusional. You can't survive in an honest world." He stepped closer. "You're right. I never did say goodbye. Goodbye, Father."

He escorted his mother off the plane as she whimpered and kept asking *why* over and over. He knew why. His father was a sick greedy bastard.

Chapter Thirty-Four

RAQUELLE PACED in Mara's apartment waiting for confirmation that everything had gone according to plan. Misha had done a one-eighty after he left the meeting. His words had destroyed her. She couldn't imagine her life without him, but instead of telling him that, she'd given him a stiff-upper-lip response with an *I love you* thrown in. *Old habits die hard.*

When she'd showed up at Mara's apartment, Mac and Dean filled her in on the plan they'd made with Misha. The heaving in her chest stopped as the pendulum of emotions swung to the other end. Titus watched her intently from the couch with his head propped on his front paws.

"Would you stop moving? You're making me seasick," Mara groaned with her head in her hands.

"Why are you so sick all the time? Did you go to the doctor?" Raquelle shook out her hands.

"Yes. We'll talk later."

She couldn't have been too sick. Her skin looked great, her cheeks were rosy, but the bags under her eyes made her look exhausted.

The waiting game was going to kill her. Then when she thought she couldn't wait another minute, the guys came barreling through the door.

She ran toward them. "Is he with you? What happened?"

"We arrested Alek but Misha's not in a good way, Raq. It takes a strong man to put his father away. He's wants you to meet over at his place later after we've swept it for bugs," Mac said briskly.

He called from the living room, "Leannan, where are you?" He found her in the kitchen making some tea and cradled her in his arms from behind rubbing her belly. For someone who had just closed the biggest case of his career, he was more concerned with Mara than anything else. It hit her. Mara's sickness all made sense.

She left Mara's apartment to seek refuge in her studio for a couple of hours, but she was too antsy and couldn't focus. Titus fell asleep at her feet, too exhausted to keep up with her. Her thoughts swirled around Misha and what he must be going through. The other outlying factor was how much his mother knew about her husband. It would change his relationship with his mother forever. Losing one parent was bad enough but losing two was unthinkable.

She gave up trying to divert her mind from anything but Misha and took an Uber across town to his brownstone. Her nerves jittered and her hands shook standing outside his place. Titus whined on the end of the leash and scratched at the door.

The door opened and a tall blond man stood on the other side, smiling at her. He looked more like Leigha than Misha.

"Hi, you must be Raquelle." He opened the door wider to let her in as Titus rushed by him. "It's nice to meet you. I'm Adrik, the attention-seeking middle child." He closed the door behind them. She put out her hand as he bent down to kiss her on both cheeks.

Hairs on the back of her neck stood on end.

"*Little one*, you came." His voice wrapped around her like a comfortable blanket.

He stood in wrinkled clothes, hands in his pockets, and grief on his face. Titus looked up at him for attention. She moved toward him and clung to his waist, burying her face in his chest. Strength had taken its leave at the door, replaced by tears of fear, joy, and regret. She sobbed as she felt his arms wrap around her and he kissed the top of her head. He took her by the hand and led her to his bedroom where they could be alone.

He sat in one of the chairs with no arms and put her in his lap, wrapping her legs around him. Pushing the hair out of her face, he said, "Why are you crying? I should be the one who's crying. I thought you wouldn't want anything to do with me after I said I didn't want to see and didn't trust you."

She sniffled. "Your words aren't what destroyed me, but with the thought that I might never see you again." She held his face in her hands. "I'm so sorry for all of this. I can't imagine what you're going through."

"He said he did it for me and my brothers, changing our names and moving to the States. But it doesn't take away the fact that he used me for his gain and now I have to start over. What put me over the edge was the fact that he put Leigha in danger. If it weren't for Dean, where would we all be? My father killed a lot of people over the years, including your father." Pain flashed in his eyes. "I wish I could bring him back for you."

She nodded. "Me too. But my papa knew who he was in bed with. It looks like a lot of people wore many masks for many reasons. But we have to move forward and put this behind us. Besides, it looks like I'm going to be an aunt. Mara's pregnant and Mac can't stop smiling about it. He's going to be unbearable in the over protection department and probably hover over her."

He smiled. "Would you like to be a mother someday so I can hover over you?" His fingers caressed her face.

"Yes, the operative word is someday. Don't you hover enough?"

"The hovering has just begun." His eyes widened with his smile.

"Do your brothers want to meet Leigha?" she asked.

"They can't wait. We've always wanted to know our sister. But everything in due time. As soon as we can, I want to take you away for a weekend without interruption. I have some more rope tricks I want to show you." His eyes sparkled.

"I'm sure you do. By the way, what happened to the art collection at the firm? Did the FBI get hold of it?"

He smiled. "It's safe and sound waiting for me to open my gallery with it. I'm still waiting for the owners to step forward to claim them. My number-one client is going to be this talented Italian goddess whose work I can't wait to share with the world."

She held him by the chin. "As long as you're not sharing anything else, we're good."

"No, I'm all yours. You've shown me the art of Eros, a lesson I'll never forget."

She laughed. "So glad you see things my way."

"Thank you," he said.

"For what?"

"For filling my bedroom with lavender. My freedom came at a very high price." His eyes darkened.

"Don't let anyone ever take your freedom. But you can take mine anytime with your rope."

He tickled her as she squirmed out of his grasp. She had finally been accepted with everything she had and all the imagined things she didn't have from a man who'd lost it all. They were quite a twosome, but a pair of hearts always trumped anyone swinging a club.

Epilogue

8 months later

"MY GOD, YOU'RE BIG." Raquelle referred to Mara's baby bump. "How's my little elephant doing in there?"

"Thank you so much for your support. This isn't easy, you know. And it's not an elephant. Although given the Highlander's size, I'm not so sure," Mara shot back.

"I know. That's why you're doing it before everyone else." Raquelle threw her arm around Mara's shoulders. "You look stunning in that dress."

They were headed out to Misha's gallery opening. The show included all of the pieces from his father's collection and Raquelle's work, along with other up-and-coming artists.

The limo dropped them off for the red-carpet event complete with flashing cameras. Misha had made sure it was a full-court press. While he had been cleared of any wrongdoing at CZR Investments, his father would be indicted on many counts. Misha needed a distraction from the circus surrounding his father's capture and imminent conviction.

Alek would need to turn state's evidence against his Russian cronies operating in the US. In return, the government would put him in the witness protection program and he would never be heard from again. In classic Alek style, he would make the feds wait until he was sure he had the deal he wanted on his terms.

Misha greeted everyone as they came through the door. His usual calm demeanor was replaced by excitement with a hint of nerves.

"*Little one.*" He held her to him and kissed her forehead. "You look beautiful as always."

She looked up at him. "And how are you holding up?"

"Okay, nervous, but praying for success. How are you doing? This is your big debut."

Contentment washed over her. "It doesn't seem as important anymore. I love to paint, but the success is taking a backseat now that I have you."

"My thoughts exactly." He held her hand and led her into the gallery.

She hadn't seen the final setup and was stunned by the arrangement. Toward the back of the gallery was an exhibition of Misha's and Leigha's photographs. The arrangement was the contrast between his rope montage and her fashion shots.

"I had no idea you were doing this. It looks fantastic." She beamed.

"I wanted to surprise you."

He had his entire masters collection set up along with her works as well as other contemporary pieces. The masters collection wasn't for sale but everything else was fair game.

"Misha," his mother said from behind them. "I want you to meet Tony."

His mother had divorced his father. She was disappointed that Misha refused to speak Russian but understood his need to cut himself off. Misha was lucky to hear from her once a week since she was out dating again. She seemed truly happy for the first time in his life.

"Nice to meet you. I hope you both enjoy the show."

"What a difference a good man can make in a woman's life," Raquelle whispered in his ear.

The event was by invitation only and MBK Global Security had been hired to keep it safe. Mac and the rest of the crew were dressed in tuxes and keeping a watch on everyone coming and going. An uneventful night would be a perfect night.

―――――――

SEAN WAS WELL aware of the image everyone had of him as a player. Appearances were deceiving and put in place for a reason. He didn't want to let anyone in after his divorce. His friends with naughty benefits plan worked just fine.

He led the evening's security team. Four of them were on duty and Peter, his IT guy extraordinaire, made a thorough check of the entire system before the show got underway. Peter moved around in a wheelchair but he knew how to work the room and the ladies. Sean had never seen anything like it. Women clamored to him in droves and the dude hooked up on a regular basis. More power to him.

He and Beck, his other partner, had the back half of the gallery while Mac and Dean managed the front end. They stayed in touch through two-way ear com devices designed to be inconspicuous. Sean wandered around the gallery without taking notice of the artwork. Besides, he had no idea what he was looking at anyway. The art world was a mystery to him and why it all cost so fucking much was an even bigger mystery. No one would catch him spending that kind of money on art.

"Everyone in position. Report out," Sean said. He stood in front of a painting of a man holding his face while screaming, kind of the way he felt tonight. Each member called in using his or her code name.

"Seven clear," Mac replied.

"Desert clear," Beck replied.

"BP clear," Dean said dead serious.

"Since when are you BP?" Sean asked.

"Since I changed it," Dean replied.

"Iceman is off duty tonight but has eyes on his tablet monitoring–" Sean didn't finish his sentence.

Mac, second in command, responded. "Wild? You still with us?"

Sean, code name Wild, stood awestruck in front of a painting of a beautiful woman.

"Wild?" Mac's voice began to register heightened alert.

Sean responded, "I'm here. Clear. Stay in position."

"What's going on? You got eyes on something?" Dean asked.

"Nothing. It's fine."

He'd know her face anywhere. The way her violet eyes always had laughter in them and a smile you could see from here to Mars. In the painting, she was looking over her shoulder and laughing at the painter. She ran through a field of wildflowers as her hair floated around her head. He couldn't turn away, struck by the sight before him.

"She's beautiful, isn't she?" Raquelle asked from behind him.

"Excuse me?" He turned around to face her.

"Jess. She could have been a model with that beautiful cocoa skin, curly long hair, and those unique violet eyes."

He looked at her dumbfounded. "How do you know her?"

"We went to college together and decided to go on vacation. She won the toss. I wanted to go to the beach but she loves the mountains. Mountains won. I took a photo of her and it called to me. I had to paint her." Raquelle smiled warmly at her fond memories.

When she looked at him, she registered the look on his face. "Do you know her?"

"Yes." He stood next to Raquelle admiring the portrait. "We grew up together. But lost track of each other over the years." The pang in his chest reminded him of what had transpired between them.

"Small world, eh?"

Before he had a chance to reply, his phone rang. "Neil, what's up?"

Neil McFadden was Mac's MI6 contact. They had done jobs for him since Mac came on board.

"I've got an extraction for you and only you," he said.

Sean was confused. "Why me?"

Neil's voice took a serious tone. "You know Afghanistan like the back of your hand. You'll be going in dark."

He had hoped never to see Afghanistan for as long as he lived. "You're going to have to get someone else. I'm done with that godforsaken hellhole."

There was silence for a moment on the other end, then Neil said, "You might want to reconsider. The person you need to get out is from your past and that's all I'm allowed to divulge at this point." Neil was firm in his response.

Sean yelled at the onlookers of the portrait, "That

painting's sold." He turned his attention back to Neil. "I got to go. I'll call you back tomorrow and we'll talk more."

He hung up and stood in front of the painting, searching for Misha.

"Seven, you got eyes on King?" They had given Misha a code name for the night.

"Yeah, what's up?" Mac said.

"Back off, it's sold." Sean said to a couple trying to see around him.

"What?" Mac asked.

"Send King my way, ASAP."

Misha came over within seconds. "What's the problem?" His face showed worry.

"I need to buy this painting."

Misha looked at him as if he was crazy. "I'm sure Raquelle will give it to you."

"No. I want to buy it," Sean said with determination.

Misha smiled. "Did you see the price tag?"

"And?" Sean stared at him.

"Got it. I'll get Gustav to write up a ticket." Misha turned to leave as Sean grabbed his arm.

"Do you have a pen and paper?" Sean requested.

"Yeah, why?" Misha handed over the pen and paper.

Sean wrote the word SOLD and tucked it in the corner of the portrait. "Because she's coming home with me tonight."

WHAT DOES the woman in the portrait have to do with Sean's past?

WILD

Chapter 1
Sean

I've spent a lifetime running from my past and never looked back. Tonight, I'm dragging it home with me. It has caught up with me this time, but I'm not sure I want to shake it loose. A past riddled with chaos and uncertainty, there's only one thing I want from it, some peace of mind.

The deadbolt unlocks and I punch the code into the keypad to my empty bachelor den. The door snicks shut and locks behind me as I place my package on the floor. My enormous television sits like a black hole above the mantel, but that is the only place for something this special. It's worth showcasing. I rarely buy artwork, but it has a piece of heart I had to cut loose years ago.

I rip the brown paper away from the canvas and set it on the mantel, covering the flat-screen television. The minute I saw her face in this portrait, she spoke to me from far away, and I had to have it. She was the one bright light in a grim past that still haunts me. I was determined not to let the events of my past drag me down, but oddly, it has dictated all my decisions.

The darkness of the living room surrounds me except for the spotlight to accent the painting. I plop down on the couch across from it. The stillness of my penthouse makes me realize that being alone had become far too familiar to me, almost comfortable. The lack of light and quiet of the night close in around me. It's too dark and too quiet. I have trouble sitting still. I hope the woman in the portrait sheds some light on my one-dimensional life because the last time I saw her; she was a girl. I wonder where she is now, who she's with, and what she's doing with her life. Losing her spark of light was one of my biggest mistakes.

The woman in the portrait looks over her shoulder at the painter and laughs without a care in the world. But I know differently. Her smile hides the pain underneath that isn't for anyone else to see. The pain of not being accepted by certain people for many reasons. None of those reasons hold merit. I saw her from the inside out. She saw me from the outside, not knowing the turbulence that lay beneath.

My phone rings, and I swipe right to send it to voicemail without looking at it. It's probably another one of my hookups. At the rate I'm going, I'll die as the forever bachelor. Nothing wrong with that, I suppose. I toss the phone, letting it bounce on the blue suede couch. Who the hell buys a blue suede couch?

I purchased it three years ago, and it looks brand new. A reminder I'm never home. Running from one job to the next, I fill the bit of free time with women I can call at the drop of a hat. After leaving the Navy, I spent years building my security company, MBK Global Security, with Beck McKenzie and Peter Bryan. I work hard. I have loyal friends and live in the greatest city on Earth, The Big Apple. But something pulls at me. What started out as an itch is turning into a full onset of hives I can't ignore. There's a void. The more I ignore the hole, the bigger it gets. Restlessness takes over. I drag my hand over my face, staring at the portrait.

When I get a closer look at the portrait of Jess, I question what happened along the way. The paint colors are vibrant and her violet eyes express light and goodness. It's a window to a past I had to run from to save her. A vivacious woman replaced the girl I remember. Hair flows around her like a cape, teasing the viewer to come and play. The innocence she radiates left my life years ago. War will do that to a man, hardening me until there's no room for light and goodness.

My phone vibrates on the couch with a muffled special ringtone I recognize as my secure line.

I sigh heavily, pick it up, and speak crisply. "Knight here."

"Sean, it's Neil McFadden." Neil, one of the big guns at Scotland Yard, heading up the MI6 division, but don't call him M.

This must be important. Neil doesn't call to see how I'm doing, and this is his second phone call of the evening. "I told you I'd call you tomorrow morning."

"You need to take that trip to Afghanistan." It's a command, not a question.

"What trip to Afghanistan?" I try for ignorance with lightness in my voice.

Irritation edges Neil's voice. "You know what trip. I understand an old friend of yours called you for a security detail. I need you to accept the assignment and leave tomorrow."

Of course, he knows. He's a spy.

"I declined the offer for a reason. Not setting foot in Afghanistan is a lifelong goal." I walk over to the window overlooking the Westside Highway. Everything on the street below is small and far away. Eight million people in this city, but loneliness is a horrible companion. It's a comfortable existence, but I've never been happy with comfortable. I always push myself to the limit.

"You're the only man for the job." Silence hangs in the air.

"You said earlier it was someone from my past. Who is it?" The only people I keep in contact with from my past are from my SEAL team and they all know how to take care of themselves.

He's running out of patience with my stall tactics. "That's on a need-to-know basis."

"Then it's not gonna happen." The edges of the phone bite into my curled fingers.

The rustle of papers comes across the phone line. "I have a hacker and potentially one other who need to be rescued, and you know Afghanistan like the back of your hand." I notice he doesn't use the word "extracted". He's done his research. The warrior in me screams louder than rational thought.

I cave. Neil knows how to play me, pulling the one card that would get me. I've always been the rescue guy. Rescuing is in my DNA thanks to growing up in a crappy home life. It's where I got my code name, Wild. I would come up with crazy plans for a rescue, but I was always under control. My temper, that's a different story.

My first rescue happened at age five. I have zero tolerance for bullies, especially when it involves girls. I had seen too much of that at home. Before I knew what was happening, my fist reared back and connected with his nose. He was never a bully around me again. That's when I had a taste of power, the power to save someone. The silk thread of fate spun around me tighter and tighter. There were so many things wrong in the house I grew up in, it was healing to feel empowered. That kind of power became my drug of choice. Each rescue took me farther away from an abusive family life where I had no control.

"Funny how you called just as I got that assignment. Coincidence? I don't think so." I know how things work with spooks. They have their fingers in everybody's business.

"Didn't you get the memo? There are no coincidences in life. After your years of training, you know that. His private jet is waiting for you. Safe travels." He hangs up.

Joining the Navy and becoming a SEAL to save people who needed saving seemed like the best fit for me, but it turned out to be a double-edged sword. Afghanistan is a place where young soldiers learn hard lessons about a life called war. It's not for the faint of heart. The weak become strong and the strong, well, the strong survive and bury fear deep. There are no words for the things I've seen and heard. The title Hell on Earth doesn't describe what really happens in the story. The only things to hold onto are sleepless nights and the shakes. No one came to save me. No one ever does. In the end, I learned it doesn't matter your skin color or beliefs, we all strive to survive and live a decent life. Living a decent life evaded the Afghan people years ago.

Fate has dictated the time to face my demons. The angel smiles at me from the painted canvas. I'll be leaving her behind again. Maybe someday I'll have the courage to find her.

Get WILD to find out what happens next.

FREE Book

I love staying in touch with my readers.
Sign up for my newsletter and receive **Silent Night**
for **FREE**
at
www.bit.ly/NLSecret

Silent Night

She must save her brother. He only sees her betrayal. Will they find love or fall prey in a deadly rescue plan?

New York City. Chloe's dream of becoming a journalist is cut short when she's unable to secure a job. So in order to make ends meet, she takes a job at J. Luc Gallery for the holidays. Her new boss is easy on the eyes and very attentive. But when her brother gets kidnapped, she must do the unthinkable.

Jean Luc has earned his galleries the hard way. As an established gallery owner, he is trusted with a unique exhibition of expensive ornaments. So when he hires Chloe's brother to install the security system, he doesn't expect to be thrown into the dangerous side of the art world.

Chloe makes a difficult choice, forcing her to betray her lover as MBK races to rescue her brother. But the plan may come together too late, leaving Jean Luc in the cold.

Can love rise above betrayal so they can find their happily ever after?

Silent Night is a novella that introduces the entire MBK Global Security team. If you like page-turning action, steamy scenes, and heart-breaking betrayals, then you'll love Kenzie Macallan's holiday story.

Please consider leaving a review

Thank you for taking the time to read Masks
Please consider leaving a review.

Reviews are so precious to writers. Writing a review helps other readers find my books and is helpful when deciding what to read next.

If you have a minute, please leave a review. Thank you in advance for taking the time to help others find Masks.

Also by Kenzie Macallan

MBK Global Security

Truths

Mara tries to shake her haunted past. Mac has a secret that could destroy what they have. Can he protect the love of his life from a ruthless killer?

Secrets- a novella

Mara wants him to leave. Mac's investigating his brother. When the Russians close in, will they make it or head for heartbreak?

Edges

Leigha's under threat. Dean's undercover. Will deadly family secrets ruin the romance of a lifetime?

Deep 8

Wild

Jess leaped into a war zone to get the story. Sean will endure hell to bring her home. Sparks fly, but will romance die on the wrong side of a bullet?

King

Jess is a hacker turned agent. Beck will become king of a diamond empire. Can two unlikely lovers survive a sinister conspiracy?

Burn

Olivia's a scientist fighting to keep her secret hidden. Declan's an ex-soldier with a tragic past and lost memories. Will the chemistry between them ignite lost love?

Acknowledgments

Thank you to everyone who stood by me while I wrote this book. Your support can't be measured. There is the ARC team, bloggers, reviewers, editors, cover design artists, and my author friends just to name a few. Without them, this book doesn't come together or get in front of other readers.

I want to thank my wonderful, patient husband who puts up with my long office hours and deadlines. He's the first one who gets to read the final copy ;)

My mother, the actress, and artist who continues to inspire me. She never stops moving or learning new things. Love you.

Elbow, friend and sister from another lifetime, fellow writer, and PR person, write on.

Nikko, my muse, who was by my side each time I sat down to write. Titus was based on him. Some parts were hard to write. May he rest in peace with Koda Bear. Now, we enjoy our grand fur baby Roxie.

About the Author

Kenzie lives with her husband in New England and is a huge dog lover. She has been fortunate enough to travel all over the world to places like Africa, Greece, Switzerland, Holland, France, England and, of course, Scotland. Edinburgh is one of her favorite places.

It's all led to an overactive imagination. Creativity seems to be part of her soul as she paints portraits, takes photographs, and bakes. Cooking seems to elude her, but she loves to garden and work out!

They have all added to her storytelling especially when writing about strong women and alpha men. She looks forward to adding to her adventures and her readers.

She loves to hear from her fans.

Join her newsletter for cover reveals, new books, deals, and giveaways.
Website: www.kenziemacallan.com

You can find her on:
BookBub: www.bookbub.com/authors/kenzie-macallan
Amazon: www.amazon.com/author/kenziemacallan
Facebook: www.facebook.com/kenziemacallan

Twitter: www.twitter.com/kenzie_macallan
Instagram: www.instagram.com/kenziemacallan
Pinterest: www.pinterest.com/kenziemacallan
TikTok: www.tiktok.com/kenziemacallan

Email: kenziemacallan@gmail.com

www.ingramcontent.com/pod-product-compliance
Lightning Source LLC
Chambersburg PA
CBHW030530270626
47155CB00024B/2631